Breakwater

ERRIN STEVENS

For my husband, Michael. Thank you. Again.

PRAISE FOR UPDRIFT & BREAKWATER

"Best mermaid book I have EVER read? Updrift by Errin Stevens."
- Ben Alderson, Top Vlogger according to *The Guardian* and *Teen Vogue*

"This book will blow away any other mermaid/siren book you've read." -
@bibliophagist_omniligent on #bookstagram

"Stevens is a treasure to be found in today's cluttered literary market."
- Peachy Keen Reviews

"If you are a fan of Mermaids and Mythical creatures, Updrift and
Breakwater need to be a must read for you. I promise you will enjoy them,
and grow attached to the characters, just like I have."
- Tracy Thomas, blogger/owner of The Pages In Between

"Told in Ms. Stevens' always elegant writing style, 'Breakwater' dives deeper
into the evocative world of sirens. Beautiful and expansive, this tale will
thrill fans as they revisit the Blakes and the rest of the siren hierarchy."
- InD'tale Magazine

"I loved this. I dreamed about it."
- Cloud S. Riser, author of *Jack & Hyde*

ACKNOWLEDGMENTS

The same associates, friends and relatives who stayed by me for my last effort also hung with me for this one, and I really don't know why you do it. But thank you, my mom especially, for pretending what I do makes sense and continuing to take my calls. I'd also like to thank Martha Moran, whose editing oversight made the final knitting up of this book both possible and an unexpected pleasure; and I harbor particular devotion in my heart for my walking pal and tamer of all writer demons, fellow author J.F. Jenkins. Finally, I cannot tell you how profoundly uplifting my fan community has become. Your heartfelt devotion to my first story and encouraging comments have been the very best part of this journey.

The shattered water made a misty din.
Great waves looked over others coming in,
And thought of doing something to the shore
That water never did to land before.

— From *Once By The Pacific*
by Robert Frost

PROLOGUE

She sensed his death and then ignored the possibility for several days. She couldn't be sure, couldn't know after all this time, could she? More than forty years had passed since she'd last seen him, and they hadn't been bonded, not truly… how could she know?

But she couldn't stop herself from thinking about it; she felt the dissolution and it was not a feeling one could confuse. But… Peter? Why?

She experienced no real grief – she'd grieved over him, over their emotional catastrophe of a marriage, when she was still with him. But there was a distinct emptiness in her now, and a sadness that one of her kind was gone, someone she'd known as well as she knew anyone. Still, she felt unsure.

When she could no longer tolerate her unease, she dove into the lake and transformed, a delicious freedom she craved especially when troubled. Lake Superior had taken some getting used to – she was less buoyant here than in the salt water back home – but her feelings were clearer when she swam. She came here when she needed to think.

What did she perceive? She sifted through her thoughts and sensations, examining each carefully. No, she was not mistaken: Peter

1

Loughlin was dead. And here, far under the water where hardly any light penetrated, she suffered for her clarity, felt her remorse more keenly. She cried both for him and for herself.

The decision she had always put off would never be made now, the one to tell him or at least get him word he had a daughter. Now he would never know he'd been a father, would never hear her apologize for leaving without telling him she was pregnant.

She liked to believe he would have forgiven her for fleeing as she had, for protecting their baby from the environment that had crippled them both. Peter's inner distress, so like her own, would have schooled him she hoped; would have helped him accept she would have stayed if she could have.

Her uncertainty dispatched, Seneca meandered toward the surface while watching the play of light on the waves rippling overhead. She slowed as she rose, unwilling to approach the world above yet, when this exit from her lake might well be her last. Twenty feet down, she paused to contemplate the most thrilling, heartbreaking endeavor she'd undertaken since running away four decades earlier.

She could no longer apologize to her dead husband, but she could find their daughter, explain to her who she was, where she came from. Knowing she would do this, Seneca wept with relief at the prospect; how many hours over how many years had she yearned for her child?

The orphanage and nuns who ran it were long gone—Seneca knew because she'd checked—but her little girl had stayed there through high school. And surely by now she was aware of what she was, although Seneca was confident the sisters had followed her directive, had kept her daughter from the ocean when she was small. She'd used all of her not inconsiderable influence to ensure they would.

Seneca surged through the last twenty feet of water, took a breath, and re-entered the lake. She flipped and then propelled herself face-up, just below the surface this time so she could watch the clouds. She felt like she was flying whenever she did this. She felt centered.

Her understanding sharpened… and the decision to go became solid and right. She headed for shore thinking about all this place had been to her and what it would mean to her to leave it. She would try to leave her fosterling, Parker, behind, although she truly didn't know if she could.

And yet the more she contemplated a return to North Carolina, the more eager she was to get on with it and go. If she had to bring Parker, well then she would.

But she would at last go to her beautiful baby, her girl. Carmen. She would find her and explain everything.

PART ONE

CHAPTER ONE

Xanthe floated thirty feet below the ocean's surface in the submerged cathedral where she typically meditated and held court. She was stationary except for her tail, which flicked periodically as she mused over the current political complications she was charged with resolving.

Things were a mess. With a committee formed to recommend government changes moving forward, Xanthe had retreated to her sanctuary to ruminate in seclusion. She still needed to find an overall direction to accommodate the cultural shifts happening under her watch.

She reflected on the recent actions of the monarchy—namely the double suicide of Queen Kenna and her son Peter, the crown prince. She needed to come up with a way to resolve the confusion their deaths had caused the siren community and normalize the power structure as quickly as possible. If she could gain some perspective, she could share it with the advisory committee and help her people heal and rebuild.

She marveled at the incongruity of it all, how a cherished member of their ranks—a prince no less—suffered such extreme loneliness he secretly kidnapped and isolated someone. And this in the context of a heretofore transparent society where bonds were protected and emotional connection revered. Unlike humans, who were given to periods of introversion that sometimes spanned years, intimacy was vital to siren survival, as necessary as food and water. What had changed so drastically in their community, implacable and stable for centuries, to produce such a situation?

Granted, Peter's cloaking ability—he could mask his identity even to his own kind—was unprecedented. If she hadn't witnessed the sequence of events leading up to Peter's suicide herself, she wouldn't have believed it could happen. Or that anyone could accomplish such a complicated deception. But he had.

If she was being objective, she'd seen other, less noticeable, signs their society was shifting, understood sirens everywhere had inaugurated an era of transition before Peter and his mother had voluntarily dissolved. Tempted as she was to dwell on the more dramatic behaviors of their former regents, she disciplined herself to focus on the larger issue at hand. Sirens everywhere had demonstrated individualistic tendencies evidencing a significant departure from tradition. Dozens of examples came to mind as she thought back, from increased assertion of individual will in matters of group governance to a new, pervasive curiosity for all things human. More and more sirens were hungry to explore the earth-bound world, and not just in groups as had been their habit.

The common thread, Xanthe realized, had to be human influence and interaction. With the advent of easy intercontinental mobility (and a human society eager for it), run-ins with their non-aquatic cousins had exploded over the past century. The relatively new practice of human/siren marriages also coincided with the arrival of these changed behaviors . . . but the marriages were a necessity Xanthe acknowledged; sirens needed the genetic diversity these unions offered. And she could not discount the raw, commanding pull humans held for her kind. Human emotional broadcasts, especially in the water, were an irresistible enticement to every siren within range, made them forget themselves as nothing else. Xanthe well knew how consorting with humans evoked a visceral, elemental response none of them would ever be able to suppress. Unlike some in her world, she knew they would be foolish to even try.

But something had to be done, and as wonderful as humans could be, her people had also experienced enough of their cruelty to explore the option of complete separation. All sirens understood the need to court human ignorance with sophisticated evasion and illusion because they knew the miracle of what humans offered—their stunning creativity, their dynamism, and their soul-drenching evocations—did not mean they could be trusted, unfortunately.

Sirens had successfully hidden from humans for centuries, but an increase in interactions threatened their secrecy and fed what many saw as a dangerous deterioration of their world. A year earlier, Xanthe and a few other officials had even hatched a plan to establish community outposts in places that would offer, if not complete seclusion, at least limited opportunity for human traffic. The idea was to create a refuge like Shaddox Island, where sirens could be at leisure and enjoy life without human interference.

In fairness the idea was also born of a need to address the problem presented by several of their young men who had developed what many felt were counter-cultural behaviors. These men had all voiced dissatisfaction with the choices available to them concerning their roles in siren society, a dissatisfaction no one had seen before. Rather than examine too closely the whys and wherefores of these sentiments, however, the decision had been made to send the group to form an outpost, one that could eventually serve as a safe congregating spot for all of them. Somewhere without a human population.

Xanthe laughed at the earnestness with which they'd chosen the location; Antarctica was as removed from siren society as it was from humans, and her government's avoidance of its people's problems struck her as comical in retrospect. The decision was a clear duck and run, with the most prominent malcontents assigned to the development task force and sent away to clear the territory. They thought such work would alleviate the men's lack of enthusiasm for pursuing an academic career or profession in one of the sciences, show them the error of their ways by committing them to manual labor. Xanthe saw the mission now as far more cowardly; rather than examine any systemic unhappiness, those who were unhappy were simply dispatched, their discontent hidden.

She thought how, in this way, sirens and humans were fundamentally alike, both races reacting cautiously or fearfully to the prospect of change even when it was too far underway to stop.

Still and all she was reluctant to believe her community's long-held stability was completely failing, still trusted things would improve if they could better avoid land dwellers and their world. She knew, given the size and prevalence of the human population, outright isolation wasn't practical and, in any case, couldn't be enforced. Sirens had always relied on human academic and financial institutions—to the betterment of both societies, Xanthe believed. They were currently too integrated to disengage.

The better approach might be to prescribe more careful interactions, although she couldn't think how this would be accomplished, either, since she could have no control over human travels.

Regardless of the changes she saw taking place, Xanthe had confidence in the order inherent in her society, knew it would not falter, and this comforted her. Even as more of them adopted individualistic habits, individual happiness was too closely tied to the overall community's well-being, and *that* wasn't going to change, not ever. So the new key to her people's stability could be working with this evolution rather than against it.

Yes. She felt the knot in her center loosen, the impossibile become possible. Her intuition told her resolution lay along the path of careful coexistence, even if she didn't yet see the specific course of action to achieve it. But she knew to trust herself, and trust she'd found the way they might all to continue to thrive.

Xanthe relaxed further and pondered the puzzle of accommodation, rightness and change. At least the problem had definition now, and a path to resolution. With consensus and help from whoever would become the new head of government, their world could find its balance.

CHAPTER TWO

Maya sat with Sylvia and Kate on the couch staring at the screen in front of them, her friends wearing the same rapt, dreamy expression she assumed she also wore. This was the fourth time in two weeks they'd convened at Sylvia's for movie night, the scope of which had narrowed to include superhero flicks only. Tonight's selection was *Superman*, which Kate declared was her new favorite.

"No argument from me," Maya pronounced. "In fact, I'm free tomorrow night, too. I could be here by seven."

Sylvia sighed. "I love this part, when she steps on his boots and he takes her flying."

"Yeeesssss," Kate hissed.

They all strained forward as Superman and Lois drifted upwards from the top of the Daily Planet, the music swelling as they ascended into the night sky, and Kate slowly released the breath she held. "The first time I saw this scene . . . well, it was so sweetly erotic I couldn't sleep for three days."

"Did you ladies want popcorn?" Gabe grinned from the doorway, and all three of them jumped. Maya shot him a venomous look while her sister, Sylvia, scrambled for the remote and punched "pause."

Kate squealed and launched herself toward her husband, no small feat given her advanced pregnancy. Once plastered to Gabe's side, she buried her face in his neck and asked, "How long have you been here?" in a muffled voice.

Sylvia rose from the couch and headed for the kitchen. "I really don't need to see this."

Maya crossed her arms over her chest. "Yes. How long *have* you been standing there, Gabe?"

"Not very." Gabe smirked, pressing his nose into Kate's hair. "Long enough to hear a lot of sighing and something about 'sweetly erotic.'"

Kate groaned and kept her face hidden. Maya tented her eyes with one hand. "I'm going to get a gun so I can shoot you, Gabriel Blake."

Gabe ignored her. He craned his head away from Kate, pretending irritation at her. "I got back twenty minutes ago," he bussed her on the cheek, "to find you *not* waiting for me at home."

"Yeah. *Superman* with the girls is my new gig when you're gone. But now that you're here," she waved a hand dismissively toward the television, "I'm no longer interested in what's-his-name. Lois can have him. Let's go home."

Gabe's low laugh sounded suggestive to Maya, but maybe that's because she made a study of other people's habits of intimacy these days. The couple wasn't staying for her brood-over, however; she watched Gabe loop an arm around Kate's neck as they walked out. "I'll see you at the bakery tomorrow, Sylvia!" Kate called over her shoulder.

In the kitchen, Sylvia rifled through cupboards while Maya sat at the table, head braced on her hands. She hated feeling jealous of her friend's good romantic fortune but still felt bitter.

"I think they're gone," Sylvia commented tonelessly, and Maya was uncharitably pleased she wasn't the only one in low humor.

"Yeah," she replied. "So let's make popcorn and finish the show. I need the distraction."

Sylvia frowned as she poured oil in a pan. "So do I."

Back on the couch with a bowl between them, they paid only partial attention to the rest of the movie. Maya knew a little of Sylvia's romantic conundrums and certainly indulged in a few of her own, which had just been made all the more unsatisfying against the backdrop of Kate and Gabe's newlywed euphoria. Maya had been seeing someone on and off for a while—which mostly meant texting and talking on the phone since her guy lived out of state. She didn't feel particularly enamored, but as she had nothing else going on she continued to talk and flirt and hope their exchanges would launch a more compelling attraction.

Sylvia was in a faux relationship, in Maya's opinion, with a man she'd met at culinary school. Maya had met Ethan and understood his appeal—he was handsome, a talented cook . . . and had charmed all of his female classmates from what she could see. Which meant Sylvia was gone on a prospect who was much less gone on her. In fairness, the guy *had* solicited Sylvia's affection, a little more than with the other girls, perhaps, although he never invited Sylvia out on an exclusive date. Her sister's joke to Maya was, "Sometimes he seems really into me." Maya had no patience for him or for Sylvia's tolerance for such weak affection. "He's a tease," she retorted.

Lately Maya knew Ethan's quirky, all-inclusive approach to romance had led to kicking, cussing—albeit private—tantrums on Sylvia's part, after which she vowed to Maya she would save her love for someone who wanted it. "I will not be a pathetic hanger-on," she insisted once after Maya made the observation she essentially served in a harem. But Maya would inevitably catch her venturing out again with the same crowd, pretending she found whatever attention Ethan tossed her way acceptable.

In rare moments of clarity Sylvia confessed her exact motivation, saying she knew she simply wanted someone to love who would love her back. And she thought Ethan could honestly be that person, although she also conceded evidence in support of this hope was thin.

Sylvia stared gloomily at the screen in front of them now and mused, "I'm an idiot."

Maya appraised her with a sideways glance. "Because you keep going out with Ethan?"

"Mm-hmm."

"Yeah. You are," Maya agreed. Her smirk faded. "But I'm no one to criticize."

"You could channel our mother for me. Help me get off this train maybe." Their mother, Alicia, always argued hard when Sylvia mooned and took the blame for Ethan's disinterest. "What you want, someone to love who will love you back, is good and worth wanting," she'd insist. "Even if Ethan's not the right one for you -

and I certainly have my own opinion on that score - do not think you're in the wrong." Maya agreed with her.

On this occasion she decided to rely on Kate's example rather than her mother's standard lecture, however. "Think of the demonstration we just had from Kate and Gabe. The one that just pissed us both off."

"I feel like too much of a jerk," Sylvia intoned. "I mean, who suffers because a friend is happy?"

Maya understood this reaction too well, since her own shaky rationalizations crashed just as hard when Kate and Gabe were around.

Kate went so far as to decimate her carefully constructed excuses out loud, although she didn't realize what she did. But she was just so dang happy, as well as annoyingly open—evangelistic even—on the wonderfulness of love and marriage.

"Feeling blue? Out of sorts?" Kate would say to introduce what had become her new life's mantra. "Get married! Have a baby!"

Maya had been Kate's best friend from the time the two were in grade school, but even she couldn't talk Kate down from her 'love-conquers-all' perch. "Can it, Blake," she told Kate irritably during their last movie fest at Sylvia's. "It's like you think you've found the cure for cancer."

Kate leaned in more closely to tease, "Maya, what's bothering you. Can't sleep? Got a hang nail?" She paused and breathed in her ear, "You know what to do."

Sylvia grit her teeth. "God. Someone please kill me." Maya swatted them both away.

At least Sylvia had the bakery now, which was a lot more than Maya had going on. SeaCakes was her sister's big bite outta life and she was rightfully proud of herself for it. Maya envied her the satisfaction of realizing a professional goal so young, not to mention the thrill of exercising skills honed since childhood. She wondered how it would feel to be competent and have a career plan. Maybe it made up for a directionless personal life, although the accomplishment didn't seem to help Sylvia figure out her troubles with Ethan.

"How's Steven these days?" Sylvia asked.

"Stuart," Maya corrected without enthusiasm. "Fine, I guess." She kept her eyes on the screen. "But he's no Superman."

Gabe hung the car keys on a hook by the door and followed Kate into the kitchen. "Did you eat already?"

"Pound cake and peanut butter. And a banana," Kate replied. Gabe grimaced and surveyed the contents of the fridge.

Kate sat down at the table and rested her chin on her palms. "How was school this week?"

Gabe had missed the fall semester of medical school while he searched for her after she'd gone missing. The university had been unwilling initially to re-admit him in the spring, but he'd spent summers in college—and some of his college career as well—engaged in studies that covered the program's first-year subject matter, something he was able to do with his father's help and because he had the disciplined, voracious intellect of all sirens. Despite his several-month absence, he first asked and then coerced those in power to let him enter the year late. He was allowed in only after serially hazing nine administrators and instructors, which he did without hesitation or compunction.

"Dry," Gabe responded, and then laughed at his own humor. "And by that I mean both the lectures and the fact that Chapel Hill is inland. I'm having a sandwich. Do you want one?"

Kate shook her head. "Have you been able to keep up? Do you wish you'd waited?"

"Nope," he said. "I mean, yes, I'm getting something out of it; and no, I don't wish I'd waited." He devoured a slice of cheese while he assembled his plate. "I have a hard time being away from you all week, and I have a hard time away from the ocean, but I'm glad I'm back on track with my evil life's plan." He looked at her adoringly. "I've got it all, you know. You, a career, our baby . . ."

"Which is taking its own sweet time coming out," Kate complained. "How long, do you think?" Gabe's sensitivities gave him a special bead on the greater happenings in life, such as when someone was going to be born or die. And since Kate's pregnancy was uncomfortable to her now she tended to ask this question often in the hopes his answer would change. "If I get a say, tonight would be ideal."

Gabe laughed sympathetically and straddled her chair to wedge himself behind her. He reached his hands around her abdomen, rested his chin on her shoulder and guessed, "Two weeks, give or take."

"Please let it be 'take.'" She let her head fall back against his shoulder.

"You're doing great," he said in her ear, "and it's almost over."

"Easy for you to say," she retorted, but she groused without rancor. Gabe cradled her stomach, running his nose along her neck and into her hair until she yawned. "Can we go to bed yet?"

Gabe moved his hands to her hips and nibbled at her neck, signaling his desire for a different kind of activity. She smiled and dropped her head forward to better accept his attention, and then frowned as her eyes lit on her pregnant middle. "I'm not actually in, ah, good form for anything too . . . well, *gratifying.*" Gabe refrained from comment, but continued nuzzling her until she reconsidered her initial refusal. "I suppose we could work something out, though. You could just, you know, lie back and think of Africa." Her frown deepened.

Gabe's muffled laughter tickled her neck. "They say sex can bring on labor, you know," he suggested, and she swiveled her head around to see if he was kidding.

"They do? If that's true, then have at me."

"Oh yeah," Gabe confirmed, continuing his seduction efforts. "We could even run over to my folks' if you want." Kate stiffened since the idea of intimacy at her in-laws' doused her enthusiasm like water over coals. Gabe's low laugh echoed down her spine.

"No, not in the house," he said huskily. "Off the pier. We could leave our clothes on the dock."

She brightened instantly. "But . . . but I *love* sex in the water!"

"Yes," Gabe replied with a lazy smile. "I know this about you." He drew his hands up the insides of her thighs. "How about it? Care for a midnight swim with your husband?"

She stood up quickly and pulled Gabe with her to the door. She stopped before they stepped out and peered at him. "Brings on labor? You're sure?"

Gabe's eyes glittered. "Absolutely." He propelled her forward until they were outside, then shut the door behind them and led her toward the ocean.

When they returned to the pier after their swim, they found towels anchoring a note from Carmen and Michael. "An invitation to stay the night," Gabe announced. Kate sighed in defeat. She should have known there was no sneaking around when it came to her mother- and father-law—even at one in the morning—but she could never completely get past her unease over the level of awareness they had of them, especially in matters of intimacy. She tried to shrug off her discomfort, knowing discretion at this point was a lost cause. "Oh, why not."

Once in bed, they lay silent for several minutes, Kate lost in her thoughts, Gabe playing with one of her hands. She stroked her stomach absently with her free hand.

"Gabe?"

"Mmm?"

"I've been wondering." She shifted to face him. "Why are you an only child? I mean did your parents ever talk about having more kids?"

"Sure they did. For a few years anyway. But Mom felt like we had a better quality of life as we were. You know, with a smaller family. And then siren women only ovulate once a year so there's less opportunity than with you people, so in general it's just not a sure thing. Something like three in ten couples don't conceive, and those who do have one, occasionally two, very rarely three children."

Kate thought back to one of their first conversations at Shaddox, when Gabe had explained siren marriage to her for the first time and how conception, at least with her kind, was part of it all. "Doesn't that interfere with their bonding?"

"Not exactly. My parents say children divert the focus of a marriage, although they think it's a worthy diversion. They say having a child gives a centering weight to the relationship. But no. Couples who give themselves to each other bond regardless of whether or not the woman conceives.

"We take child rearing pretty seriously, though," Gabe continued, "and bringing up baby is more exhausting than living without such a responsibility. I'm sure you remember when your mom and John had Everett. That's why my mom was ultimately glad to just have me to chase after." He flashed her a wicked grin. "She says I wore her out."

She sniffed. "You were an ideal kid. You were smart and well-mannered, an all-around 'good' boy."

Gabe's grimace was playful. "My folks might argue with you. But in that I didn't end up a disaffected criminal, it was because Carmen and Michael and I were pretty close." Kate smiled fondly, wondering how anyone could *not* want to be by him all the time. "Mom assures me it was trying enough with just one of me," he concluded.

"Well. I don't know what I think about that," Kate said, "about having only one, I mean. I always assumed I'd have a couple, and now I wonder."

"Which is not a decision we need to make tonight," Gabe finished with a yawn.

"I suppose not." Kate shifted deeper into the covers.

They talked quietly for a few more minutes, about how they hoped to be attentive, involved parents, and then they discussed home improvement projects they wanted to start that weekend. Finally Kate relinquished her hold on consciousness and drifted away.

CHAPTER THREE

Simon Blake hacked at his Wall of Siberia, as he called it, with methodical, annihilating blows.

He liked the Siberia metaphor because it relied literally on polar opposite land masses for definition, with him chipping away in Antarctica and Siberia residing on the other end of the planet. Regardless, both were cold as hell. Both were uninhabited and isolated, true ends of the earth.

He stopped to admire his work as he switched his pick to his other hand. Between the ten male sirens exiled there, they'd excavated over a mile of frozen rock, all of it underwater, in little more than eight months. Not including the four months when he and his crew were land-bound—because it was simply too freakin' cold and dark to work in the sea—he'd been in this godforsaken place almost a year. He and his companions had become very good at digging out caves.

In a way, the work was a relief, a haven for his restless nature, which had threatened him and apparently everyone in polite siren society before he'd come here. The physical exertion was total, and just as it exhausted his body, he found it calmed his mind. He knew his companions felt the same way.

And his brother, Aiden, was with him, which made their group's seclusion tolerable, even occasionally fun. All ten miscreants assembled shared the destructive bent that had resulted in their nomination for this project, and they all understood and accepted one another because of this. Each of them, via parallel paths of misbehavior, had demonstrated a like inability to relax into the more traditional choices offered young men in their world, and as their rebelliousness increased, so had their willful disregard for community norms. The chance to escape those norms and expectations had been a relief for all of them.

They'd almost finished here and planned to return to Griffins Bay next week. It was unclear what would happen next, if the same crew would be dispatched to prepare another outpost somewhere else, or if they would be expected to resolve their differences of opinion with leadership and reintegrate. Xanthe had hinted more than once she hoped each of them would take a mate, the idea being they would settle down more happily if this were the case.

Simon didn't have any real enthusiasm for the idea, but he wasn't opposed, either. In fact he attributed some of his angst to his desire for companionship, maybe specifically with a wife. He didn't want the life that came with this set-up, however, where he and whoever he married would retire into some bland, lethally boring existence revolving around 'the good of the community.'

He was ashamed to feel this way. He understood the agreeable, supportive way his kind lived together—something he was proud of—was a function of each individual putting the collective first. He had benefited from this support his entire life, and he admired the many sirens who dedicated themselves happily to the cause and felt fulfilled doing so.

He even agreed with Xanthe on this issue; especially when measured against the selfishness they saw too often in human society, his people's choices seemed not only practical but praiseworthy. The underlying desire to support a nurturing environment carried with it a spiritual beauty, one revered by every siren on the planet, himself included.

While he was unsure of its provenance, however, his dissatisfaction was genuine. It was also, in everyone's opinion including his own, a drag. Time and again when presented with the opportunity to make a choice to cement his role in siren society, he'd refused. When encouraged to follow a course of study benefiting siren-kind down the line, he chose otherwise.

When asked to attend Carmen's social gatherings, where he might meet his mate, he flat out fled in the other direction.

Anything that carried the scent of compliance had him resisting.

This last effort, the one meant to help him find a wife, especially bothered him after the fact. He liked the idea of bonding with someone, finding a person to share his life with; in fact he longed for the intimacy and emotional fulfillment his old school friends enjoyed with their spouses. But he could not shake the belief he would eventually hate it, was certain the sameness his relationship would have with that of everyone around him would grate on him and become oppressive. The idea of being made to live in a box, even if the box was very nice, irritated him. He continued to dig in his heels.

Xanthe had even taken time from her duties to question him last year in Griffins Bay, not unkindly. "You feel so at odds with your nature?"

Simon always weighed his responses carefully with Xanthe, and he'd been wary on this particular occasion. "Nothing so drastic. The deal is I don't like the choices I have, but I'm not on fire to do anything else, either."

"Hmm," Xanthe mused. "I'm trying to understand and failing, although you sound a little like a human adolescent."

Simon snorted. "Yeah, except I'm 34." He relaxed his stance and conceded. "But your analogy intrigues me. There's something to it, although I don't know what." His ensuing laugh was short.

Xanthe studied him thoughtfully. "I've been discussing this very issue with the committee. We believe there's a link, and not just with you. Meaning you're not the only one of us with existential problems these days, although the others are younger. Across the board, except with the oldest among us, we've seen more unrest, an appetite for independence from each other we've never experienced before. This at a time when our interactions with humans has also grown, so we suspect a correlation."

Simon smiled and cocked his head. "I'll go study adolescent human psychology then," he offered. "Maybe that can be my practical contribution."

Xanthe's frustration flared. "Your practical contribution would be to find your equilibrium, to choose your purpose. We want to feel your contentment, not your turmoil."

Simon's smile faded. "I'm sorry," he responded, and he meant it.

"If I could change, I would." He didn't want to feel his unrest, either, much less share it, so he'd understood. He even agreed with her.

He'd come closest to resolution here, clearing in Antarctica for future habitation. The insulation from judgment back home, as well as the grueling physical labor the project entailed, had expended his discontent to the point it disappeared, something the folks back home had noticed even from their limited phone and email interactions. For a time during and because of their work, he and his coworkers had also lost the "problem" moniker they'd all earned, since societal integration was not expected of them when they were on site; and because hacking away at all that ice was, after all, for the greater good. The effort so placated everyone, Xanthe issued an open invitation to Simon to take his team back whenever they felt inclined, even if it was just to blow off more steam. Which Simon found funny, since she made the offer while they were still there the first time.

"You guys were brave to do what you did and everyone appreciates your efforts," she assured him over the phone. "If you want to work on the next stage of development, you have first right of refusal."

Simon had discussed this conversation a couple of times with his brother afterwards, not really caring one way or the other at the time what role they might play in Antarctica's future. "I'm not sure I'd come back," Aiden confessed.

"I know," Simon agreed. "I feel good about what we've done, but I'm not cut out for this permanently."

Aiden chuckled. "We should request detail in Hawaii next time."

Simon clapped his brother on the back. "Yeah, how Hawaii lost out to Antarctica, I'll never get. I mean, who do they think will actually live in this ice bucket?"

The brothers shook their heads, although privately Simon understood perfectly why the South Pole development was underway. Sirens needed a place other than Shaddox away from the human world, to maybe forestall the pace of their community's disintegration. Everyone knew the value of avoidance in these times, the need to skirt around the residual problems attending those sometimes troublesome, habitually addictive interactions with their biped counterparts. Like everyone these days, Simon just wished their haven and their home could be one and the same.

CHAPTER FOUR

Sylvia walked into her SeaCakes kitchen and scanned the pretty, well-ordered space with pride. She unashamedly adored every part of her job, even cleaning the utility shelves and trolling through the expiration dates of the ingredients in her pantry. She poured herself a cup of coffee and then retrieved the doughs she'd set in the cooler to proof the previous afternoon.

She loved this first-morning quiet, where she and her store woke up together, so much she made sure she was always the first one in. Today would be busy, however, and she'd asked Kate to join her early.

She heard the bell ring over the front door. "I'm back in the kitchen!" she yelled.

She'd come to depend on Kate these past months, certainly for her work ethic but maybe more for her friendship. Although they'd known each other since they were girls—Kate was best friends with Sylvia's younger sister, Maya—they'd only recently spent time one-on-one after she'd hired Kate to help juggle the a.m. crowd. Kate now also pitched in occasionally in the afternoon or to decorate cakes. She'd shown talent for the latter, and while not yet as adept as Sylvia, she was good and getting better. Sylvia was extra pleased by Kate's interest in icing since she shared Sylvia's design aesthetic, which seemed to be the engine behind SeaCakes' growing popularity.

Sylvia relied on Kate more than her friend knew.

The job was more than just a paycheck to Kate, as well, something Sylvia would have perceived even if Kate hadn't confessed her motivations several weeks back. "I'm more restless than I thought I'd be without my magazine job, and working here really helps. Maybe it's because I was a captive, but I got so tired of just gardening and reading." Her glance toward Sylvia was an apology. "I know that sounds crazy."

"Do you miss the city, or working in an office?"

"A little, but not really. I'm mostly way up for being a wild and free newlywed. But I wonder what I'll have to go back to in a few years. That's what I worry about at night." She paused to study the brightening sky outside the café window. "I also feel like I walked away from something I shouldn't have, like I'm a fool for giving up my career."

"You didn't quit," Sylvia countered. "You got into the field you wanted, no small feat. Then you got kidnapped—hardly your fault. And you and Gabe were always on some kind of forever radar, weren't you? You don't have to see yourself as down for the count, I don't think, more like you're taking a break, having a baby. And I think you'll be happier in the garden this time, with all your peeps close-by."

Kate slumped into a café chair. "Yeah, but I was too new to leave when I did. If I'd stayed even a few more years, I think I'd have more options. None of the women out there who were where I wanted to be checked out in their first year of employment to get married and have a baby."

"I don't know anything about that," Sylvia conceded, "and I do think it's smart to have some sort of oar in the water these days in case your boat springs a leak. Or you get kidnapped and have to build a life afterwards. What did your boss say when you called?"

"Oh, everyone was wonderful. They were worried of course . . . and Janice—she was my manager—regretted she hadn't been able to hold my job. She invited me to keep in touch, said she'd keep her eyes open for another spot. But I told her location was going to be an issue for me moving forward. I didn't even mention I was pregnant."

"Maybe you should have."

Kate's regarded her doubtfully. "Maybe. But doing that job with an infant . . ."

Sylvia understood. She was, after all, Alicia's daughter and indoctrinated into her rigid views on parenting. Kate had heard Alicia's opinion almost as often as Sylvia had: "Don't even think about having a child you cannot care for. And don't park your kids in daycare all day every day." Sylvia didn't disagree, although the cost of supporting a household was daunting without two incomes, as far as she could tell.

Although she knew this wasn't Kate's problem. "I'm sure you can still find a way to do what you want."

Kate rose to fill the salt shakers and didn't look Sylvia's way when she next spoke. "Okay so I do have an idea to float by you."

"Let's hear it."

"I ran a tiny little cooking and lifestyle blog outside of work before leaving. And I've been collecting photos and article ideas to get it up and running again." She rushed her next words like she feared Sylvia would interrupt. "There's a lot of fabulous stuff already out there, I know, but I had a loyal following and I can't stop thinking about it, what I would do, how it could create income. My goal is to stay just a little professionally active, but my blog could actually be my dream job." She hesitated before continuing. "I'm telling you about it because I'd love to do a tie-in with the bakery and promote it here."

Sylvia nodded slowly. "I think it's a *great* idea."

Kate squealed and clasped her hands. "Really? Do you mean it? I'll bring it up with Aunt Dana—I mean your partner—if you're open to it. And I'll work up a bunch of articles so you can all see how everything would look first."

"I'm sure Dana will be all over it, but yeah, run it by her. She—and Will, too—will probably have some advice for you. And I know they'll support you."

Kate looked like she might actually tear up from happiness. "You're going to be fine," Sylvia assured her, and she believed what she said. "As far as I can tell, everyone wrestles with work-family issues. You'll figure things out."

Kate laughed. "You sound like my husband."

"You know, I want one of those," Sylvia griped.

"It'll happen," Kate promised. "For now I'm going to school on you, sister. I mean look at you, a twenty-something with your own business—you're doing great and it's what you want and are good at.

The rest of us are trying to find ourselves while you're already out here killing it."

Sylvia smiled. "Thanks. I love it, as you know. I can't believe I landed my own business right out of school. Well, I'm only part owner, but still." She loaded sugar pourers on a tray. "I love every little thing about this place, even scrubbing sinks and refilling sugar." She laughed, tapping one of the containers in front of her. "Not to sound all Polly Anna, but this doesn't feel like work. My biggest challenge is leaving it. I mean shutting my brain down at night, so I can fall asleep."

"I know what you mean. I have to do a crossword puzzle, or play a game on my phone to turn my wakey-wakey switch off."

"I've got a better one for you since you're a foodie," Sylvia offered. She leaned forward as if to share a salacious secret. "I review what I ate during the day, starting with breakfast." She leaned back and beamed.

"So . . . what? You relive that first bite of cinnamon roll and bliss out?"

"Pretty much! Actually, I relive the whole experience, like the burst of sweetness I got from the honey in a piece of baklava, and the dark, rich coffee I swallowed after, how the flavors and scents blended, what I ate for lunch and then dinner . . . and then I'm too caught up in that little dream to feel anxious about everything I didn't get to."

"Mmmm . . ." Kate closed her eyes. "I could do that, remember each thing I ate and then forget about absolutely every other worry."

"Exactly. It's a great way to let go. When I remember the cookie or bread or soup or whatever and how I felt eating them, I quit obsessing. Then I fall asleep."

"I love it and I'm going to steal it. Sounds like a lot more fun than puzzles."

"My gift to you." Sylvia gestured expansively. "Let me know how it works."

Kate sidled to one of the pastry cases. "So, in order to prepare, so I have something to think about tonight . . ." She nabbed a brioche and raised it as she would a glass in a toast. "Care to join me?"

Sylvia smiled but shook her head and shooed Kate off. "Go for it. We've only got a half hour until we open and then it's a hurricane, as you know. *I've* got work to do."

CHAPTER FIVE

One week after his return from Antarctica and just before dawn, Simon decided to swim alone, to stretch his muscles as well as escape the undercurrent of expectation pulling at him around the Blake home where he and his brother were staying.

Have you thought about what you want to do next? Do you feel more resolved about your future? Are you ready to settle down?

Yes, no and no, he thought. He was tired of the constant inquiries, even though everyone who badgered him meant well.

He'd come to Griffins Bay to meet with Xanthe; and so he and Aiden could review their charts with Carmen, who believed the activity would inspire them to integrate better this time around. They also wanted to relax and enjoy the North Carolina coastline for a few days, something he and Aiden had done every summer since they were boys.

On the return swim north, the whole Antarctica team had reviewed ways to keep working together and protect their comfortable separation from siren society. Everyone expressed enthusiasm over the proposal to form an inland construction company, which they knew would be a cinch given their recent experience. They agreed to reconvene the following month and discuss logistics. Once back, the crew dispersed to visit family or to Shaddox while Simon and Aiden set up camp at Carmen and Michael's, just like old times.

Lacking an inland construction job or another off-shore assignment, however, Simon felt like his life was in a holding pattern once again, which left him vulnerable to the angst he'd battled prior to his stint on the ice cap. This morning, he'd awoken especially restless. He rose quietly in the dark so as not to disturb the rest of the house and walked outside to the back of the Blakes' wrap-around porch. He stopped briefly to pet Soley, who greeted him sleepily from his blanket by the door. The dog padded away afterwards, down the steps toward the back gate. Simon braced his hands on the balustrade and surveyed the ocean.

Only a hint of gray light seeped into the sky from the eastern horizon. Simon scanned the path to the pier, which extended down several flights of stairs and past a series of sculptural, wave-like walls lining the walkway and dock. From the elevated plot of land where the house was situated, he had a panoramic view of the back lawn, the ocean to the east, and shoreline stretching south to Griffins Bay. The ocean called to him hard this morning, promising the unfettered freedom he craved after so many days of wearying questions and advice from siren leadership. He pushed away from the railing and headed for the water.

He stilled when he heard the metallic click of the back gate. Sylvia Wilkes had just let herself in and was crouched down to participate in a love fest with the dog. "Time for our walk, big guy," she said as she rose from her crouch. He knew the sky was too dark for her to see into the shadows where he stood, but his siren abilities allowed him to see her clearly. He retreated against the siding to continue observing her.

He remembered her from high school. He and Aiden pulled a prank one summer, one they'd thought was so clever at the time and really wasn't. Sylvia had been there picnicking on the beach with her family, along with the Blakes, and Kate and Cara. Simon and Aiden decided to shock their elders by breaching where everyone might see. They made it quick so they couldn't be identified, or so they thought; and they knew Anna, Carmen and Michael could handle the humans if any of them saw too much, which was part of the fun. Michael swam out to them right away and pretty much scared them straight . . . but Simon recalled seeing Sylvia afterwards. He'd thought she was pretty in a generic kind of way and given her no more consideration thereafter.

He was more interested this time, and reached with his senses.

Sylvia was lost in her own musings and believed she was alone. Consequently she talked to herself and even sang, which Simon found endearing. Soley lay at her feet and rolled onto his back, hoping for a longer tummy rub. "Look at you, scruffy old man," she said as she complied. "Here, I brought you half an egg sandwich. Don't tell on me for feeding you scraps." Soley thumped his tail, bolted her offering, then whined and squirmed in a shameless bid for more of her caresses. Sylvia laughed at him and pet his head. "Such a big, bad guard dog you are," she teased. "I'll end up protecting you out there."

Simon grinned, a little in response to her play with Soley but more for her particular exuberance. He felt the stirrings of fascination within him as he continued to watch her interplay with the dog, her essence a subtle pull that had him tensed and poised to walk closer to her. A tickle of sensation like a waft of perfume reached him as she continued talking, and it both gratified him and left him wanting. He inclined his body forward.

Her draw intensified until he felt he had to see her at closer range, to talk with her and feel her responses directly, perhaps touch her. He even stuttered forward two steps . . . and then clamped down on his compulsion to pursue and engage. He wasn't interested in Sylvia, not really. He couldn't—or rather wouldn't—risk such a threat to his equilibrium. He drew a deep breath and retreated further into the shadows instead. Sylvia attached Soley's leash and exited through the gate.

Simon strode in the opposite direction, removing his clothes as he progressed down the walkway to the pier. At the end of the dock he dove into the dark, cool water and transformed. Ah. This was better. He glided out to sea toward freedom and away from the fetters everyone on land seemed ready to put on him.

What a delicious pleasure this was, no practicalities to consider, no schedule to keep. He gave his siren self free rein, pushing himself faster and faster until he exhausted himself, chasing a particular release he needed this morning.

And there it was: a powerful, liquid detachment from the

stultifying inactivity of soil-based life. Ahhhh. How he missed this, the physical demands accompanying the excavation of all that frozen rock. In order to feel stable since his return, he'd had to exert himself with gargantuan daily swims, or by hunting for multiple families until he depleted the colossal stamina he'd acquired while developing the South Pole outpost. All sirens were strong, but Simon and his crew returned from their project in crazy good shape, something he should have expected from what was essentially an extended strength-training regimen. His body now demanded he use it, and Simon, in the course of one week, had become addicted to his daily, self-imposed ironman effort.

He thought of Xanthe and Carmen's suggestions for him and tried to manufacture some excitement for what they wanted. "You should do what you feel called to do," Xanthe had advised, "which hopefully means settling in, taking your place among us." Her instructions, while not insensitive, carried the overtones of reproach, which never failed to abrade his independent streak. He'd stiffened in offense and barely refrained from walking away, regardless of how rude that would have been.

His aunt Carmen had been the more tentative of the two, because she was more sympathetic by nature and because their families had socialized often while he and Aiden were small. Consequently her approach to him tended toward the maternal, where she worried more about his happiness than others' approval. She'd even smoothed his bangs, just as she did with her son Gabe, when she offered her own encouragement.

"You'll find your way, Simon. And I know you want more individual choice than you feel you have. I get that—I really do. But I think in this case the cart should go before the horse. It will help you adjust, make you content." She flashed Xanthe a quick smile. Her purpose dawned on Simon, then, and he shook his head at her.

"What a sneak you are," but a smile softened his admonishment.

"We're having a party in two weeks," Carmen continued as if he hadn't spoken, "and I've invited several women I think you'll like, all bright, attractive and talented. You should come."

Simon cocked an eyebrow. "You mean you don't already have someone picked out?"

Xanthe had scrutinized him during Carmen's speech and must have intuited his resistance because she had an opinion. "Maybe a human, Carmen. Someone different from us, who would help Simon feel like his future is less prescribed." Her expression brightened. "Doesn't Solange Hokeman have two sisters? One just opened a new bakery in town, right?"

Simon responded with a hard stare at both of them. Marrying a human would be no different at all, he thought. He'd still be jammed into a house and some boring job and pushed to produce progeny. No thanks.

Carmen's glared at Xanthe. "Sylvia Wilkes is lovely, of course, as is Maya. But we can't co-opt an entire human family. It's too risky from an exposure standpoint. And don't forget Solange already married Luke Hokeman." Her expression darkened further. "Please remember this is *my* area of expertise, Xanthe. I prefer to spread the love. So to speak." She faced Simon again.

Simon raised his hands. "I feel more advice coming, ladies, and I'm good for today." He kissed his aunt's cheek, then nodded politely at Xanthe.

He paused at the front door. "I might be ready to go traditional," he offered, and he sincerely thought it could be true. "That gig in Antarctica did something for me, took my issues on vacation. It did for all of us." He looked out at the ocean. "But I want more time." He exited before Carmen or Xanthe could respond.

CHAPTER SIX

Sylvia stepped through the front door of SeaCakes anticipating what had become a cherished routine. She breathed in the familiar scents of chocolate, lemon, vanilla and butter as she took a cursory visual inventory of her little kingdom and smiled with pride at what they'd accomplished here, from the shining pastry cases to the vibrantly colored walls and softly glowing countertops to her ultimate pride and joy: the freshly outfitted, professional kitchen. The clock on the wall read four a.m.

She put the coffee on and pulled out her supplies. She loved being alone at the café at this hour, the quiet and dark of the outside world wrapping around her like a hug from the universe. She felt insulated and protected and . . . like she was in some personal state of grace. Later she would go for her walk, and when she returned, her sleepy bakery would be transformed by sunshine and the activity of whatever helpers were scheduled to come that morning. But not now.

In culinary school so many of the other students began their days in a frenzy, blaring their music and illuminating every square inch of the kitchen with harsh fluorescent overheads. Sylvia found the practice barbaric. She left the storefront dark and the phones off when she came in, turning on only the pendant lights over her workspace, the only noise that of the coffee maker gurgling. She relished this particular quiet, the only time of the day she was certain to have it.

She worked on the yeasted items first—the brioches and rolls and fritters and yeast cakes—because they took extra time. When she'd dealt with those, she mixed the quick breads, then assembled her fruit tarts. She'd frost last.

She'd first opened SeaCakes for breakfast-only but expanded her offerings two months later to include lunch, which was attracting a growing number of regulars. She even took the occasional catering gig after hours, which burdened her staff although they all enjoyed the extra revenue. But at only five hundred square feet, she was at capacity now, and if business picked up any further they'd have a space problem. For the moment her crew could just keep up, thankfully.

She worried over this issue more than she should. Because more growth would mean . . . what? Everyone had to work all the time and would hate the place? She wished she could freeze their current operations; protect the brisk, pleasant rhythm of her days.

Still she felt fortunate and thanked her lucky stars or ghosts of dead relatives or whatever power had helped her get here. She was also grateful to have skipped the struggles so many of her peers experienced as they fought for jobs and endeavored to launch themselves.

Sylvia had always known she wanted this, had always longed to work in a kitchen. From before she could remember her mother would set her up with some cooking task, usually peeling vegetables or stirring a batter, jobs Sylvia understood were given more to keep her out of her mother's way. But Syliva hadn't cared, had worked to make herself genuinely useful anyway, even as a little girl.

By the time she was ten, she'd settled her affections solidly on baking, so much so she experimented in the kitchen every day to the exclusion of athletic and social activities, and sometimes to the detriment of her grades. Alicia and Jeremy intervened enough to make sure she kept up, but they never truly pushed her to excel academically, not like they did with her sisters. Sylvia questioned them about this only once.

"You've already found something to carry you, honey," her mother had told her. "Maya and Solange aren't as decided. They need options."

Sylvia harbored no resentment for the extra attention her sisters received over schoolwork. In fact, she was a little proud of herself, because unlike Solange the academic whiz or Maya the über athlete, Sylvia was encouraged for what she did now instead of what she might do in the future. She was even smug, thinking she was more evolved and her parents knew it, and like maybe her talents counted for more. *Lots of kids strive for good grades and athletic stardom. It takes a special kind of stubborn to go for broke over custards and genoise*, she reasoned.

Finished with her morning prep, she hung her apron by the sink and headed out for her daily seaside walk.

The ocean put her in a contemplative frame of mind, with thoughts of her work and personal life tumbling in her head like driftwood in a meandering current. She wished she could think about things of no consequence—the pretty sunrise, the sound of the waves or refreshing breeze on her skin—but she couldn't. Her hopes and frustrations welled up and clammored around in her mind without resolution.

She considered her outwardly independent life, how pleased she was with her freedoms and the future she was building. But she acknowledged how, despite all her satisfaction, she was lonely . . . and Ethan was proving no help. She felt a new decision looming on that front, a threat of decisiveness she thought she wanted but feared at the same time. Still, something like resolve coalesced inside her. She could swear it came from the ocean.

Who's the guy you're after?

She cringed at the memory she called forth of Ethan. Dashing, solicitous, flirtatious, remote Ethan. Whose anemic courting in no way warranted her continued hopes for an actual relationship.

Wow. Three years and he's never once made a move?

This one made her defensive. *Not exactly. No. But maybe he would if—*

What a loser.

She had no comeback for that one. The waves were almost right, too . . . except she suspected she was the real loser in this situation. She was the one who'd spent years dreaming about one-sided what-ifs over someone who hadn't responded. Her sisters could scold her for her idiocy—like she didn't know on her own she was chasing after the wrong guy—and insist on a no-Ethan diet. But their advice hadn't stuck. She needed a different motivation.

Which was plainly in front of her if she looked at her life honestly. Her schedule really didn't give her a ton of free time; and when she was working and busy . . . well, she realized she didn't brood, or even think much at all about Ethan. That was telling. Instructive, too, if she'd quit berating herself for gushing every time Ethan called or stopped by.

She didn't have it in her to be rude, nor could she quell the surge of hope she felt every time Ethan called or showed up at the café. But. If she must fall at Ethan's feet maybe she could divert herself with work when he wasn't available? Yes, yes she could. She was never the one to seek him out and initiate their flirtations anyway, so if she started to obsess over him—or rather what he represented to her—she could distract herself, whip up something time-consuming like laminated French pastries or a really complicated cake. She laughed at herself. Only she would think to cure herself with croissants.

But cure herself she would, and to celebrate her decision, she deleted Ethan's number from her contact list on her phone. *Take that.* She returned to the bakery lighter on the inside and very pleased with her bid for improved mental health.

She found her partners, Dana and Will Fletcher, waiting for her at one of the café tables.

The Fletchers had been a godsend after her graduation from culinary school. They'd approached her with a proposal to open SeaCakes, run it exactly as she envisioned, and they offered her part ownership with only a small cash investment on her part. Their families were longtime friends, too—Dana was Kate's aunt—which led Sylvia to believe she could entrust them with the biggest dream of her life. Her larger worries over what she thought of as the Fletchers' 'executive-itis' had not manifested. At least so far.

"Thought we'd hold a quick company meeting," Dana explained after a brief hug. "And don't worry, we'll stay to help with the morning stampede."

After a review of the previous month's sales and sorting out the upcoming staff schedule, Will asked Sylvia if she had any new products in the works. "Are you inventing the next multi-million dollar snack cake back there?" Sylvia thought he looked overly keen, and she immediately tensed.

"I wouldn't go that far." She forced her expression to relax. "I confess to playing with confections a little, using sea salt, of course. It's the only thing we don't offer. Chocolates, I mean."

"How close are you? Can we sample with customers yet? If they're a hit, we could think about a mail order business . . ." Will began a search on his laptop.

Sylvia placed a hand on his arm. "Will, I have all I can say grace over as we are—in fact we could plug in another part-time worker *today*. I also don't think our facility can handle a candy line on top what we already do, at least not to any scale."

She hoped she didn't sound like she was complaining. She liked her creative explorations in the kitchen . . . but a whole new line? For mail order? The prospect sank like a frozen lump of granite in her stomach. Even if she could squeeze production into their existing space—which was doubtful—she refused to overload the staff.

She'd dreaded just this type of impasse when she'd signed on. Her reluctance underscored a key difference in their partnership, one she'd noticed during their first conversation and here it was: she didn't care about profitability in the same way Will and Dana did. She believed SeaCakes was successful because it provided a little income, offered yummy pastries and a nice place to eat them. Whereas fooling around with new recipes was idle pleasure in her world, it was a business opportunity in theirs.

Dana relieved her with her very next comment, thank goodness. "We don't want to change the operations we have," she assured her. "We won't ruin SeaCakes for you, Sylvia."

"No we won't," Will agreed. "We'll rent another kitchen if it comes to that. You'd be in charge of the look and taste of the chocolates, and then train someone else to ride herd."

Sylvia's concerns bled out of her like melting snow under a brilliant warm sun. Lucky her, she'd landed partners who worked up spreadsheets as easily as she made muffins, and yet their talents imprisoned no one.

Will stretched before he rose to leave. "We can't afford to be overwhelmed either, Sylvia. So we won't be." He winked at his wife and gathered his things.

Dana patted her pregnant middle with a wry grimace. "Yep."

Her optimism restored, Sylvia leaned her elbows on the table and grinned. "Okay. I'll play hard with some chocolate, make a few things for us to try. And we'll sample at the bakery to get a feel for what people like."

Will promised to look for fill-in help, estimating he'd have candidates for Sylvia to interview within the week. He checked his phone and leaned down to kiss Dana's cheek. "I'll leave you ladies to it. See you at home, hon."

Dana stayed to work the cash register during breakfast and sat down immediately afterwards to put her feet up. "I'm beat, and I'm not up for dealing with the lunch crowd. How about we call in the other pregnant lady to help?"

Sylvia chuckled. "You go on home, Dana. I'll text Kate."

CHAPTER SEVEN

During the final hour of their drive to North Carolina, Parker watched Seneca slowly fall apart.

The dynamic was familiar at first: Seneca—who'd never been chatty—was eerily quiet. Then she was *deathly* quiet, more than Parker had ever seen her, and was this normal? She made a few verbal forays as a test, or maybe to prod Seneca back to planet earth.

"Where will we stay when we get there?"

Seneca didn't answer. Or indicate she'd even heard her.

"Will I go to school our first week?"

Again, no response.

Okay, if polite conversation wasn't going to work . . . "So I stole money at that convenience store a ways back and I see the police are following us."

Nothing. Seneca looked like she was carved out of stone, just maintained her trance-like stare over the steering wheel.

Which Parker considered funny until . . . until she realized she might cry. Seneca's silence, so ordinary at first, darkened and then expanded to push all the air from the car. And something related to it preyed upon Parker now, draining away every sunny thought or hope she contained. All her meager joy spilled out of her like a waterfall, leaving her empty and bereft and on the verge of hysteria.

Just before desolation crushed her and she broke down however, Seneca seized her hand. "I'm sorry. I'm anxious, and I'm compromising you and I don't mean to." Parker was a little soothed. Seneca returned her attention to the road but kept her grip on Parker's hand.

The intense quiet between them lost its menace. Instead of feeling desolate and alone, Parker now began to feel she was part of an elite, two-person combat team headed into enemy territory . . . and she was essential, not peripheral, to their success. Comforted, she relaxed in her seat and allowed herself to observe Seneca's strange behavior without worry over the personal consequences.

If they'd been around others, Seneca would have drawn a crowd. Her former stillness was interrupted by small, nerve-like twitches; accompanied by a piercing, erratic attention to visual details they passed. A bird alighting on an overhead wire, a café sign advertising all-you-can-eat fish, droplets sprayed from the compromised head of an in-ground sprinkler system—all received brief, intense scrutiny. Like they were targets Seneca apprehended in the crosshairs of the scope of a gun.

And the small quirks Parker had always associated with Seneca— her attractive energy, the silvery quality her eyes sometimes had and the erstwhile iridescence of her skin—all manifested more prominently now. Parker remained quiet to allow Seneca her concentration, but also to examine her as her fascination demanded.

Seneca turned her cutting gaze to Parker, and the impact caused Parker's breath to catch in her throat.

Her next words came off like an accusation. "You're seeing quite a lot today. But then I've always shared more of myself with you." Seneca veered into a parking lot in front of the beach and turned off the car. Her face when she turned toward Parker again was lit with a savage, frightening joy. "I'm about to tell you those secrets I mentioned, and you're going to have to trust me. But you're not to worry, okay?"

Parker experienced a stab of alarm because Seneca had lost every bit of softness she associated with her. Instead, she seemed shiny and brittle and possibly dangerous.

But Parker wanted answers. "Yes. Okay."

The closer they came to the water, the more frenetic and strange Seneca seemed to her. She would walk a few paces then skip sideways or lurch forward in a sprint, her gaze darting furtively between Parker and the surf. She was excited but fretful, as if she was hungry and on her way to a banquet where she'd have to steal her dinner. She laughed in fits and starts, pleaded with Parker to hurry and tugged on her hand, urged her to go faster.

When they entered the ocean, Seneca calmed and again became someone Parker recognized.

Peace—emanating from Seneca—blanketed her the deeper they went. Seneca was now assured, and her confidence was a balm after the mania of the last two hours. She hummed, and her song was . . . peculiar, hypnotic. Lovely. Like Seneca herself. A sense of cohesion Parker craved from Seneca settled easily within her now, ridding her of everything except anticipation. Seneca pulled them until they reached the last depth Parker's feet could touch. Then she released her.

Their sundresses lifted and floated away, which seemed the most natural, freeing thing to Parker. She followed the slow, dreamy drift of the garments as they disappeared and felt her own awareness, just as boneless, float away with them.

Seneca was talking now in words not spoken aloud but still there. And Parker turned both her eyes and thoughts to the dream unfolding before her.

Watch me, darling.

As she spoke, Seneca's appearance altered more profoundly. Her glistening skin flushed to a deeper hue, her irises reformed and sharpened. Parker watched raptly as Seneca sank beneath the surface.

She arched backwards and began to twist in lazy, sinuous circles around Parker's legs. The world outside the two of them disappeared, until all Parker heard was her own respiration, the beat of her heart; and all she saw was Seneca who was fast losing her resemblance to the woman Parker knew. In a few discreet pulses and twists, she saw Seneca's lower body fuse and lengthen. Her skin became opalescent. Her lower body now had . . . scales. By the time Parker reached out to touch her, Seneca was no longer human at all, but the embodiment of a fairy tale she read as a child.

Come.

Parker followed the shimmering, diaphanous fluke, diving to grasp for a hold on the beautiful creature that was and wasn't Seneca.

Although Seneca's transformation was shocking, her expression held Parker's attention most. Her coloring and her floating hair made an enigma of her facial features, punctuating the play of emotions that rippled across them. The seawater itself seemed to carry Seneca's intent—her great love for her new foster daughter, her compulsive need for a particular kind of emotional feedback Parker was unable to withhold. Her heart filled with a longing so intense, she thought she might burst. At which point Seneca became violently possessive, her stare a command for control over her, and for her utter devotion and allegiance. Parker gave it in full and without reservation, regardless of any potential harm she might suffer.

She didn't suffer, however. Instead, their bond compounded the further they swam, and rather than feel emptied and spiritless, Parker was sated with a sense of Seneca's devotion to her, her protection a sweet echo in and around her. *You are my own dear child. I will keep and defend you always.* The words filled her with euphoria.

When the two surfaced for air, sunlight flashed on Seneca's lower half, now a glistening, powerful length of nacre scales and gossamer fins.

"I finally understand," Parker whispered.

"Yes, darling."

"No one back home knows?"

Seneca shook her head. "And this is what you cannot reveal."

"Because you would be hunted," Parker guessed.

"Because we would all be destroyed."

Parker frowned. "I don't understand."

"You will. Later. For now, don't be afraid."

"I'm not," Parker answered sharply, then more gently, "not if we're together."

Seneca's response was to take Parker by the hand and pull her under the waves again. *Let me show you my beautiful world.*

Carmen was on edge. She stared out the back windows of her home and paced and fidgeted while her eyes were drawn again and again to the shallower waters bordering the shoreline north of the public beach. She couldn't shake the feeling something was out there, something she needed to investigate.

Michael stuck his head out of the kitchen doorway. "What are you looking at? Hankering for a swim?"

"Maybe," she responded uncertainly. He came to her side and scanned the same stretch of water she did.

"What do you see?"

"I'm not sure. Something out there calls to me."

Michael silently joined his perceptions to hers. "I don't sense anything. But let's go have a look."

Carmen relaxed into him and smiled. "Don't you have a ton of papers to correct?"

"Yes. And I'd rather swim away."

She laughed, but then frowned as she looked again to the beach. "I hope it's nothing serious . . ."

". . . but it might be," Michael surmised. He squeezed her. "C'mon. Let's check this whatever-it-is out."

They both felt the presence exerting its pull once they were in the water. When they paused to take stock, Carmen silently asked Michael to be vigilant. *I don't think we're in danger, but we should be careful.* Michael agreed.

People were in the water at this hour although so not far out, but she and Michael surfaced discreetly and projected illusions of dolphins to be safe. Although Carmen longed for the security of deeper water, she kept looking toward the beach. *We need to be closer in*, Carmen admitted after several minutes. They swam toward shore.

A hundred yards later she and Michael both locked in on the source of her disquiet: a female siren swimming with a teenage human girl. The water was too murky to see the pair clearly. Carmen called to them.

They turned around, and the siren called out. *Carmen.*

A slow recognition crept through her. She concentrated hard on the adult form swimming her way and resisted the idea forming in her mind, because it felt outrageous. *No. It can't be*, she thought even as her perceptions insisted otherwise. Michael put a hand on her arm and consequently became lost in the throes of the same shocking speculation she was.

When she could no longer negate her sense of conviction, Carmen turned to face her husband. She felt wild and unanchored when she vomited the words, *My mother. Sweet heaven. It's my mother.*

CHAPTER EIGHT

Sylvia leaned on the end pastry case to watch Kate lick sugar glaze from her fingers. She loved seeing people enjoy the goodies she made. "The idea people can't eat their way to happiness is so not true. I mean, just look at you."

"Ha. I can't wait until *you're* the most pregnant thing on the planet," Kate retorted. "I'll be there to push you right off the Cliff of Indulgence, and that's a promise."

Maya carried a tray from the back to replenish the display platters, which had been depleted during the afternoon rush. "Don't listen to her, Sylvia. I've seen Kate's sweet tooth and believe me, this is *not* about her pregnancy."

"Believe me, a constant need for éclairs *is*," Kate countered. She looked forlornly at her empty plate and then at the tray Maya had set on the counter. "Maybe I could just look at another one, maybe smell it." She cast another covetous glance at a particular tray.

Sylvia didn't hesitate to retrieve an éclair for her. She knew these visits were a necessary distraction for Kate from her discomfort; and everyone—even childless friends like her and Maya—took pains to soothe her these days. Maya's presence this week—she'd elected to help out at SeaCakes over her spring break—was giving Kate a much-needed lift.

Kate shifted uncomfortably in her chair and then shifted again, then one more time before glaring at her distended stomach.

She huffed. "Look at me—and by that I mean please *don't*—I'm as big as a barn. And I'm eying up another pastry." She looked sharply at Sylvia. "Don't even *think* about telling me no." Maya snickered.

"Honey," Sylvia admonished. "Like I would do that to you." She set a small plate before Kate and then took the chair opposite her at the café table. Maya remained behind the counter and leaned forward on folded arms.

Kate nodded her approval. "Good call." Her gaze caressed her treat for several seconds. She picked it up, breathed in, bit down, and chewed it reverently. "I'm just going to have to change how I think of myself," she said after she'd swallowed. She kept her eyes on her éclair. "In fact, I've decided to embrace my inner fat chick. I'd much rather eat your doughnuts than be thin."

Sylvia chuckled. "You're not fat. You're due like any minute now. You're just real, real pregnant, girl."

"I'm just real, real huge," Kate groused. "I can't tell you guys how weird it is to outgrow not just your clothes, but your husband's too . . . and then just keep right on growing. I hope I'll shrink back down to something like normal after, but I can't see how I ever will."

Sylvia propped her chin on a hand as she reached across the table with her other to pat Kate's forearm. She'd been one of the evil co-conspirators in getting Kate to wear maternity clothes a few weeks ago when Kate was—inexplicably to her mind—reluctant. Their mothers, Alicia and Cara, had explained things to her.

"She thinks she won't get any bigger—and won't stay as big as she is so long—if she wears 'normal' clothes," Cara had informed her.

Her own mother, Alicia, who had been like a second mother to Kate growing up, concurred. "Pregnancy feels about like alien possession, especially the first time. You have no idea how you're going to feel or look after you've birthed the little darling, and by the end of it you can't even hope for normal again. You just pray you don't look like a beluga although you think you might."

"She'll feel better—and look better too, by the way—if she's comfortable," Cara promised, "and that pretty much means maternity wear." She held out two shopping bags for Sylvia to take. "Would you be willing to suggest, maybe because Kate will be in front of customers at your bakery, she might try these out?" Sylvia had reluctantly agreed.

She'd quickly pawned the job off on Maya, though. She was Kate's best friend, after all, and known as a straightforward, get-'er-done kind of gal. But she could have used a little more diplomacy, Sylvia thought. Maya had simply tossed the bags at Kate's feet and told her, "You look homeless. Wear something that fits."

To everyone's relief Kate hadn't argued. Rather than look hurt or outraged at Maya's callousness, she'd said nothing, just headed calmly to change in the back restroom. When she reappeared looking loads better, she closed her eyes and stuck her hands in front of her to forestall their compliments. "If our moms are bugging you guys about it, they're probably talking to everyone else in town, too. Anyone who'll listen, that is. Can't have that." Kate smiled an apology at Sylvia, completely ignoring Maya. "I'm sorry they put you up to this."

Sylvia brought herself back to the present. "At least you're not having twins like your aunt Dana," she ventured. She rose to take Kate's empty plate back to the kitchen.

Kate brightened at the comment. "She *is* way more enormous than me. Which sadly I dig."

Sylvia checked the clock on the wall. "Uh-oh—we forgot to close. Maya, will you dump the coffee while I lock the door?" Two men walked in as she turned around.

"Sorry guys, but we're closed."

Kate's eyes went round. "Simon?"

"It is," one of the men said. Then gesturing toward Kate's midsection, "And congratulations. I heard you and Gabe finally caught up with each other." He dipped his head toward his brother. "Do you remember Aiden?"

"Sort of. We all hung out on the beach a thousand years ago." She cast a furtive glance toward Sylvia and Maya. "You guys were what, 16 or 17? You're, ah, more tricked out these days . . ."

Good way to put it, Sylvia thought. The two were massively fit.

But she suspected her adrenaline was up for a different reason. The men practically vibrated with a bigger-than-life vitality, and their beauty . . . whoa Nellie. Like maybe they were aliens come to make pets out of them all, but they forgot to add a few imperfections to their person costumes. They were also too intense, too hungry, too appealing; and they activated a kind of implosion in the store—of light, oxygen, sensations and feelings—*everything* gravitated toward them.

Sylvia wanted to give them whatever they wished for, Simon in particular. He stared at her as if she were someone unspeakably dear to him. Her heart stretched in response, a soft ache that deepened with each step he took toward her. He wanted her adoration? He could have it. Her full attention? She was riveted.

A tiny grain of consciousness asserted itself, however, mostly because she feared she looked like a drooling idiot. She got hold of herself enough to peek at Maya, which relieved her some; Sylvia wasn't the only one caught up in the guys' appropriation of the place. Kate babbled earnestly, although nothing she said made a lick of sense. She might as well have been speaking Swahili.

"Since I'm married to one of you Gabe says I've built up 'immunity' and thank goodness because I see what's going on and not to be a nosey parker but I don't think soliciting here is a great idea . . ."

Aside from Kate, however, the entire store seemed caught up in an emotional vortex, with Simon and Aiden at the center of it.

"Are you guys hungry?" she managed, determined to overcome their collective catatonia, or at least pretend to overcome it. Her words came from some buried cache of normalcy she didn't actually feel, and her movements felt mechanical and forced. But she retrieved two small plates. "What can I get you?"

Simon winced . . . and she felt his withdrawal. Ouch. He pushed his glasses up his nose to study offerings in the case. Aiden still stood by the door, clutching the handle, and Sylvia dimly perceived some tortuous exchange underway between him and Maya. She decided she couldn't do anything about Aiden, but she'd make one last grab for control from the guy in front of her. She cleared her throat. "It's Simon, right? I'm Sylvia."

Aiden, whose eyes never left Maya, offered a gritty smile and said, "You can call him Ishmael," which drew a withering look from his brother.

Sylvia tore her attention away from Simon long enough to insist on Maya's help. "Wake. Up," she grated.

Maya's gaze dropped to the floor for several seconds and she addressed Kate. "Ishmael?" she inquired.

Kate, who'd been digging for her phone, answered over her shoulder as she marched toward the door with her cell engaged. "First line in Moby Dick. Look it up. I'm going outside to make a call—back in a sec."

Sylvia returned her focus on Simon. "I have a talent for choosing for people—what will make people happy, I mean. If you want help?" He raised his gaze . . . and she became lost in it once again. She drew a deep breath and held it. "Try the apple fritters," she squeaked.

"Done," Kate said as she re-entered the cafe. "An apple fritter it is. What's Aiden having?" She came to Sylvia's side, shouldered her out of the way and put the plates back on the shelf. She grabbed a to-go bag.

Aiden continued to concentrate on Maya, who had started to perspire. She backed up until she reached the counter behind her, which she gripped with both hands. "Same," he murmured, frowning at Maya's shift away.

Kate dropped two fritters into the sack and slid around the counter to hand them off. "On the house," she announced brusquely as she offered the bag to Simon. He accepted it but barely looked at her, and no one else moved. "Thanks for coming by. Now scoot," she tried, shooing the air with her hands. Still no response. She placed a hand on Simon's forearm. "Simon . . ." she pleaded.

Reluctantly, Simon tore his attention from Sylvia to stare at Kate's hand on his arm. He fisted the bakery bag. "Come on, Aiden. Time to go." He paused before he stepped out, however, and handed the fritters to Aiden. He turned around, his expression pensive as he considered Sylvia again. He walked to stand in front of her, studied her features, and then placed his palms on either side of her face.

Kate's vision dimmed, and black dots floated in front of her eyes before she remembered to breathe again. When she finally inhaled, she sank into a nearby chair, knowing the course of her friend's life was about to alter, and that she was powerless to intervene.

Simon ran his hands lightly down Sylvia's arms to rest at her wrists, frowning in concentration. Sylvia tilted her face toward him and closed her eyes. Kate felt everything vicariously, but time relaxed for her and her sense of worry dissipated. When Simon stepped away from Sylvia, her stare over his shoulder was blank, unfocused. Kate came to her senses more quickly . . . and she wondered what suggestion Simon had made.

Simon retrieved the bag of fritters from Aiden and raised it in farewell. "Thanks for the treats." The door closed behind the two men and several seconds of stunned silence ensued.

"Wow," Maya said. "Those guys were . . . were really something."

Sylvia looked up at her, awareness returning to her features as she frowned at her sister. "What guys?" Which answered Kate's question about what Simon had been up to. He'd wiped her memory. "Oh, brother," Kate muttered.

Maya was incredulous. "Sylvia. Don't be an idiot."

"Drop it," Kate commanded, giving Maya a quelling stare. "It's the heat, or fatigue. Or something. But leave her alone." To Kate's surprise, Maya listened to her, maybe because she felt self-conscious, maybe to placate her because she was pregnant. Kate milked that possibility with the comment they should hurry to get out of there so she could put her feet up. They finished the rest of their closing duties without conversation. Kate and Maya remained agitated. Sylvia, Kate noticed, was calm and smiling.

"Well. That was interesting," Aiden said as they walked away. But he appeared shaken.

"I take it you're into Maya?" Simon asked, trying to sound cavalier, although he was too rattled to pull it off. Aiden didn't respond. He didn't need to—Simon understood too well what his brother felt. After another block Aiden commented, "That was a bad idea." He frowned.

Simon wondered if he should apologize, like he'd done something wrong although he wasn't sure what. He defended himself anyway. "I was just curious. I didn't think things would get out of hand."

Aiden's response lacked conviction. "They didn't exactly. But if we're going to follow orders from on high, we should steer clear of SeaCakes. Or *I'd* better steer clear if Maya's going to be around."

Simon couldn't disagree. "I barely held myself together and all I want to do is go back."

"Yeah. I know." They finished their walk back to Carmen and Michael's in silence and by some miracle didn't return to SeaCakes.

CHAPTER NINE

The presence of a siren stranger in the water—along with the human girl adding to her mystique—attracted sirens from several miles around. Carmen first sensed and then saw everyone congregating as they tracked her, drawn to the same source of tension she was. Their curiosity increased the closer they came, until they were in a frenzy of anticipation. She realized she and Michael contributed to the draw; they had served siren government going on two decades now and their emotional signatures were well known. By now she figured every siren on the Eastern Seaboard knew them by feel as well as by sight.

Seneca was causing the real stir, however, and her familiarity added to the enigma. Once the group reached a closer proximity, some among them offered small recognitions—Carmen caught snippets of conjecture among sirens who'd attended Peter Loughlin's wedding some forty years earlier. But they couldn't have said why this event came to mind, didn't automatically know how to assign their memories.

Her cousin, Lydia, approached in advance of the others. Lydia was worried about her, which Carmen appreciated. She also sensed a commonality with the stranger in their waters, and she couldn't attribute her perceptions, either. But as she got closer to Carmen, awareness dawned. Carmen heard the same fragmented thoughts she did from the others.

. . . decades ago at court . . . a distant royal cousin, I think . . . I remember her from Peter Loughlin's wedding . . . Carmen became even more anxious as the speculations thickened to a deafening level.

I'll take charge of the human girl, Lydia offered, *and I'll ask the others to keep back so you can concentrate.* Carmen thanked her.

With all the drama and excitement agitating their environment, the crowd on the periphery refused to vacate the area, but they did respect Lydia's request to retreat. The human girl also leaked worry— from a fear Carmen would usurp Seneca's affections, and what an odd concern to have. When Lydia led the girl away, her extraneous emanations and the chattering of the siren onlookers cleared enough so Carmen and Seneca could at last focus on each other.

She stopped in front of the woman who had birthed her, and a terrible thrill twisted in her gut. A shimmering recognition hung between them, one they'd both accepted but not yet acknowledged.

Carmen. You're my Carmen.

The spectators twitched forward as they scented the flood of turmoil Carmen and Seneca gave off. Carmen was dimly aware their audience extended their hungry senses toward them, to catch every nuance of the exchange underway, she was sure . . . but she ceased to care.

It's Peter Loughlin's estranged wife! Carmen heard the words ripple through the crowd, and then almost instantly the ocean teemed with a subsequent announcement, one she was too shocked to fully comprehend.

Carmen is Peter and Seneca's daughter!

The knowledge spread with the impact of a high-voltage electric current until the sea around them trembled.

Carmen experienced a thousand things at once, all of them insubstantial and surreal. Lightheaded, she scanned Seneca's features for commonalities first, unwilling to recognize her as her mother until she had something to tie the assertion to. And her inspection helped; she saw herself and her son Gabriel in Seneca's eyes, in the width of her brow.

Acceptance, as weightless and delicate as a butterfly, alit within her, bringing with it a pure, uncomplicated happiness. For the first time in her adult life she knew a biological connection she had coveted in others, something she'd felt incomplete without when she was growing up. It was an elixir she wanted more of, and she searched Seneca's physique and mannerisms for validation. Seneca reached forward to clasp her hands.

Carmen was astonished at the effect this had on her. Her mother's touch. She realized she'd been carrying an obstruction in her heart her whole life, something like a railroad spike hammered in so long she hadn't noticed it was there. Removed, Carmen felt life-giving blood and oxygen flooding into previously dead tissue.

She also knew a growing anger for a betrayal she'd never fully felt until this moment, for never having been claimed by parents who loved her. *How could you?* she whispered, followed by *Why? Why didn't you return for me?*

Her sorrow bled into the surrounding water like a black dye, wrapping everyone within the vicinity in a haze of disquiet. If not for her fragile hope—because her mother wanted to be here, had come here seeking her out—Carmen would have fallen into grief and brought those in attendance with her. As it was, the watching contingent of sirens fidgeted and fretted and hoped for her, and they strained to be closer to the rich drama feeding their senses.

When Seneca's response registered, it obliterated Carmen's emanations with a heavier sadness. Some of the sirens started to keen.

Seneca's decision still tormented her, and Carmen knew the pain she'd borne was the heavier burden between them. *I couldn't stay, and it killed me. Imagine what it would take for you to leave your own child with strangers. Then you'll understand what it was like for me, what I did.* She recalled her remorse freshly now, and an ancient despair dimmed the remaining light around them.

Why? Carmen had to know. *Why did you leave, and why did you come now?*

Seneca's bitterness exploded from her. *I had no choice, Carmen!* And then she recalled the time in her life before Carmen was born, sharing her last agonizing exchange with Carmen's father, then the fear for the future of any child she would birth in the palace. She remembered her terror at the prospect of a solitary, fugitive life but how she forced herself to leave before Peter or Kenna knew of her pregnancy, before Carmen's heartbeat announced her condition. She showed Carmen all she overcame to protect her from the deprivations that had destroyed both her and Peter.

Seneca then recalled sitting on a ledge, one which jutted from the cave she'd chosen to give birth in. She relived the first minutes of Carmen's life, how she'd run her mouth and nose back and forth across her infant's forehead, kissing her and crooning to her, telling her how much she loved her. She looked hard at Carmen when she delivered the memory of handing her over at the orphanage, her despair so intense Carmen attempted to break contact with her. Seneca wouldn't let her.

We cannot afford not to know each other, and I'll wait no longer to be by you. Which means I must tell you what happened.

Oh, but the price for reconnection was high. Seneca's outpouring rubbed like sandpaper on the underside of Carmen's skin until she writhed. Still Seneca would not free her from their exchange. Only after she'd shared the whole of her story did she relax her hold, ending her remembrance on a positive recollection that was no less devastating to Carmen.

It was my greatest joy, naming you. Carmen. My song.

At last her mother had related all, and her sentiments flowed sweetly, like a caress after a beating. Carmen's body spasmed as she reacted to both the anguish over the separation they'd each endured, and then gratitude for the gift of comprehension her mother had delivered. She was aware of the aftershocks of their exchange pulsing through every other siren gathered.

I came because I felt your father's dissolution, Seneca explained at last. *I always thought I'd find him, tell him we had a daughter. But I could never decide how to do it without risking them taking you. I feel wretched he never knew. When he died I had to find you. I had to tell you who you are.*

Carmen was past the ability to express herself in words. But her mother was reaching, wanted to hear Carmen's story from her side, so she shared what she could, concepts and flashes of memories mostly. As she calmed a little, she could recall for her mother a dozen experiences during her childhood with the nuns, their genuine love for her, how they'd cared for her when she was sick, and her many attempts to sneak around their interdiction against the ocean. She reflected on her ignorance and confusion over who and what she was, sharing how very strange and different she was from the other girls and the shame this brought her. All her hypersensitivity, her insuperable obsession with the sea, the 'mind-reading'—she hid her alternative reality from everyone. When she thought of her husband, Carmen became centered enough to form a coherent sentence.

Michael was the one who showed me.

She recalled her first glimpse of him as he and two of his friends rough-housed on the beach. She'd crouched at the top of a hill with her arms around her knees, far enough away to think she was hidden. The distance made his features—and she'd presumed hers as well—indistinct, but Michael had looked directly at her when she focused on him. She'd run back to her room, shaken and sweaty and hungrier than she'd ever been to swim. She didn't sleep for the next four days.

Early on the fifth morning, when the moon was still high and she couldn't survive another minute of her own restlessness, she rose from her bed and left her suite. With something like prescience, she crept through the silent halls without encountering a soul, pausing before the Mother Superior's chambers in a fit of fear she would be stopped.

But she was in the clear. She attuned herself to the life behind the door, heard the steady heartbeat and slow breaths of sleep, and felt no shame over her sensitivity for the first time in memory. She even imagined planting a dream, of a gentle rolling swell far out on the sea, with people like her singing to deepen and extend the woman's slumber. After that she sauntered out the front door.

She had known Michael would be waiting for her in the sea, and she'd entered the water with absolute certainty. He'd come to her, and she transformed the moment they touched.

Michael made everything okay, made everything make sense. I left with him that night.

Her narrative tantalized. Even those who knew a little of Carmen's past became eager for details, but Carmen waved everyone away. *That's a story for another time. I need to hear more from . . . from my mother.*

For the next hour, Seneca shared all she knew—about Carmen's grandparents and other family, and most helpfully about her Illyrian heritage.

When I first transformed and saw myself, I wondered why my skin changed color. No one else's did, Carmen told her. She lifted her hand to touch her mother's face, a deeper hue than her own, and Seneca covered the hand with her own to hold it there.

Did you ever visit them? The Illyrians? Seneca asked.

Never, Carmen replied. *After you left the palace, there were hard feelings, and they retreated back to their old customs of seclusion. No one sees them.*

Carmen felt a struggle within Seneca because of their contact, how the intensity of their connection discomfited her. *I've only recently learned to tolerate touch again,* Seneca explained. *You should know that I was . . . I am . . . broken.*

Carmen was confused. *I sense nothing wrong.* Seneca didn't reply, but shared memories of interactions long ago when she could not engage, communicating her one-time inability to accept and reciprocate emotions. And with this confession, Carmen at last truly understood the impetus behind Seneca's refusal to stay at Shaddox.

Your royal upbringing caused this. Seneca nodded slowly.

By now they were both exhausted, and Carmen suggested they take a break to recuperate. Then she asked Michael to take her home. She was over the worst of her shock but reeling from the cocktail of sensations still racing through her, and she badly wanted insulation from the emotional chatter emanating from the crowd.

The others were persistent, however. She focused unwillingly on their intentions as she turned away. And before she could escape, their newest proclamation covered her like a cage.

The word 'queen' was suggested lightly at first, vague and pungent and insubstantial for all of two seconds before everyone grabbed onto it like a lifeline. Even Michael succumbed.

Carmen. You were Peter's only offspring.

The unwanted awareness washed through her, of what they now wanted from her and the implications this run-in with her mother might have. She retreated from the group, sick with the idea she had just lost herself. *No. You cannot think . . .* she began. But they *did* think.

She would not stay still to negotiate this issue, to say she might be the one to save them all from uncertainty. Not when the idea felt like it might kill her. She didn't even care if everyone was right. Without a word, she twisted away from the gathering, propelling herself in one powerful thrust toward the murky waters further offshore.

Michael let her go. *She'll return,* he promised everyone. Then he waved away the onlookers, telling a few to go to the palace, find Xanthe and report what they'd seen. He invited Seneca to follow him to the house. *She just needs time,* he assured her. *We'll figure everything out when she comes back.* He then accompanied the remaining entourage—

Lydia and Parker included—to the house where everyone dispersed to rest.

Late that afternoon, Michael met Seneca, Parker and Lydia in the kitchen where they began to pull together a meal. He asked Lydia to play hostess while he saw to Carmen, which Lydia was happy to do. She enlisted Parker's help to keep the girl occupied and, Michael suspected, to manage the anxiety the girl felt.

He called Xanthe, who had by then learned of the day's developments from one of the witnesses. Consequently his question was short and to the point: Carmen was Peter's daughter, and did that mean she was next in line for the throne?

"She is," Xanthe stated. She asked how Carmen was coping.

"I'm not sure. She swam off . . . and I can feel her unease."

Xanthe sighed. "Well, yes, of course. That's a pretty big shock." She promised to come as quickly as possible. "Would you please call Gabriel and ask him to come as well?" Michael promised to gather everyone for an impromptu summit.

Kate stared at her phone for a full minute after hanging up with her father-in-law, wondering if she'd heard him correctly. Gabe needed to meet at their house to discuss Carmen's ascension to the siren throne? He'd said Gabe's future—and hers, for that matter—were now on the table because of royal succession laws.

She must have misheard.

But then no one would make something like that up. She called Gabe on his cell.

"Honey, did you just ignore a call from your dad?"

"Yeah. I was in class, but I stepped out when I saw it was you. Everything okay?" Kate knew he expected her to go into labor, and although he disliked talking on the phone—or rather what he called the pseudo-intimacy of wire-talk—he answered promptly when she called these days.

"Well . . ." Kate floundered, wondering how to best relay what she considered outrageous news. Ending with the realization Peter, i.e. Gabe's *grandfather*, had kidnapped her last year, which made both his obsession with her and Gabe's mortal fight with him all the more bizarre.

But her hesitation made Gabe anxious. "What is it?" he insisted. Kate decided to deliver the news unadorned.

"Apparently your mom being adopted and all . . . well, see, her biological mother found her today, and it's someone named Seneca Loughlin?" She paused when she heard Gabe suck in his breath.

"Seneca *Loughlin?* Are you *sure* you heard that name right?"

"Pretty sure," Kate confirmed. "Just got off the phone with Michael. He's called a summit with Xanthe at your parents' house. I take it you understand why."

"Yeah. And wow. Here I was thinking it was something little, like you're about to have our baby. Who, by the way, will literally be a prince."

Kate didn't know how to respond to such an assertion, so she didn't. Her questions hung silent and oppressive between them.

"Seneca was Peter's wife. Remember, the one who was too emotionally broken to hold up her end of the deal, went nuts and took off?"

Kate sank back in her chair, the import of today's events finally dawning on her. "I thought she died," she said dully.

"We all thought that." He blew out a breath. "Look, class is just out. I'll be there in a couple hours, pick you up and we'll head to my folks'."

Kate hesitated. "I don't think I should be party to a high-level siren government meeting, Gabe."

"If they're discussing our family and royal titles and where we're going to live, you should be there, Kate."

"Ah. I see. Come get me then and we'll go face the music." She hoped she sounded unruffled, but her mind reeled. "I mean we just got our little life back . . ."

Gabe's voice softened. "It'll be okay, honey. I promise"

Kate smiled. "We'll figure it all out, right?"

"Yes. Yes we will."

CHAPTER TEN

Duncan Fleming knew he'd enjoyed his role as interim head of government too much because he didn't want to give it up. Not ever. The more time he spent immersed in policymaking—and more specifically, mandating policy—the more certain he was this was the job for him, no matter what the transitional committee recommended. He'd been viceroy to the recently deceased queen and her son and had, in his opinion, shouldered the biggest governmental load ever. He had soldiered on better than anyone else could have, had run the entire siren bureaucracy perfectly.

He was young for a viceroy, just sixty; but then his youth had also factored into his initial invitation to join the palace staff thirty years earlier. He was chosen then and appreciated now for the modern perspective he brought to government affairs, a function of his age as well as his experience with human politics. Duncan cut his professional teeth first as a student in the human university system— *not* in biology but political science and consequently *not* with other sirens—and then as an aide to a prominent U.S. senator. Along with the Blake family, which represented the siren community's most visible foot forward in the human world, Duncan was among a select group who had navigated the murky universe where human and siren ideologies overlapped. This endeavor had enhanced his image with other sirens both inside and outside his government.

He further elevated his standing with the exploration and then adoption of technologies few in his world wanted any part of. Sirens were among the last societies on earth to embrace telephones, because they distrusted the physical distance accompanying communication on such devices. The advent of computers, cell phones and other remote communications technologies had no place in the intimate discourse that formed the basis of siren interaction, they believed. In fact, in the little his people collectively studied humans, they saw justification for their distaste; although touted as a means to stay connected, too often individuals in the physical company of friends or family engaged in their electronics, choosing to text remote friends instead of converse with real ones. Such practices were abhorrent to sirens because they diluted the richer, more substantive interactions on which they thrived.

Duncan understood—he was a siren after all—but he craved the advancement new technologies afforded. He didn't deny the emotional distancing problem, but he'd urged his colleagues to adopt several practices anyway for efficiency purposes. "I suggest we use the technologies as their manufacturers recommend, which is to facilitate business, not replace personal relationships." And with a great deal of revulsion and a few hard-core dissenters, his recommendations were slowly integrated.

His marriage to Isabel tempered the unpopularity his pro-technology stance created. She also completed his appearance of viability for higher office because she was from an old, traditional family and a comforting presence to those who disliked the extent to which Duncan mimicked human behaviors. Isabel and her family eschewed contact with humans according to the beliefs of most sirens in their milieu, where interactions were a little feared and as a precaution avoided. Isabel counterbalanced Duncan's modern-only sensibilities and softened his political image into something more comfortable for broader siren society.

He knew of no precedent for a vice regent taking the throne. Canada, where a proxy monarch eventually assumed political leadership, had flirted with the concept, although the outcome there had been a representative government where elected officials replaced the royals, and titles such as "King" went by the wayside.

Duncan was gunning for more pomp and circumstance. He remained romantically attached to the ceremony of it all—the robes, the crowns and other showy adornments of an actual throne-sitter. He thought governing without these trappings would have all the charm and personality of an actuarial job.

Best of all, his siren subjects agreed on the value of having a regent around. Xanthe and the transition committee's inquiry had confirmed his people preferred ritual and ceremony to argumentative, divisive elections. From the committee's standpoint, the trick now was to comply with succession laws, since the next in line to the throne suffered from dementia and the heir after him was still a baby.

But. At least the community would not make the mistake humans had, chucking all their beautiful traditions for base and flavorless political ideals. Duncan worried a little over the decision to incorporate *some* elements of democratic rule although, as Xanthe had suggested, "There's no reason it can't be pretty."

Duncan wanted to command the link between the old ways and new, and he hoped his recent accomplishments would help him transcend the small matter of succession protocol, where ruling preference went only to the genetically designated.

He had reason to be hopeful, he believed. He'd often reached outside the norm even as a child, in a way his parents had found worrisome but inspiring, too. His interests had consistently veered toward the not-exactly mainstream, usually as a device for avoiding his humiliating lack of competency in athletics. Hard as he tried, he'd shown no talent for physical contests, and human entertainments provided an alternative to this insufficiency. He'd started out with mystery novels and nonfiction works covering historical naval battles or political intrigue. When the electronics industry came out with software games that let him build cities and move armies and blow things up when he was frustrated . . . well, he'd thought nothing could be more wonderful.

His parents had let him go his own way, concluding he had an independent streak no one understood, themselves included. A desperate, manic light came over his mother's face when she described him to neighbors; how independent he was, how agile his mind. He was destined for greatness. They condoned his quirky education—political science was not considered true science—for the same reasons. Duncan stated early on he wanted to be among people

of influence, hoped to wield it himself some day, and his mother and
father released him to his ambition without censure.

CHAPTER ELEVEN

Xanthe arrived at Michael and Carmen's well after everyone else, which gave those who'd come earlier a chance to discuss the afternoon's events more casually. Kate noticed the resemblance between Carmen, Gabe and Seneca right away, and it softened the perceived havoc Seneca had wreaked on Kate's personal life. She was so clearly related, not just physically but also according to something less easy to define—her mannerisms, maybe, or how she talked. But she was one of them, and within minutes of watching her converse with Gabe, Kate thought of her as one of the gang.

Parker, on the other hand, struggled with the day's developments. Kate understood her concerns from talking with Lydia, who'd shared how she feared over her adopted status with a "real" daughter now on the scene. Kate sympathized, perhaps because she'd lost her father at a young age and had suffered the emotional instability of a similar childhood tragedy.

When Xanthe entered the room, all chatter ceased, and the gathering took on the solemnity of an impending funeral. Carmen looked like that was her take. Each couple shifted to some unspoken hierarchical position without being asked; Carmen, Michael, Gabe and Kate stood closest to Xanthe, while and Seneca, Parker, Cara and

John made up the next tier. The rest of the attendees hung back by the walls.

Gabe appeared to take everyone's measure before whispering in her ear, "I'm glad Seneca came back. But I don't want to move." Xanthe answered him as if he'd addressed the whole group.

"And yet all of us here will have to make concessions. You will be expected to accommodate and adapt along with everyone else."

Gabe stood tall. "I already delayed going to medical school once because of our," and he gestured around him, "royalty problems."

"No," Xanthe disagreed. "You delayed because Kate was taken from you. You would have gone after her regardless of who took her."

"Well. Sure. But no one other than our prince could have kidnapped her, or succeeded in hiding her as long as he did, and it was because of his position. So the issue isn't independent."

"You're arguing semantics," Xanthe said irritably. "The immediate issue is Seneca's return and how it will influence succession to the throne."

Carmen placed a hand on Gabe's shoulder before speaking up. "I understand Gabe's concerns, Xanthe, because if we define succession according to tradition, the monarchy will come first to me and then him. And that has implications for his family."

Kate found Xanthe's regard toward them more sympathetic this time. "Yes, but he assumes the designation will require him to forego the life he envisions, which isn't true. Let's talk about the monarchy first and we'll get to what comes next. Neither Gabe and Kate nor you and Michael need to give up life as you know it." Gabe and Kate exchanged looks of relief.

Michael cleared his throat. "I researched the question of succession again for tonight's meeting, and the description was pretty clear. Carmen is queen by function of lineage, straight up. Do you think there's any other way to look at this, Xanthe?"

"No," she answered. "Not according to everything I've read, and not as we've decided to treat the monarchy moving forward. You and John were on the same committee I was, Michael. You heard the rationale for dissolving the institution and shifting to a democracy. The community has no appetite for any change in how we govern."

"Right. We talked more in terms of removing the more oppressive customs—to protect the aristocracy from the isolation driving its members to desperate acts. I think this still needs to be addressed."

Xanthe addressed Carmen. "Do you dispute your claim to the throne?"

"I don't," Carmen said slowly, "although I have the same reservations Michael has. But I know the existence of the monarchy holds more than superficial value." She smiled at her husband. "I'd also like to point out how keeping the crown because our community wants it is a democratic decision in and of itself."

Xanthe appeared satisfied. "Good. At least we agree on premise. Now we just need to go over the details, starting with residency. How do you two feel about ruling from Shaddox?"

Michael and Carmen regarded each other when Carmen answered. "I think we should move, conduct our business from the palace, where the king and queen have always lived. I love my home, but Shaddox is set up for governing, with systems and staff and a thousand other things, security included." She offered everyone a sad smile. "Although we have done our fair share of facilitating from here."

Michael discreetly clasped her hand. "It wouldn't make sense to stay here." He said to Xanthe, "But thank you for considering that option for us."

"Which brings us to the question of where you two will live," Xanthe said, facing Gabe and Kate.

"We three," Kate rejoined quietly.

"While I attend medical school," Gabe added.

"Of course." Xanthe smiled. "I mean you and your family, including your children, and while Gabe completes his degree. Would you be interested in moving here and taking over?" She asked this question the same way she might have suggested sandwiches for lunch or recommended they try the lemonade. "If you need to think about it, fine. But I can see such a situation working out well for all concerned, you included."

Gabe's expression was pained. "I don't know we would be the best choice for . . ."

"You would be centrally located, Gabe, but not at the community's beck and call," Xanthe reminded him. She included Kate in her brief smile. "Please remember how your parents managed independent lives while also performing diplomatic work."

The first thing Kate thought of was Carmen's astrological

mapping and its attendant matchmaking commitment, which she felt woefully under-qualified to take on. Because she was tucked into Gabe's side and they were holding hands, he read her concern in an instant.

"Would those duties include hosting meet-and-greets for potential mates?" he inquired. He looked to his mother. "And although Kate is intuitive for a human, I don't think we can saddle her with charting for our people." Kate released her gratitude like a blast of heat. "Thank you," she whispered fervently.

Xanthe ignored her. "You would be unable to chart?" she asked Gabe.

"Ah . . . no. Just . . . no." Gabe shuddered. "I've never studied how, so I don't have the training. Or aptitude. Or any interest whatsoever."

His mother frowned disapprovingly at him but took the responsibility off the table with her next comment. "I'll continue charting," she asserted, "although I wouldn't mind training someone else to take over." She glanced speculatively at Seneca. "As for the matchmaking events, I believe Kate and Gabe could and should do that part."

"Excellent," Xanthe said, ignoring the gasps of protest from the newly elected. Michael gave his son a warning look. "Be grateful you're not being dispatched to South America or something, Gabe. This way you'll have your families around you to help with the baby, and you can finish your program in Chapel Hill."

Kate capitulated first, offering those gathered her reluctant acceptance. "Fine. We'll do it."

"I suppose," Gabe said with a grimace. Xanthe beamed as if her new recruits were eager.

"Your lack of enthusiasm will only make the work unpleasant for you and negatively impact the success of your gatherings," she advised. "You'd be well served to adopt a more positive approach." She turned toward the rest of the group. "We should send out a formal announcement concerning Carmen's succession. The coronation will take place in a month."

Carmen's eyes widened in alarm. "Four weeks to leave here and move to Shaddox? And you realize, don't you, that I have no idea how to be queen?"

Xanthe's brusque demeanor softened in an instant. "You are my longtime friend, Carmen. I couldn't ask for a better person, a better family, to lead us right now. And you're going to be a wonderful queen."

Xanthe left first, citing urgent obligations at Shaddox. Gabe and Kate were next as Kate could no longer smother her yawns. John and Cara departed to collect their son, Everett, from Jeremy and Alicia's house; and finally Seneca and Parker excused themselves after Seneca saw Parker literally swaying on her feet from fatigue.

Michael and Carmen refilled their champagne flutes—they'd enjoyed several well-meaning toasts to their success after Xanthe's final pronouncement—and meandered to the porch swing at the back of the house, where they sat to sip and gaze at the stars and the ocean.

"I wonder how many more evenings like this we'll have," Carmen remarked.

"Not many, I'm sure. How are you?" Michael asked.

Carmen laughed sadly. "I have no idea. I can't decide if the whole situation is momentous or absurd."

"It might be a little absurd. But in a way the changes will only be as serious as we make them. I mean we'll take things one step at a time, and I think we'll find as we go we're still us, still living the life we want."

"One can hope." Carmen leaned against him and considered the sea. Its infinite expanse, along with her husband's steady presence, calmed her.

"You're right, of course," she said after a while. "We're just a regular old queen and her consort, assuming rule after a routine suicide took out the last monarch. No need to get all excited."

Michael chuckled and stroked her hair. "See, that's the way to go at this," he said. "Use your humor like that and you'll have everyone eating out of your hand."

She frowned. "I just hope I don't screw everything up." She took another sip from her glass and shared her next opinion with more confidence. "Our society is becoming more complex, and interactions with humans more of a factor. None of us can predict all changes coming."

"If it weren't humans, it would be something else, Carmen. And that you recognize it speaks well for you already." He craned away to see her face. "You know you won't be going it alone, right? You will have many, many good people to help you."

"You being one of them," Carmen replied. She remained quiet again for a few minutes before muttering, "But I know we can do this."

"We *can* do this," Michael confirmed. "You're going to be great."

"Well, whatever the outcome, I *will* do it. And I promise to give it my very, level best effort."

"Then you have nothing to worry about."

She snuggled further into his side and contemplated the waves, the sky, and the soft roar of an ocean that was the cradle and wilder home of their people. As they swayed in the swing, she allowed the familiar vista to center her, and when she felt ready, rose and pulled Michael up with her by the hand. She led them silently to the guesthouse by the pier, closing only the screen door. She opened the windows on her way to the bedroom so she could fall asleep with a breeze caressing her skin and the sound of the water around her.

CHAPTER TWELVE

Duncan was livid. How could they, after all he'd done, so casually inform him his services as head of the siren government were no longer needed? And to make way for the likes of Carmen Blake no less, who he regarded as a glorified fortune teller. *She* was to be crowned ruler? The idea was ludicrous. She either suffered from extreme ignorance or hubris, probably both, if she thought she could fill his shoes. As far as he knew, Carmen had spent her adult life as a stay-at-home mom and erstwhile technical writer. Oh, and she was the community's head matchmaker. He guffawed. Anyone, in Duncan's opinion, could do what she did. No one, her least of all, could make the gears of their government turn as he could, not as they needed to.

Gabriel Blake's insertion into the equation concerned him, too, as he was basically just out of diapers and equally unqualified to have an opinion on matters of state. Much less participate. Also, Gabe was a behavioral wild card, evidenced by the killing revenge he demonstrated in his fight with Peter Loughlin a few short months ago. Duncan emitted a humorless laugh as he wondered how Gabe felt when he learned he'd murdered his own grandfather.

Maybe murder was too strong a word, as Peter didn't actually succumb to injuries Gabe inflicted. But still. The two were engaged in mortal combat, and Gabe would have ended him if he could have. Duncan grit his teeth, disgusted with every component of the news he'd just been given.

He surveyed his office with all its updated appointments and technology enhancements. He alone among the ruling class—among all his people if he thought about it—understood the value of connectivity, of building a competent technological infrastructure within the palace. He wondered if the new regime would dismantle everything. Probably, the cretins.

He certainly couldn't stay here any longer, not in this frame of mind and seething with scorn and outrage toward the person who was to be his new boss. If anyone ventured near him right now, he'd be ejected out the door before the Blake team left the mainland, and then what would he have for career options?

No. He would give himself some time away to either come to terms with the new situation or create an out for himself, preferably one where he could keep a modicum of influence and power. He penned a note to Xanthe: he was overwrought from his responsibilities and taking a leave. He promised to call without specifying when. Oh, and good luck with the transition. He sealed the note, left it for the courier and began packing for a trek inland. The ocean was no place for him now, not if he wanted to hide his anger.

He fretted for several minutes over how to handle the challenge of human interaction, which he still struggled to withstand despite his years at an inland university and in Washington. He never became adept—was certainly never comfortable—with non-sirens, and he feared human encounters would trouble him as much as they ever had. In the past he'd had his wife nearby to support him . . . on his own, he consistently skated on the edge of freakishness, too overcome to engage "normally," and he never did achieve the graceful social image he strove for.

He rummaged in a cabinet along the wall for his personal items and came across a small digital music player. One of his coworkers had given it to him following the successful install of a palace-wide wireless system he'd fought for with reluctant support from his staff. The gift was given tongue in cheek, delivered with the decree that since he was their technology guru he should own the latest personal devices, too. No one, including himself, saw the appeal of a contraption plugging your ears and cutting you off from everyone else in the room.

Now Duncan speculated how he could put the player to good use. Even if he were to wear only one of the ear buds, the distraction might let him disengage enough to avoid over-absorption in a conversation, maybe forestall the catatonia he fought against in human company or take the edge off his intensity. He tucked the device into his travel sack.

As an afterthought, he left Isabel a message. He hadn't informed her of his day-to-day plans in a very long time, decades perhaps. But he needed to leave the water for a while to nurse his grudges and he didn't know how long he'd be away. He'd look better if he informed his wife.

He got her voice mail, thank God. "Isabel, it's me. They've found a blood heir to the throne . . . and I can't stay and watch. I'm going to take some time off, get out of here. I'll be in touch."

"How'd it go?" Carmen asked Xanthe when she returned from the palace. "Anyone else as shocked as I was we still have a Loughlin or two running around?"

"It went well," Xanthe said brightly. Carmen thought she equivocated and raised an eyebrow. "Okay almost everyone was happy. Grateful our traditions will live on."

"Almost?"

"Just . . . except for the viceroy. Do you remember Duncan Fleming?"

"I've never spent much time with him, but we're acquainted."

"He's done a wonderful job running things since the Peter and Kenna debacle," Xanthe continued, "and he's got an impressive record of service to the crown . . ."

"But?"

"He was not pleased," Xanthe confessed. "I think he's been too immersed in the emergency of the situation . . . and he doesn't believe a lay person, someone who hasn't been part of governing this past year, can step in."

Carmen's laugh was humorless. "I respect that. I actually agree with him."

"Now-now," Xanthe reproved. "You're going to do just fine. If I didn't believe in you, I would not support our plan. You know that."

"I suppose," Carmen mused, although she didn't agree at all. "But you have to admit scads of people are more qualified. And I really don't look forward to making an idiot of myself in public. I don't blame Duncan for his lack of confidence."

"He's right to care so deeply about our government," Xanthe said sharply. "He is wrong to judge the direction we're taking."

"Should I remove him?"

"Maybe. But not yet. He was extremely disappointed—I felt more than a little anger from him, too—but I respect the job he's done. We should give him a chance to come around." Her expression belied her lack of confidence. "I believe he will."

"We'll table the issue for now, then," Carmen concluded. "He sounds like he could help me, so I'd prefer his support."

"I think that's wise. And I think you'll be able to work together."

CHAPTER THIRTEEN

Sylvia opened the gate to Carmen and Michael's back yard to retrieve Soley. She took him with her each morning at Carmen's insistence, "as a protection against ruffians and sea monsters," she'd joked. Sylvia had never felt unsafe walking alone and was in no way inclined to give up her peaceful, solitary jaunts by the water. But Carmen was adamant, at first asking her not to go at all, which she'd refused to do. Instead, she ended up with the dog.

Soley jumped so his paws landed on Sylvia's stomach, a habit nobody had tried seriously to break him of. Sylvia didn't deter him, either, scratching behind his ears, feeding him bits of bacon, and cooing over him for being such a good boy. His indiscriminate appetite for attention—not just from friends and family, but from strangers and disinterested passersby too—pretty much negated his value as a protector in Sylvia's opinion, although lately she suspected Carmen might be right about those sea monsters.

"You're one rotten guard dog," Sylvia scolded.

She connected Soley's leash before giving him a final scrub on his neck and leading him out the gate. Her anticipation rose the closer they got to the ocean.

The character of these walks had altered over the past three weeks and she didn't know why. Maybe she was more worried about work than she realized? She'd always daydreamed on these strolls, but she'd finish them alert and inspired. No longer. Now she left the beach each morning anesthetized, her senses sluggish and mind distracted well into the afternoon. And the catharsis she achieved relied not on introspection, but on bits of hallucination, usually centered on a picture she imagined of a landless ocean, with her lost in it feeling . . . what, exactly? Something like longing, except it made her happy.

Once back at work, her saline preoccupations stayed with her until evening and fragmented her attention span in a way others—Kate especially—had noticed. Sylvia didn't care. She still hurried from her bed each morning to chase her fantasy and hope this time more would be revealed. She stopped for a conch shell at the edge of the surf, put it to her ear and smiled.

From the water Simon heard Soley bark and dimly sensed the human presence with him. By design, he was too far from shore for a stronger sense of her. He stopped swimming, however, and examined the tickle of compulsion he felt, permitting his senses to reach toward Sylvia in what felt like a full-on tease.

He should leave well enough alone today but he wouldn't. He turned toward land and propelled himself steadily, stealthily toward shore.

At this pre-dawn hour, the beach was deserted save for the object of his desire and her dog. Simon entered the shallows, careful not to splash or draw attention to himself. When he was near enough to get caught—she could have seen him had she looked over her shoulder—he poked his head above the surface.

He followed Sylvia here every day in spite of his attempts to drive himself too far from shore to catch her, an effort he made each morning that never worked. Even if he was too far away to feel her presence, he knew she'd be here and he always turned around.

And he knew she looked for him, or rather evidence of him. So far, he'd been careful to avoid direct interaction. So far.

He dropped back a dozen yards, a small stand against his troublesome fascination. What an idiot, because here he still was. He choked on a laugh, which caused both Sylvia and the dog to stop and look his way just after he ducked down again. Oh, he was really pushing it now. He should just breach and say something like, "Hey! Look! Siren, over here!" Sylvia's hopeful expression faded and she resumed her walk.

He knew staying to engage her was as good as pursuing her, which objectively he did not want to do. He surveyed his convictions for more evidence he shouldn't be here and found it; he *didn't* want a commitment right now, no matter how terrific Sylvia's appeal.

He still kept right on following.

Okay. No need to assume the worst here. No one else was around, and he didn't *have* to feel trapped. In fact, given his flawless record on the marriage avoidance front to date he had nothing to worry about.

So he wouldn't worry. Maybe he could even play a little, as long as he kept to the water and she kept out of it.

Yes. He'd stay, just with him immersed and her on the sand. He could satisfy his curiosity and then leave.

Bad idea. He should leave *now*.

He headed away from her but stopped after only a few seconds. He felt another trace of longing—hers, not his—which proved harder to dismiss. Why did she have it? He turned back. Again.

He could do this if he was careful, he reasoned, moving as close as he dared, whereupon his thoughts, increasingly sabotaged by Sylvia's sweet, unwitting summons, became a slippery slope of rationalizations. He realized his actions could have only one outcome but disregarded his pesky internal warnings.

Of course I feel drawn to her, he thought. Humans have always been irresistible to sirens, and he was a siren. Nothing more to it than that. *Keep justifying*, he told himself. *Another ten minutes of this and you'll be on your knees holding up a ring.*

But apparently he was staying. And he didn't *have* to take her swimming, and at least she was alone. The risk was minimal, really . . . He thought no more about leaving. He could control the situation, he believed. He hoped.

He swam alongside her from twenty feet out, taking care to stay outside her field of vision. The more he watched and felt her, the more compelling he found her. He inched closer with each stroke and noticed the blossoming of a kind of euphoric frenzy within him the nearer he got. At some point he caught the scent of vanilla . . . and he yearned for her so strongly his heart seized.

Vanilla and human and salty air wafted his way again, and his eyes rolled back in his head as pleasure blanketed him. This must be why people give up their freedom to couple up.

He became less careful now, willing her to turn around and see him. She didn't, but . . . screw it. He wanted to flirt.

He swam until the underside of his tail brushed sand and his topside broke the water's surface. Soley barked excitedly, and Sylvia stopped walking. Simon gave the dog a silent command to return home, which worked flawlessly. Soley made off at a dead run toward the Blakes'.

Sylvia didn't appear to notice Soley's departure, instead approaching the edge of the tide and scanning the section of water he occupied. "Hello?" she called. "Is someone there?" Simon felt a predatory thrill of anticipation.

He wasn't about to answer honestly, of course; he did *not* want to suffer any repercussions from Xanthe or her ilk over his antics this morning. So he worked to deepen her reverie, locating the seam in her consciousness between awareness and meditation and loosening the laces. Which worked beautifully. Despite her quick step backwards (To leave? He couldn't think of anything more awful . . .), her face was alight with hope.

Just a harmless sea dude, come to check you out, he offered.

Her attention to where he swam became absolute, her affinity for him a flower unfurling under a warm sun. Which hit him from head to toe like an opiate wash that took away his desire for independence in just one rinse.

I keep thinking about you.

Oh, God, she was too darling. But her allure was about to pull him onto the beach, which was such a no-no.

At least she believed him to be a dream, meaning he could still proceed under the illusion of autonomy, if only out of habit. She took a deliberate step toward the waves, and he panicked.

Stop!

She did, although she appeared to disapprove of the idea. Still, he couldn't afford to let her enter the water, not if he wanted to stay out of trouble. Because if she was this addictive on land, he'd lose his mind in the intensity of the ocean, might haul her off somewhere more private. Or worse, accidentally drown her. So, no.

He made an emergency foray into her mind, easing apart the last of where outer awareness and inner contemplation met. He felt her focus shift internally and watched her inch back from the surf, albeit reluctantly. Still, she maintained that crucial separation of the elements and kept her feet dry. She began a slow-paced stroll again, following the meandering pattern formed by the tide to stay just at the water's edge. Simon swam slightly behind her and tried to make the most of her hypnosis. He asked her about herself.

She was the middle sister of three in the Wilkes family, and shyer than her siblings, who she thought were amazing. By comparison, Sylvia had felt little in the way of personal accomplishment growing up, sandwiched as she was between Solange the raving beauty and super student; and Maya the athlete extraordinaire who was also wicked smart. She loved to bake, to make something sweet and satisfying for people who came to her cafe. She said she had a secret ability to guess what someone needed and provide it to them. Her goal was for them to leave happy.

You're talking about more than giving someone a treat, Simon observed.

"Yes. I feel like what I do is make people feel comforted and loved. That's my true intention, I think. Not just to rock the texture of my pastries and cakes, which I also do." Her smile was so bright it hurt. She became thoughtful again before going on. "The goodies are the delivery mechanism."

That's beautiful. You make me want to eat for you. His tone grew sly. *What would you give me?* Like he didn't already know.

She focused on him . . . and he felt her intuition, felt her skill. She did have the very talent she described; her thoughtfulness reached into him, found the hint she sought, and then before she withdrew she planted an expectation of pleasure like a born enchantress. He'd met sirens less intuitively competent.

"You should try my apple fritters," she suggested.

He had to laugh. *Yes. Yes, I should.*

He wanted to stay here and talk with her all day, but she'd be late if he kept her any longer. He steeled himself against regret, to remove her memory of him, which he could hardly make himself do . . . and when he couldn't quite accomplish it, he realized he would need to touch her. How was he going to pull that off? He wouldn't be able to make himself swim away. He tried again from where he was. No go.

And here he'd been doing so well; he hadn't left the water, hadn't even really appeared to her except as a swirl on the surface of the ocean.

Sylvia, stay there. I'll come to you.

She stilled. He made himself think of something other than what he was about to do: the bright, teal-green underside of an iceberg and the swirl of snow in a harsh wind on the Antarctic plain, like an eddy of sand . . . and he touched the tops of her feet. Oh, she would be lovely to hold. With desperate focus on the slide show running in his head, he instructed her not to see him, and to forget him, or at least forget their time together this morning. He felt this last hour fade into her subconscious and almost wept. But he'd done what he wanted, and he'd kept his promise to Xanthe. Due to an absolute miracle he couldn't explain, he jettisoned himself away and swam like a missile toward deep water.

He didn't know how Xanthe and the Blakes interacted and touched humans and appeared normal.

He was a mess of competing resolves, but he no longer lied to himself about skipping Sylvia's sunrise stroll. He knew he'd be back tomorrow for her. Simon pushed himself further from shore and fought hard to reaffirm his former convictions about women and the independent future he envisioned for himself. Maybe he could expend his fascination in the next encounter or the one after that . . . Far away from the attraction she wielded at close range, Simon could believe she would exert no lasting hold.

Well, he almost believed.

"As for me, I am tormented by an everlasting itch for things remote. I love to sail forbidden seas, and land on barbarous coasts."

– from *Moby Dick*, Herman Melville

PART TWO

CHAPTER FOURTEEN

Duncan was convinced they'd sent someone after him. They must have. He'd left weeks ago, and by now Xanthe would know he'd gone . . . wouldn't she? He'd never worked closely with her—she'd once thanked him for being so competent she hardly needed to check in, which had been true. The Loughlin suicides had taken her away from the palace almost constantly in the past year, hence his solo heroics running their government. He also presumed Carmen's myriad inadequacies required a lot from the community's senior advisor, so she'd certainly been in Griffins Bay much of this time, propping up her neophyte . . . so *maybe* she was unaware of his departure?

But he'd left abruptly and without reassurances, nor did he promise to return. In fact he'd left without talking to anyone, so by now, someone at the palace must have started wondering. If he were Xanthe, he would have dispatched a sleuth.

Which posed a risk he couldn't afford to take yet; he was still disgusted, furious even, with the decision to replace him. And he still needed to bolster his efforts here.

He spent a lot of time scanning passersby.

He checked first to see if anyone made a study of him, and then searched for words like 'treason'' and phrases like 'banish the feckless bastard' in whatever he could catch of people's thoughts. The constant vigilance exhausted him, but he was all alone out here and had to look out for himself. And he wanted to know right away if another siren hunted him.

Of course, if the follower could cloak he might not clue in, although to his knowledge sirens couldn't completely hide from each other, Peter Loughlin being the exception. Peter was thankfully dead, though; and the only other legitimate cloaker he knew was Gabe . . . whose cloaking abilities had been strong enough, but he doubted Xanthe would have sent someone so erratic and untried.

Would she have sent a human?

No. He'd see through a human in an instant, as she would know. So. Maybe they had taken him at his word, assumed he needed a break and was simply taking one. *Maybe.* Duncan browsed his surroundings again and, as usual, intuited nothing. For the first time in several days, he allowed himself to relax.

He wasn't unhappy with his progress. He'd made his way inland—going far enough to deter casual visits from his sea-dwelling brethren—and practiced his siren's call to build an interim community. He found he was rusty at socializing with humans, something he'd struggled with when he'd lived among them but now seemed to have lost the facility for altogether. He attracted easily enough, but lacked the ability to engage his new fans in the casual way he wanted, so they would accept him as one of their own. He wanted to feel part of, not like a freak attraction at a carnival.

The music player and ear bud in one ear helped from his side of the social equation; it divided his focus so he was not completely absorbed in the people he tried to interact with. Consequently, it cut down on his catatonia, and this meant he responded quicker to their questions and comments. He also learned by reading the humans he spoke with that it minimized the hungry intensity of his stare, which helped normalize his affect, as well.

It didn't negate all of the antisocial cues he gave off, however. His paranoia over being followed, for instance, made him appear shifty, and he worked to control his urge to skulk and constantly look around and behind him. He decided he needed an additional distraction, one to divert humans not just soften his own tendency toward fixation and speechlessness.

He chose smoking.

He couldn't really smoke—no siren could. Their bodies simply refused to allow inhalation of anything so dirty into their lungs. But he found he could hold a lit cigarette, wave the glowing tip as he gestured in conversation, and effectively confuse the more off-putting signals he exhibited.

Part of smoking's appeal was the shock factor; many couldn't believe he indulged in such a politically incorrect habit, and so casually. He never asked if he could light up or if his smoke bothered someone, which he knew insulted many of the folks he met. In fact distaste often overrode fascination and more than a few retreated in the first few minutes, which was fine by Duncan. He was just separating the wheat from the chaff, he believed, and those who disregarded their misgivings to engage with him were susceptible, suggestible. Those were the people he wanted more from.

"You, Julian, show promise," he'd told the most vulnerable, tenaciously adoring fan he attracted. "A technology and business professional, you say? I may have an opportunity for you. Stop by my office tomorrow if you want to talk." He handed the young man his card, then insisted he leave, because otherwise he wouldn't have ever.

As Julian walked away, Duncan again had the impression someone followed him, so he checked his surroundings once more . . . and felt a swell of anger when his scan revealed nothing. He would have preferred validation—a person or concrete evidence he was right to be concerned. He was tired of looking over his shoulder.

He'd prefer to confront an informant. He shouldn't want to, shouldn't wish he could tell one of his kind exactly how he felt about Xanthe's spurious decisions regarding siren rule and his position—or lack of it—in the new hierarchy. He clenched then unclenched his fists.

He regretted his new penchant for aggression, had always taken pride in his civility. He believed he should continue to uphold his high standards of conduct even among the more barbaric beings he relied on for company here in spite of his justifiable outrage. He straightened, smoothed his shirtfront and resumed walking. He forced his mind away from vengeance and onto the more refined outcomes he hoped to realize with his land-bound efforts. He resisted the urge to turn again and see if he was being watched, reminding himself he soon would have no need to worry about spies. Because he would be so entrenched in a community of his own making, whatever other sirens saw and reported wouldn't matter. He stopped, smiled at a jogger and lit his next cigarette.

Xanthe pressed the heels of her hands to her eyes and leaned against the wall of Duncan's office at Shaddox. She'd been so embroiled in the peripheral dramas surrounding their new government structure and Carmen's ascension to the throne, she hadn't physically met with Duncan since thanking him for his interim service. Which had been . . . how many weeks ago? She should have paid better attention.

As far as she could tell, no one had heard from Duncan since she'd told him about Carmen. And while she didn't suspect foul play, she was worried. Community members—especially high-ranking ones like Duncan—didn't leave unless they were forced to or they died. Since Duncan fit into neither category, she wondered about his motivations and how susceptible he was to deviance. Of course she was no longer as trusting as she'd once been. The catastrophe that had ensued the last time a ruler went off the deep end amplified her musings like a 10,000-watt subwoofer.

She called Isabel to ask if she knew anything . . . and then wished she'd visited in person. Isabel knew something, was too nervous and anxious to end their conversation. She did no more than answer Xanthe's questions, and Xanthe couldn't search her feelings as she would have face-to-face. How she despised the weak, insufficient communications technology afforded.

Duncan had not returned and had not tried to contact his wife. Isabel knew he was alive and had gone inland, but she didn't know where.

This last piece of information most alarmed her. Duncan could be nourished by humans; and the frenzy their proximity caused was mitigated out of the water, meaning he could conceivably function near them, although he'd had a harder time than most trying to pass on land before. And again, why would he try? What would he gain from an extended stay so far from home? She decided to call on Isabel personally.

CHAPTER FIFTEEN

Isabel dropped the phone after hanging up with Xanthe and walked directly out the door, taking nothing with her. For all she knew, Xanthe was already on her way.

She exited their palace apartments and hurried to the nearest tunnel leading to the ocean, transforming the second she hit the water. She made the open sea in under a minute.

She slowed only after she was well away from the island. She hoped she'd escaped notice—and since no one had followed her she thought she had. She relaxed her pace. She replayed the events of the past hour, reliving the flood of terror that had prompted her last-minute decision to run.

Evading Xanthe on the phone was one thing, but an interrogation in her actual presence was unthinkable, and she was sure to show up after Isabel's clumsy, artless responses. In Xanthe's company Isabel's knowledge would have spilled out of her like the tide and damned both her and her husband. Because she could not excuse her cowardice and silence all these weeks, could think of no way to prettily couch Duncan's parting sentiments or actions. He strongly disapproved of the incoming regent. His lack of respect was so profound as to be treasonous, was certainly grounds for dismissal.

Isabel would have destroyed him—as well as their entire life—if tested by a powerful intuitive like Xanthe. And she couldn't live with such a prospect, not when she wasn't absolutely certain Duncan wouldn't come around. She headed for shore.

Meaning Xanthe found Isabel and Duncan's apartments deserted. Nothing looked out of order—their personal effects were still there—but Xanthe felt traces of Isabel's anxiety. She concentrated on these and extended her senses. Was she elsewhere in the castle?

She wasn't. Meaning Isabel had fled, which was bona fide cause for concern. She'd apparently left in a hurry, left anxious, and hadn't taken anything with her . . . so Xanthe had to acknowledge her concern for Duncan's stability was unfortunately warranted.

She experienced a raw flare of irritation, something which used to happen rarely but she experienced more and more frequently of late. She placed a hand on her solar plexus and took a breath, hoping to exorcise through willpower the displeasure her negative conclusions provoked. She called the guards, one of whom had seen Isabel head toward an exit tunnel, and she pivoted away in disgust. Now she had two missing sirens on her hands. And an intuitive knowledge they were engaged in deceit.

Gabriel Blake wasn't going to like this, but Xanthe needed a cloaker to track Duncan down.

She retreated to her office to call him, pausing to rest her forehead against the door. She so wished her job was less complicated, or that at least she still understood it. As delicious as humans were, their world had become a persistent aggravation to her, and while she felt she'd always coped professionally, she no longer wanted to. Nor did her dissatisfaction leave her when she went home at the end of each day. But. After the Flemings were sorted out and the monarchy settled . . .

Maybe she would take a year off. Yes. She would work through this one issue and take a long-overdue, necessary vacation. She reached for her phone.

CHAPTER SIXTEEN

Sylvia no longer came away from her morning stroll all calm and centered, which had been *the* purpose of this habit when she'd started it. These days she arrived at work not relaxed, not collected, not insulated from the chaos of customers who came to SeaCakes harried and hungry and usually late for something. Whatever had happened the past five mornings—and she could in no way identify what that was—left her abuzz with nervous energy. As well as a little trigger-happy on the temper front. Once her sanctuary, SeaCakes in the morning became a ball-peen hammer applied to an oil barrel she wore over her head.

She didn't sleep well, either, and her appetite was just gone. This morning she'd hesitated before getting up, feeling empty and vaguely nauseous. She wondered if she'd contracted the flu. But the prospect of the beach and what she might find today compelled her to rise. She was exhausted but she rushed anyway. "Craziness, I'm your girl," she muttered.

The routine was familiar by now. She walked with Soley toward Griffins Bay from the Blakes'. She sank into a reverie she was eager to have but could not recall once she had it. She always felt as if she'd had a conversation with someone important to her, like a dead relative come back to give her vital advice, although she also had the impression she'd been on a date, one where she wanted the guy to hold her hand and kiss her goodnight but he never did. She joked with Soley they were on their way to see her sea monster, and as soon as the words left her mouth a familiar lethargy settled over her.

She stopped at the place she knew she was supposed to. She scanned the water expectantly.

She saw nothing at first, and she looked harder for some irregularity in the waves, her breathing shallow, her heart rate increased as she searched hungrily for . . . what? Her awareness declined, but today she fought her usual trance.

She just wanted to understand why she was driven to return here each day, to recall something—*anything*—to explain why she felt so nuts. Whatever drew her here had turned her morning meditation into her a.m. anxiety attack.

Twice earlier in the week the universe gifted her with brief insights during sleep, flash visuals she saw like pictures under a strobe light, never long enough to fully recognize much less understand. She glimpsed the tail of a silvery green fish with a wide, graceful fluke; and the face of a man she knew but couldn't place. She also had vicarious memories she could not ascribe. A blast of cold on her skin, images of ice floes and sea lions, or an endless desert of snow viewed from a barren shoreline. She felt these images in a new dimension, where her senses became tangled or interchangeable. She saw the cold, for instance, and smelled the night. She flickered through sensations of salt and sunshine and other things like anemones and seashells with an expanded capacity for experiencing them.

Sylvia.

The almost-image called to her in a dream she couldn't fully excavate from her subconscious. She scrutinized the water again, seeing only endless gray waves under a lighter, pre-dawn gray sky. Her sea monster did not surface.

She waited. Nothing took shape in the water although her belief in her phantom experience did solidify . . . and kept her rooted where she stood.

Whatever had occurred here—and *something* had—it had shaken her world, and not just when she was by the ocean. In every area of her life, she'd been catapulted out of some foggy self-absorption she hadn't known she was in, where nothing familiar to her made sense any longer and very little of it was still acceptable. Her insistence on autonomy in particular took a beating, since she now felt compelled to share her experiences. She wanted to think through her daily conundrums with another, rejoice in her accomplishments both petty and significant. The result of her ruminations was a profound, uncomfortable expansion of how she saw herself, and she found the takeaway unflattering.

Still she looked inward and picked at herself. And on top of the physical discomfort this brought—the nausea, the sleeplessness—her ongoing self-critique eroded her confidence. She likened her recent composure to the crust of a mountain fissured by rivulets of lava about to rupture it. One of these days she was going to spew her chaos all over everything. And she couldn't do one single thing to stop herself.

By comparison her former unenlightened outlook was ever so preferable. She badly wanted it back.

In the new hyperawareness that characterized her days, she looked at choices she'd once made without question, ones governing everything from friendships to romance to her professional life. Primarily she examined her own refusal to accept help or even much in the way of encouragement from others, and she wondered if these choices were not the show of strength she'd once believed. They'd perhaps been a habit enabling her to hold herself above it all. Which made her past attempts at intimacy seem weak and pathetic.

I'm protecting something I shouldn't, she thought. *A too-narrow definition of independence. And I'm feeding my own loneliness.* How tiresome and unattractive. More importantly, how miserable.

She considered how she might engineer a better program, maybe actually share herself with someone. During these morning walks she'd risked more than she ever had and in return experienced true communion with another . . . and she wanted more of it. When she dreamed of romance now, she hoped for a man strong enough to lean on, not just someone she could prove her strength to; and she'd convinced herself someone out there would hold her when she was unsure, would love her in spite of her deficiencies.

Yes. She was the author of her solitude and had the power to rewrite herself. For starters she wanted to connect with the marine instigator of her changed way of thinking, even if the experience hurt her. Which highlighted the fear behind her daily quests to this place, how she might find her companion was nonexistent. She did not want to discover he was imaginary or, perhaps worse, that he was real but didn't care what happened to her. She predicted exactly how raw and exposed she'd feel then. Her hunger-cum-fear for the truth had her teetering between anticipation and dread each day. Meaning hope, not despair, robbed her of her appetite and disrupted her sleep, which she almost found funny.

As she studied a dark shape lurking near the shore, a prickling sensation like the brush of a light electric current ran down her back and along her limbs. Ah, relief was on its way. He was coming. Soley's barking broke through her reverie before he abruptly stopped. He ran back toward the Blakes'. Sylvia returned her gaze to the shallows.

The shadow under the waves twisted, and Sylvia again felt her perceptions narrow and her awareness recede. She almost remembered this! She concentrated harder to try and force the recognition buried within her. She leaned toward the ocean. Maybe she should wade in . . .

Sylvia. Wait. I'll come to you.

She made a sudden decision. No. She didn't want to comply, didn't want to almost know what was happening this time. She took a deliberate step forward, and then another. The warning to remain on shore felt hollow anyway.

A silvery glint under the surface, a flash of iridescent scales. *No. It's a bad idea . . .*

She ignored him and entered the surf, everything in her focused on the hypnotic whorl that revealed fins and scales.

And a human face.

When the water reached her knees, her yearning intensified. By God she was going to figure out what was going on. When the creature next swirled where she could see it, she charged it.

Aw. Hell. She'd waded in. And nothing, not descriptions he'd heard from other sirens, not his own suspicions about how he would feel—nothing could have prepared Simon for Sylvia entering the water with him.

He was a fool to think he could have engaged her and left. Granted, before now he'd flirted from a distance, had only gone to her at the end of their exchange. Hidden in the tide, he'd reached out of the water to touch her feet, and even that brief contact had gutted him.

But he *had* left afterwards, in spite of her pull and despite his wish she would remember him. Serial interactions like theirs were forbidden because repeat efforts to dim human perception failed with ongoing exposure. He'd ignored this risk—couldn't help himself—and reinforced her awareness of him every morning. He could tell each time his efforts to tamper with her memory were losing effectiveness, although she still hadn't quite remembered him. Until this morning.

So today would have been the day his house of cards fell down anyway, he reasoned. Their connection had become too strong to subvert, and her belief in their affinity was at play before she immersed herself.

She ran right to him. He transformed instantly, standing just in time to catch her full against him.

His breath shuddered from him at the contact and he stumbled, the onslaught of sensations she triggered all but toppling him. Now her face pressed into his chest, her hands spread across his back in an insistent hold that offered everything he wanted, her only request to keep her with him. He held her and promised her more—his body to lean on, his strength to support her, endearments to reassure her. He could deny her nothing, and yet his capitulation felt to him like triumph.

He could no longer retreat from her. As compelling as their walks had been—and he waited for them like an addict waits for his fix—he'd still told himself Sylvia was a sideshow to the rest of his life. What a ridiculous thing to think. He would never let her go.

An urgent warning worried the edges of his thoughts, but he ignored it. He was so caught up in the euphoria of discovery, how he had found something bigger than his rebellion and unease, was soon to be free of it entirely. He would bond with Sylvia no matter the consequences.

A litany of adorations echoed between them, confirming their intentions and feeding their desire for one another. Sylvia clung to him sweetly now, her cheek against his neck, her heart beating against his. He whispered in her ear how they would be in the days ahead, described the island he would take her to. Shaddox, with its hidden coves they could swim to, just the two of them. Her name rolled through his mind with beautiful fluidity. *Sylvia. Sylvia Wilkes.*

His insistent, cautionary voice finally insinuated itself. Wilkes. The family of sisters Carmen told him to avoid because one had already married in. She would not want this.

Xanthe would disallow it.

They had to get away from here, leave so they could complete their bonding without interference. He closed his eyes in frustration because this meant a delay. He needed a few hours, maybe a day, to arrange a getaway.

But he was convinced he could devise their escape and determined to protect their opportunity to do it, so he prepared to send her away. He gripped Sylvia's arms. "Go back to the bakery," he instructed, even as it sickened him to utter the words. "Remember nothing of this exchange and go. I'll come for you there." He lurched away gracelessly, forcing distance between them by concentrating on the outcome he wanted.

Once at the house, he dried off and grabbed a pair of jeans from the front closet. For the first time in his adult life he understood how couples withstood the "small" existence he'd disparaged. He could think of nothing he wanted more than a future with Sylvia—a modest home with or without kids where they returned to each other at the end of the day, where they spent the night in each other's arms and shared inanities and corn flakes for breakfast. The image of the repetitive, too-dull existence that had fueled his avoidance of this path . . . now he could imagine nothing more fulfilling, and he wanted it badly enough to defy his queen. Wanted it badly enough to risk banishment. He toweled his hair as he approached his brother, who sat on the couch reading.

"How was your date?" Aiden asked snidely.

Simon swatted him on the back of his head. "Let's go. I need you to get the guys together to set me up with some supplies. They can swim to Antarctica faster than I'll be able to travel. You're gonna be my man on the ground back here, facilitating."

"And then?" Aiden asked watchfully.

"Then I want you with me while I check out that bakery again."

Aiden snorted, kept his eyes on his magazine and made no move to get up. "You want to check out the baker again, you mean."

"Get up. Otherwise I'll go alone."

Aiden leaned his head back to look at him. "You're in a bad way, aren't you." He sighed. "And I'm assuming you can't be trusted to run off leash, maybe keep me out of this?" He lost his smirk. "Is Sylvia working alone today?"

Simon answered his real question. "I don't know if Maya's there." He pulled on a fresh shirt. "But it doesn't matter. I'm going."

Aiden tossed his magazine on the cushion beside him, took his legs off the coffee table and stood. "If Maya's there, I am no longer your babysitter," he warned. Simon didn't respond, which seemed to make Aiden nervous. "Seriously, who's on fire?"

"Come on. I'll tell you on the way."

CHAPTER SEVENTEEN

Isabel located Duncan after a two-week quest, one that left her exhausted and depressed and on the verge of a nervous breakdown. She'd followed his trail to Raleigh through perseverance and a singular need to prove herself capable. But she'd found herself ill-equipped to defend against the tidal wave of human need she encountered on the way.

Which was no one's fault but hers. Her attempts at subtlety became a spectacular fail, drawing scores of people instead of a discreet few each time she sent out what she thought was a gentle inquiry on whether or not anyone in the area had seen Duncan. Humans flocked to her like hummingbirds to nectar, sometimes forming a circle around her fifteen bodies deep. At which point a sort of switch flipped inside her, and her circumstances devolved into the most brutal cycle of solicitation she could imagine—with needy admirers, unmet demands for intimacy, and the escalation of a truly caustic level of frustration, since no one got what they wanted. She couldn't send out the smallest tendril of perception without getting caught in this suffocating vortex, and she couldn't get away without feeling like someone had stuck a big straw in her and sucked out her insides.

In the end she'd used her speed and agility to escape these disasters despite interdictions against supernatural demonstrations. She didn't care, was just grateful for the abilities that gave her an out.

She so wished she were not alone on this mission. She wondered at the abilities of sirens who did this, who could reach out to humans without falling apart and without creating a mob. She wondered how much practice she would need to interact fluently, not that she was on fire to improve herself in this area. She had persevered this far, though, and would continue on until she found him. Because she had to. Her complicity in Duncan's strangeness demanded her current effort.

But sweet heaven, she struggled to follow through. She recommitted herself a dozen times each day by anticipating the profound relief—maybe even redemption—she would experience when she found Duncan and talked him back into compliance. And she developed a better routine for escaping her devotees when their intensity became intolerable, an illegal one but she no longer guilted herself over the practice. One showy, improbable leap up and away dislodged her from the center of any gathering, and her sprint afterwards . . . well, humans couldn't see her, she went so fast. Which meant they couldn't follow her, either, which was the whole point. Of course she couldn't afford to return and edit their perceptions as she should have.

She knew she defied community law with every single one of these exhibitions, understood she had established herself as a conscious memory with dozens of coastal residents; but she couldn't figure out how not to create these throngs, and once in them had no other way out of them. She hoped no one understood what they saw and guessed most people later treated the experience as if they hadn't had it. Following her sudden departures, Isabel observed them from a distance to reassure herself all was not a disaster. And she was reassured when she felt the incremental release of her crowd's collective pull. She saw them come back to themselves, could sense how self-conscious they were over their deliriums and then the edge of shame they felt over losing control. Her favorite human humiliation was the belief their participation reflected a weak intelligence, which made no sense. Why did they correlate instinct with poor intellect? Humans must value a very particular definition of sanity, one that did not include falling into a thrall and begging for a mermaid's affection, which she maybe understood a little if she thought of her own society's rules of comportment. At any rate, she believed she was dismissed as a fantasy, a daydream had while out on a walk. She continued to look for her husband.

The relentless, unbuffered demand from all these human encounters wore on her, however. Alone and unable to either moderate these exchanges or meet her need for emotional connection, she languished, spending more and more of each day huddled and crying. She longed for the comfort of home. Her regrets and hope for relief were the only inducements strong enough to drive her . . . and when she encountered a dead end, she truly despaired. If she couldn't pick up his trail, she would have to go back, perhaps feel demoralized and defeated for the rest of her long life. She wished for failure even as she worked against the possibility.

Mid-morning on her fourteenth day she stumbled across a lead at a café, having checked out several since she knew how thoroughly Duncan enjoyed the human caffeine habit. A man in the corner, a regular if the proliferation of personal items strewn around him were an indication, stared at her strangely. When she returned his gaze, she caught what interested him; the man had made a comparison between her and someone he'd met.

That skin. Something about her eyes is just like his.

The man rose from his seat and leaned toward her as she approached despite her attempts to edit her appeal. Conversation around them stopped and Isabel braced herself, recognizing the lost expressions blooming on the faces around her. Alarms tripped inside her head.

She had to make this quick. She clasped the man's forearm. *Where?* she asked tersely.

The man swayed with desire for her and took precious seconds to answer. "He asked if I knew anyone in Raleigh," he managed. Isabel felt a sickening swell of panic as others in the cafe started to shuffle her way. "Will you sit with me? Talk with me for a while?"

Isabel released him, closed her eyes and swallowed. Raleigh. So far from the ocean. She turned and ran from the establishment before the encroaching horde made exit impossible.

Once outside, she followed a riverway to Raleigh.

She found Duncan at a public park, walking in measured paces along one of the sidewalks. He surveyed passersby with a hungry regard Isabel found creepy. Many sidled away from him. He startled when she stepped in front of him and placed her hand on his chest. "We need to talk."

And then she was dumbstruck.

His appearance appalled her. His hair was longer and in disarray, his clothing an edgy, messy contrast to his usual crisp business attire. He wore one ear bud connected to a device tucked in his pocket, the wires hanging down the front of his shirt . . . and she could hear the buzz of heavy metal it emitted from five feet away. His eyes, distorted behind his thick-rimmed glasses, looked manic.

Disturbed, Isabel thought, earning her a frown of disapproval from Duncan.

She skittered backwards when she noticed the lit cigarette in one of his hands. A cigarette! Why would he carry it when he couldn't possibly smoke? She retreated another pace, feeling the stirrings of actual fear. Like he might unsafe.

He probably was, Isabel thought, and she slid into despondency. She'd made a mistake coming here after all.

She studied him for some hint encouragement, any small negation of her worries. Finding none, she curved around herself, cradling her middle with both arms. She had hoped to feel happy reconnecting with another of her kind, but she didn't. She saw only aversion in Duncan's regard, felt no rush of unity. And because she'd expected welcome, she now felt even more desolate and alone, something she would not have believed possible. She turned to walk away.

Duncan was not happy to see his wife. Needy and dependent as she was, he would not have predicted she would undertake a solo mission to seek him out, especially here, leagues from the ocean. He also had no intention of accommodating her no matter why she'd come, could not have cared less how distressed and tired she was.

She should have known better than to expect solace from him.

He looked heavenward and sighed. He didn't want her by him, but couldn't afford to have her running back to Xanthe or Carmen, either, to share how she'd failed to connect with someone who was supposed to adore her, maybe highlight his apathy and preference for isolation. He couldn't risk the scrutiny, at least not yet. So he tried to summon residual affection for his wife, to comfort her for appearance's sake and draw her into his confidence.

He couldn't manufacture true empathy, but he did manage to pity her, because she'd become so deluded and trusting she thought she could still influence him. He gripped her arm to stop her from leaving and smiled, which probably came across as a grimace. The contact between his hand and her arm made his upcoming pitch feel even more distasteful, but at least he could use it to read her.

Ah, success. He noted how, in her misery, even his weak, unwilling outreach soothed her; and while she had no confidence they would ever understand one another again, his small attempt swayed her as he hoped. She hesitated, reconsidered her decision to go home now. *Maybe he'll be open to talking after all?* She hoped to heal them both, cleanse them of what were to her serious transgressions. Even if they would part ways afterwards—and Isabel foresaw no resurrection of their marriage, thank God—she thought she had a duty to maybe stay and finish what she'd started.

Her rally made him instantly regret his attempt at comfort because her questions bubbled forth incautiously. "What are you doing this far inland?" she blurted. Even committed to her course of action, she struggled not to cry. "Why did you run away, and why are you . . ." she swept a hand up and down his frame, "dressed so strangely?" She bit back the rest of her accusations and hoped he would somehow acquit himself.

Through the touch he maintained on her arm, he read all of her: how she was weary from her search and concerned over what would happen. She was needy after her lonely sojourn to find him. She thought surely he shared her distress, having isolated himself as he had this far from the sea, with no one they knew, and without any social facility with humans. By now—especially in the presence of her own longing—he should be eager for the support they could offer one another.

Duncan sighed. So much to address . . . and he shook his head. "Not here. I'll take you someplace we can talk." He turned abruptly along one of the public paths and gestured without enthusiasm for her to follow.

CHAPTER EIGHTEEN

Duncan had been empire-building.

He led them into a multi-use high rise containing businesses on the lower level and condominiums above. Their first stop was a main-floor office suite, fronted by a frosted glass door which bore the signage, "Fleming Communications." He placed a hand at the small of Isabel's back to direct her through the entrance. "Good afternoon, everyone," he said crisply as he guided them through the galley of employees who'd stood in greeting.

Their expressions were her first clue something was seriously amiss—vacant and bright and branded, as far as she could tell, on the face of every person who worked there. Conversation ceased as workers from every corner rose to offer Duncan something that felt like homage. He shuddered with pleasure . . . and Isabel understood how Duncan had tolerated being alone all these weeks. He'd replaced his community with a human fan club, one he'd somehow mass-enthralled to wait on him even when he wasn't present. How had he managed it?

She was reluctantly impressed. "You've done all this in so little time?" she asked.

Duncan's gaze made a quick tour of their surroundings before returning to her. He straightened proudly and his smile was smug. "Yes. It's impressive, don't you think?"

"Very nice," she murmured, frowning again as she noted the weird, fervent devotion of one of his aides who'd approached with messages. "They're like trained dogs," she commented.

They passed several sections of low, cleanly styled cubicles as they made their way toward a rear suite, and as they walked, Isabel watched in astonishment as each employee either bowed or *curtsied* as they passed. Their deference, which felt engineered and strange, put her off, although she couldn't deny the fulfillment accompanying the deluge of human adoration. It was directed at her husband but intense enough to reach into her, as well. And unanchored as she was thanks to Duncan's painful dissociation from her, the human attention soothed, blanketing her like warm water in the middle of a frozen current. She felt almost stable for the first time since she'd left Shaddox.

They stopped at a set of double hung, carved wooden doors reminiscent of the entrance into the royal offices at Shaddox. A human male who Isabel judged to be in his mid-twenties rose obediently from a nearby desk at their approach. Unlike his dazed colleagues at the front, he offered her a clear, clean smile and, once he'd greeted his employer, his full attention.

In fact he looked aware, which bothered her. What did he know, and what was he allowed to remember that he shouldn't? Wasn't he released, as most working humans were, to the great, wide world at the end of each day, and didn't he talk with others about his boss, a strange man with a compelling presence and the power to influence?

Her concern intensified. What was Duncan doing with these people? The aide from the desk offered his outstretched hand, which she hesitated to take because the emotional output around her felt tainted. Everyone's heady adulation aside, she didn't want to want to actually touch one of them and ingest whatever contagion they might impart. She looked to Duncan for answers as the human spoke to her.

"I'm Julian, Duncan's office manager." He bowed. "Welcome to Fleming Communications."

"This is my wife, Isabel." Duncan urged her to shake Julian's hand and so she did . . . and she promptly learned several things at once, all of them troubling. Julian wasn't being influenced, at least not like the others; and he had a pretty good idea something mystical was attached to Duncan. A laugh caught in her throat as she apprehended his suspicion Duncan was an alien, because how cute. He apparently admired her husband for his ability to inspire a crowd and attract beautiful women. He believed Duncan was teaching him to command the same kind of attention.

She also read in Julian an undercurrent of hopefulness she found especially heartbreaking. Julian had been, until recently, a self-loathing slob, was reformed because he'd taken pointers from Duncan on how to appear and interact with other humans. Duncan, the most socially maladjusted being she'd ever known, a guy so compromised he had to an wear ear bud and pretend to smoke to withstand the most casual interactions. She smiled sadly. If only Julian knew. This poor young man was being duped, and Isabel turned to accuse Duncan of playing his underling false.

You perpetrate a lie. Why?

Duncan shrugged and answered her aloud. "I cannot be recognized as I should at home, but here, I am royalty." He inclined his head toward his assistant. "Julian serves as an intermediary for me. He helps manage and cultivate my business."

At last Isabel understood Duncan's motivation, and it horrified her. In all the scenarios she'd imagined—over why Duncan had abandoned their marriage and left his prestigious job or fled Shaddox as he had—she'd never, never thought he craved the throne. She tugged her hand from Julian's to better concentrate on what she now saw as a very serious problem indeed.

"Then you left to avoid exposure. And you can't intend to return," she stated.

Duncan's anger flared, and his response bit like a striking cobra. "*I* should have succeeded Peter. Xanthe and that ridiculous committee should have been at my feet after all I did. Instead, they chose an idiot half-breed, someone who probably can't even find the assembly hall."

Isabel gasped and pressed a fist to her chest in an attempt to loosen the compression on her lungs. When she could breathe again, she said, "Carmen has served us faithfully, and she is Peter Loughlin's daughter." Duncan glared, and a stab of pain squeezed her again, causing her to hunch her shoulders, a gesture Duncan mirrored, albeit weakly. His expression changed from fury to surprise, and then to Isabel's relief, the constriction in her heart subsided.

The knot in her chest disappeared and the relief nearly caused her to faint. What had just happened to her? She assigned her discomfort to her own state of mind, a response to the anguish she'd lived with these past weeks over her loneliness and failed marriage. As her breathing normalized, she thought perhaps she'd finally achieved catharsis, and a physical release from the stress she'd been carrying. Grateful, she closed her eyes and breathed for several seconds. Within moments she felt completely well and ready to resume her inquiry, although she wondered what she would gain by it. How could she, one lone siren, stop the catastrophe Duncan courted with his treasonous ambitions? She resolved to try.

Before she could continue, Duncan shook his head. "We should have this conversation in my office." He faced Julian, who paid rapt attention to their exchange, and smiled as he would at a puppy. "Hold my calls, please." He led them toward his office, pausing to turn around just before closing the doors behind them. "Also, please book a room at the Brenlow for my wife."

"Yes sir," Julian replied, watching them retreat. She kept eye contact with him over her shoulder as Duncan pulled her away, because something in Julian's regard bothered her. She couldn't quite identify what, or why she had a sudden, dim intuition she was in danger. She searched Duncan's expression, which no longer reflected disdain. In fact, he smiled indulgently at her and emanated a disturbing aura of anticipation. Like he was flirting with the idea of killing her, or something equally beyond her ability to identify.

She turned to Julian again, and confirmed her suspicion; he pitied her. Her face fell as the last of her optimism disappeared into the ether. The bravery she'd so recently claimed—over getting here and confronting Duncan—meant nothing. Because if Duncan's most devoted follower was concerned about her enough to show it, she was lost.

After reserving a suite at the Brenlow—for an indeterminate length of stay and on Fleming Communication's dime—Julian contemplated Duncan's closed office door before forcing his eyes back to his computer screen.

As he typed, he mentally reviewed the interaction he'd just witnessed between his boss and his wife, which made him think more on the enigma of Duncan Fleming. This time, his conclusions felt like they had integrity.

He'd been surprised to hear the term "wife" come from Duncan's lips because the man had not behaved as if he was married, especially given the near constant entourage of hopeful females he had attending him. He guessed Isabel didn't know about them. He also surmised she signaled some sort of problem, because she hadn't been around, for one. And she was emotionally strung out and appeared fragile. Too fragile.

Duncan had never mentioned her, didn't wear a ring, and even with Isabel here didn't seem to care much about her.

Maybe his kind, hailing from planet whatever, treated marriage differently? Not for the first time Julian wondered if he wasn't the biggest nutcase alive for his outrageous speculations. He could even laugh at himself for them; but he'd long ago quit trying to talk himself out of his whacky suspicions over Duncan's origins, mostly because the guy was clearly different—off the map different—but also because Duncan had told him outright he "wasn't from 'round these parts." Ha. As if that wasn't as obvious as snowflakes in July. The thing was, Duncan had just shown another side of himself, a new facet to his ambitions and dealings with people, which Julian had always found bizarre but in keeping with his overall strangeness. And he hadn't seen any harm come from Duncan's desire for deference so far.

Duncan's anger when Isabel confronted him disturbed him, however. Julian just plain didn't like how he'd behaved, had never seen so clearly the extent of the man's self-absorption or lack of consideration for others. He couldn't imagine any Southern gentleman treating a woman that way no matter how he felt about her, certainly not in public and definitely not his wife. Julian's allegiance aside—and even unaware of the specifics—Isabel had Julian's complete sympathy. Duncan had just earned his disapproval.

The situation bore watching, because Duncan and seemed downright mean—that fervent gleam in his eye when Isabel had clutched her chest . . . well, he couldn't afford to think about it too much. Julian feared he'd never recover his former admiration, which was the only glue holding him to his newly improved self-esteem.

Again, what he'd just seen could have been an aberration. But he was pretty sure Isabel had just signed up for a whole lotta misery.

Duncan closed his office doors behind him and leaned against them. He was too excited to speak.

Isabel thought her freak-out and chest pain were in response to the revelation Duncan had wanted Carmen's job.

Duncan knew the real reason.

What an amazing discovery! When his frustration swelled in her presence—when he openly shared the festering resentment he'd harbored all these months—his anger exacted unexpected consequences. And while he found the release cathartic, how his reaction manifested in Isabel excited him.

Perhaps if he'd previously lowered himself to indulge in such base emotions he would have discovered the physical effects of malevolence sooner. Because *he'd* caused Isabel's heart constriction and resulting pain. In fact her symptoms had echoed in his own body. He wondered if his own discomfort would have intensified if he'd continued. Probably, given his sympathetic siren nature. He would think on it later.

Now he had to address the threat Isabel posed to his campaign.

He told her, without warmth, to make herself comfortable, which she did by pacing nervously away from him. Her anxiety mounted as Duncan once again stonewalled her emotional outreach efforts. He refused to enlighten her further. He defended nothing, explained nothing: not his reasons for running, not his physical persona, not his strange devolution into solitude. After a stretch of tense silence following her barrage of questions, Isabel—predictably—approached him, reaching with her hands and her senses to try and force an understanding between them. He again denied her inquiry, recoiled in fact. He walked away from her to stand behind his desk. Isabel slumped onto the couch.

Duncan removed his ear bud. Then he lit a cigarette.

Isabel relaxed further into the sofa, too tired to think anymore. She'd been prepared for Duncan's anger, knew he was disappointed in the leadership change at the palace. And she'd expected his surprise at seeing her, his astonishment over how far she'd come to find him.

She did not anticipate his complete detachment—from her, from their bond, from his former friends and colleagues and even his siren home. She realized she'd been counting on his regret over running away, for abandoning their life together. More than anything she wanted him to harbor some kindness for her, had assumed they would have an open, honest conversation about his recent activities and their bond. Even if their marriage was irreparable, Isabel had believed they could still help each other heal.

She would mend nothing and no one here, not him, not herself, not his intentions toward their people. She'd come seeking apologies and remorse for the choices he'd made. She received indifference. Her sense of irrelevance twisted in her gut like rotten roe.

Moreover, she was not strong enough to weather a break-up with Duncan if her existence meant nothing to him, if their entire time together was no longer worth any consideration at all. Her singular sense of purpose, which had carried her through to this point, had been compromised by the grueling process to get here, and she had no reserves to withstand Duncan's galling lack of concern.

Her head lolled onto the cushion behind her, and she watched the light change outside the window. She contemplated walking away and accepting the disappointment of all their loose ends. As things looked, she might as well. Which was a kind of relief: she could no longer berate herself for Duncan's noncompliance with siren customs or agonize over her failed marriage—she'd gotten herself here, came prepared to confess and confront. She'd made the hard choices and was willing to sacrifice herself to try and make things right.

But Duncan was not capable of the same, meaning her sacrifices furthered no one's interests.

At least she'd tried, and now she could go home with a clear conscience. She wanted to go home. She rose to leave.

To her astonishment, Duncan stopped her. "Please stay."

A mere hour ago, he would have been delighted to see her take off, but as she broadcast her acceptance of their marital demise, she also made known her intent to side against him; to report his actions to Xanthe and Carmen and possibly see him removed from Raleigh. She didn't realize the effect this would have on him.

"I'm not ready for you to go back and report me to siren leadership on this," he stated.

She shrugged. "You should have thought of the consequences when you concocted your schemes."

She watched a look of calculation followed by a kind of hollow sympathy pass over his features, and what was that? They both knew he couldn't lie to her, that he felt nothing but distaste for her any longer.

But he surprised her by asking for her help . . . and God love her, she was so emotionally depleted and vulnerable, the mere suggestion he might need her elicited sympathy.

"I realize what it took for you to come," he stated. "You were brave to embark on this little errand all alone, I'll give you that. And although you know I'm not happy to see you, staying an extra day or two to learn more about my operations is a good idea, no? Anyway. I've figured out how we can help one another."

A sense of obligation spilled from her like a thick, smoky incense, one that cloyed and irritated the back of her throat. She wished she didn't feel it. She felt her old devotion chafe against her recent bid for independence . . . and she felt trapped.

She didn't fully hear what he said to her now, intent as she was on the tip of his cigarette, which calmed her as he moved it to and fro.

Duncan's words were a confusion of wants—shallow wants in her opinion—cloaked under a veneer of sincerity she found disgusting, like his honest desire for her help even though he fundamentally wished her away. So if not for that fire-kissed spot waving through the air, she would have risen and gone home. But she didn't. She badly wanted to watch how the blaze orange tip softened to gray; and she really had to see the silky, sheer smoke curl upward from those dainty, riveting embers until it dissipated into the ceiling. When a long section of ash detached from Duncan's wand and sifted down like tiny petals, she realized she was completely at ease. She didn't need to leave after all. She needed to stay.

She felt an expansive love for all living things including her husband, who she was inclined to forgive everything. She smiled indulgently at the excuses he offered her now.

His attire wasn't bizarre, just a ruse to fit in with human society, which he needed since he had no one else. He'd been under tremendous pressure this past year, surely she was aware, and the prospect of blindly accepting his replacement, having had no say in the matter when he more than anyone should have been consulted . .

. well, she could also understand his dissatisfaction, couldn't she? He would never risk sharing his displeasure at such a delicate time in their government's transition, so of course he left. Shame on her for thinking badly of him.

He was happy and relaxed, and he was excited about his life. He wanted her to feel the same way, and she could if she would do something for him. Something little and easy, and it would make their separation more comfortable for her.

Of course their marriage was over, but this was for the best. The cooperation he sought wasn't anything harmful. No, just a way for him to structure a better life for himself. If she allowed him to finish his work here, they could part friends and she would be free.

What was it? Nothing difficult. Something she would enjoy, in fact. He wanted her help with a documentary, one profiling her and, no, she wouldn't need to do anything other than be herself.

For what purpose? Well, I want it more for insurance than actual use, a warning, you know, but nothing to fret about since no one will be hurt. He might not ever need to use it.

Yes, he knew he'd misbehaved, and he wanted to establish a different home for himself, clear the path for the new monarch to rule unimpeded back home. She would help everyone if she stayed. Carmen would be grateful, and they all would end up happier, didn't she see? *Isabel, darling, we're setting each other free, and isn't it wonderful.*

Yes, Duncan. Yes, it's wonderful.

For the first time in a long while, Isabel felt useful and wanted . . . and her relief undid her. Duncan's couldn't disguise the holes in his warmth, but for now, she reveled in something like closeness, and in the promise, however weak, of redemption.

Of course I'll help you, Duncan.

CHAPTER NINETEEN

Maya wheeled a bin of volleyballs to an isolated area of the gym to practice her serves. She stretched her serving arm and shoulder as she eyed the box she'd outlined on the wall with athletic tape.

Loosening up felt good. Her season was long over, but she still liked to keep a training schedule for fitness reasons and to stay fresh for the coaching job she'd been hired for next summer. She was also at a loss over what to do with herself since her college volleyball career was officially over, and she felt better keeping up some sort of athletic routine. She'd participated in sports so intensely from the time she was ten—gotten the scholarship, played for the most elite women's team in the country—and now questioned if there was anything left in her life to replace what she'd always done, always been. She took her first serve, aiming at her box. It hit wide and left.

She'd returned to campus from Griffins Bay a few hours ago after hurrying home to see Gabe and Kate's new baby. Their little boy—Henry—had contemplated her with squinty, intelligent eyes and a comical tuft of black hair that had endeared him to her in about two seconds. Kate had been a trooper, electing to go through the ordeal sans pain medication and surrounded by family. Maya thought she was crazy and told her so.

"What's with the heroics? I think you should take all the help you can get from our pharmaceutical friends. And I wouldn't tell my in-laws I was in labor much less let them in the room."

Kate gave her an enigmatic smile, an annoyingly common occurrence since her marriage to Gabe, and Maya knew she wouldn't get a straight answer. She understood marriage entailed a special intimacy in which friends weren't included, even best friends. But she felt an edge to Kate's withholding and believed her secrets created more distance than they needed to.

"Trust me, Maya," Kate replied. "By the time you get to the end of your pregnancy, your body hasn't been your own for so long . . . having people around, well, it's like you're loaning out a shirt or something. No big deal." She looked at Gabe, who was holding their newborn son in his arms and cooing. "And as for pain management, my husband's presence helped." Maya snorted.

To cap it all off her sister, Sylvia, had been floating around like sleeping beauty although her story went the opposite direction, where a prince's kiss caused her to be all dreamy and semi-conscious instead of awake. When asked, Sylvia reported, "Nope. Not seeing anyone new." Ethan was the same as ever although she hadn't been out with him in a while. Maya smelled a rat. "You just seem so happy and settled all of the sudden," Maya commented suspiciously. "And kind of checked out."

"What, I can't be happy and checked out?" Sylvia asked, and her smile came off infuriatingly like Kate's. Like they both were in on some massive private joke she didn't get.

"Not if nothing's up," Maya countered with a probing stare. "It just seems like you've met someone, that's all." Sylvia assured her she hadn't.

On her drive back to campus, Maya attempted to pick apart her discontent. It wasn't that she didn't want her friend to be happy or her sister to find love. It was that she suddenly felt left behind. While Kate was barreling through college and becoming a wife—and now mother—Maya had gone to school and played volleyball. While Sylvia learned a trade and opened a business like a regulation grown-up, Maya had remained stuck in the same routine she'd been in since junior high. And while she her choices were admirable in their own way, seeing evidence of Kate and Sylvia's forward progress underscored her own lack of it, as well as the fact that she really didn't know what she wanted to do next. She thought about the complexity of Sylvia's business and her new air of self-assurance; and Maya had held Kate's baby—her *baby*—in her arms not three hours earlier. Maya saw herself as a long way from being either a professional success or a mother.

Her parents had borne the brunt of her festering insecurity. The day before, Jeremy, mostly in an effort to make conversation, had asked how school was going and if she knew what she wanted to do after graduation. Maya had instigated an argument that had her father throwing down his paper and leaving the room. "Don't you sass me, young lady!" Jeremy warned as he stomped away.

Alicia came to investigate and Maya had treated her no better. "What on earth was that about?"

Maya huffed. "He was riding me about my plans for the future. And I told him to mind his own business."

"Maya Jaqueline, your father was not 'riding' you," Alicia chided. "You're a senior in college—one he worked hard to get you to, I might add—and he's your father. He has a right to ask about what's next."

Maya crossed her arms and glared. "Well, *I don't know*, Mother! How's that for an answer?!" She'd stormed away.

Now back at school for six more weeks of same-ol'-same-ol' before graduating, Maya reconsidered her response. She'd actually given her father's question a great deal of thought, she just hadn't felt prepared to talk about it when he asked. She'd never been a true wunderkind in the classroom, but she was a strong student with an aptitude for science. Given her background in athletics, she'd been considering sports medicine, had even reached out to a couple of medical school programs to make inquiries. She'd also enrolled herself in a preparatory course for the MCAT over the summer and scheduled to take the test next August.

She told no one about this, mostly because she half expected to fall flat on her behind and fail and in that scenario the fewer people who knew the better. But the bigger influence ended up being her own self-doubt over the vocation itself. Since adolescence, she'd excelled in volleyball thanks to rigorous practice, native talent, and genetics, since height helped a girl at the net. And once she'd gotten a taste of athletic accomplishment, she'd chased that opportunity to the end of the line, chased it like a rabid dog.

She'd had a great last season at Penn State, but when it ended, it had left a gaping, empty void . . . and she felt like someone had died. Maybe her. And whereas at every other time of transition in her life she'd had some new athletic agenda to pursue, her choices from here on out were not enough in her estimation. Sure, she might try out for the Olympic team or take a look at a professional league, but those options felt like a sideshow and were not consistent with what she saw as progress, or respectable adult living. She wanted something to replace the consuming role sports had played in her life up to now, not re-enact the same achievements over and over again.

Medical school sounded and felt suitably ambitious, where if she made it through she would feel proud of herself again. The desire also exposed an inner need she found unattractive, especially when she thought of her smart, capable sisters and her friend, Kate; these women, after all, had accepted themselves without seven years of school and the sleep deprivation and poverty becoming a doctor entailed.

So why couldn't Maya see herself the same way?

She would have to think more on the subject before explaining herself, either to her family or in an acceptance interview. She hoped she would come up with a better answer than the one she had now, which was that she felt ornery and insecure and wanted something "big" to take her mind off all that.

On the other hand, the endeavor did interest her, and she honestly craved the fascination the area of study offered. Too, helping others be healthy sounded a lot better than improving her offensive stats on a volleyball court.

Maya finished her workout and headed back to her apartment. Her phone notified her of a text as she left the athletic center and she dug it out of her bag as she walked. Stuart was coming to town next weekend. Could she pick him up at the airport? She stopped walking and began a reply. When she was half way through a suitably flirtatious, light response, she hesitated and frowned at her message. She hadn't thought about Stuart much the past two days, and not at all during the past hour, one she'd spent ruminating hard over her future. Why was that?

If she was reaching for a meaningful, grown-up existence, her casual romance with Stuart hadn't been among her considerations, which didn't sit well with her. She lost the lighthearted vein of her reply, deleted what she'd written and spent several seconds considering how she really wanted to answer him. When nothing surfaced, she decided she'd had enough introspection for one day. She turned her phone off and tucked it in her bag. She'd get back to Stuart later.

CHAPTER TWENTY

Sylvia went about her tasks at SeaCakes in a frenzy of anticipation. She was so keyed up after her morning walk, she couldn't focus. And in contrast to her normally efficient, methodical work habits, today she moved around the bakery erratically and created chaos instead of order as she passed. She made simple errors at the cash register, put dishes in the refrigerator instead of on their shelves, and she accidentally poured syrup in the soap dispenser by the sink. She was distant with customers and co-workers alike, and more than one person expressed concern after an interaction.

She was cognizant of her misfires but did nothing to improve herself, was only aware something big had happened and something even bigger was coming, would be here any minute. Kate had dropped by to help with minor tasks around the café and for a dose of adult company, although she'd brought Henry with her. She sat with him at one of the tables by the window now and tracked Sylvia warily. Maya, who'd also scooted home for the weekend, followed her antics with equal distrust. Both did their best to cover for her with patrons, but Sylvia couldn't be induced to care.

By early afternoon, Kate and Maya were too exasperated with her to keep silent. "How much did you drink last night?" Maya demanded, followed by, "Go home and sleep it off, Sylvia. You're a walking disaster."

Kate huffed. "Seriously." The bell over the door jingled.

Sylvia floated from the kitchen to find two men from a build-a-better-soldier government breeding program standing at the front of her store. Although even gymed up, they were too tentative and slouchy to be true fitness gods . . . and their nerdy eyeglasses suggested they spent their days in academia somewhere instead of pumping iron. Like they maybe studied astrophysics for fun, might even know Stephen Hawking personally.

She also thought she knew them from somewhere, although there was no way. She would have remembered these two, wouldn't she?

Their possible exercise addiction and MENSA affiliation aside, they commanded the room, and they were so familiar Sylvia struggled to place them and felt foolish when she couldn't. But neither could she shake the conviction she'd met them.

And she was so star-struck she didn't even manage a polite welcome. Her eyes flickered to Maya.

Heh. Maya was equally rattled. And as an athlete in a prestigious university program, she'd met all kinds of famous and influential people . . . but even she was flummoxed, although unlike Sylvia, she *did* know who these guys were. Or rather she knew one of them.

"Aiden," Maya whispered hoarsely. She stared hard at the one on the right and didn't even glance at his friend when she acknowledged him. "Simon." How did she know them? Sylvia shook her head to clear it and squeezed her eyes shut.

When she opened them, she focused on a spot between the pair, hoping she could normalize if she didn't look directly at them. She especially couldn't look at the one Maya had called Simon.

"Can I help you?" she managed blandly as she moved toward the counter. Simon crept forward like a thief and she froze mid-stride. She fought—literally fought—the urge to run to him.

She didn't win, or at least didn't win completely, as her plan to avoid eye contact failed. She reluctantly raised her gaze; and awareness covered her senses like a velvet blanket. The same stupor she experienced by the water each morning.

His expression—intense, devoted, and too familiar—devastated her. He was here for her, she realized. Which siphoned every last molecule of air from her body.

You know me.

She heard his voice like a whisper inside her head. They *had* met before.

Yes.

His name was Simon Blake.

Yes.

He knew what she felt all those mornings on the beach.

Yes, love.

An icy, liquid joy spidered through her veins, leaving her lightheaded and desperately hopeful. He was why she'd lost her appetite and couldn't sleep. He was the undefined something she'd waded into the surf earlier to confront.

He closed the distance between them and settled his hands atop her hips. He greeted her companions without looking away. "Maya, Kate." How courteous of him to say hello. She'd forgotten anyone else was there. She registered Kate's response in the most peripheral manner possible.

"Oh. God." And then, "Ah, Simon? Aiden?" She shifted Henry to her other arm and frantically patted around the base of her chair for her purse. "You both know this isn't a good idea, right?" No one acknowledged her.

Kate continued to chatter as she fumbled with her cell phone. "Maya and Sylvia, you should know I've seen this situation before and it isn't good. You girls are about to have your whole lives . . . well, I'm sure this is *not* a sanctioned visit. C'mon, Carmen. Pick-up-pick-up." When Henry began to fuss, she stood and bounced. "Where *is* everyone?" Then more loudly, "I'm calling John now, and that is a threat." Again, she spoke into a vacuum.

Sylvia thought of her friend like she would a cartoon character, one performing on a television running two or three rooms away. Her words and urgency were muffled and inconsequential. White noise to the real drama underway.

Because Sylvia was embroiled in the most profound emotional exchange of her life.

Want streamed from her unchecked, like a physical substance Simon literally pulled out of her. His own longing flowed back like an ocean tide, one that encompassed and lifted her on its swells before it ebbed and gathered strength for the next rush. Sylvia stared into his eyes and cared for nothing except the desire he uncovered, for the promises he hinted at; and she didn't care how little they knew each other, or how they were seconds from a public display that could get them arrested.

Maya's drama intruded only briefly. A blast of bitter regret from Aiden encroached on Sylvia's daydream just enough for her to surface and notice him. Maybe his problem was the pastry counter separating him and Maya? Maybe if he and Maya could touch as she and Simon did, they'd feel more settled. Because they'd understand how gloriously simple this whole proposition was.

"John!" Kate exclaimed into her phone. "Simon and Aiden just came into SeaCakes and they're, well, you know, *talking* to Maya and Sylvia except no one's saying much if you know what I mean and, oh my, well, Simon is holding Sylvia's wrist and saying 'come away with me' and all that and maybe it's all fine and good but I'm just not sure . . ." Kate paused for John's response. "Great! *Hurry!*"

In a tiny area of her brain, Sylvia admitted Kate was wise to be concerned about what was going on. Simon *was* here to seduce her, and she was all for it. But he accepted her responses to him so earnestly, with such pure intention and care he endeared himself with each passing second. He took her hands in his with something like reverence, his touch as sincere as her own mother's . . . and she was lost for him.

So she couldn't care if their attraction was sudden or she if felt overtaken. This was the explanation she'd searched for these past weeks, this was the resolution she'd have given anything to realize.

Inside her, she heard Simon's words, which now were edged with panic. *We have to get out of here. Kate called reinforcements, and they'll be here any minute.*

And wasn't this conversation exactly like the ones on the beach with her sea monster?

I'd drag you away and explain later if it wouldn't look so bad. Will you walk out of here with me?

Sylvia felt as if a million tiny snowflakes had just landed on her skin—light, scintillating points of sensation that caused her to shiver and smile. She placed her palm against Simon's chest, drew a breath to speak . . . and had a vision comprised of several images in rapid succession.

Icebergs. A sea lion. A humpback whale surfacing to breathe. Scenarios so surprising she pulled away. "Wha . . . ?"

"Sylvia," Simon insisted, and his voice was rich and resonant. He folded her hands between his and drew her attention up to his face. "Come with me. Please."

Kate cleared her throat and squeaked, "Why doesn't everyone sit down while I get us some cookies?"

Aiden and Maya didn't budge. Simon continued to look straight at Sylvia but said, "Hey, Kate. Why don't you get out of here, take Henry to your mother's." Sylvia snickered.

Kate scowled, which Sylvia found amusing. "No one's listening to you, Kate," she said carelessly.

But Simon cared more than he let on, because he murmured urgently to her about John and others being on their way. "Sylvia, we have to take off *now.*"

Her response was immediate and without reservation. "Yes." Should she have asked about specifics? Maybe, but she knew everything in this moment she needed to. They'd talk once they were away. Of course she'd call Dana and Will from the road, and while they wouldn't like it, they'd cover SeaCakes for her until she got back. She didn't even consider contacting her family.

"Let's go," she told him. Simon answered her with a smile so bright her heart fluttered.

Kate kept trying. She continued her arguments as Sylvia and Simon—who remained oblivious to her—passed her on their way to the front of the store; and Maya and Aiden . . . well, they were engaged in a stare-down Kate couldn't have penetrated with a bundle of lit dynamite.

She understood she talked to nobody but herself. She also knew she needed to make the effort she did.

She wondered for a fraction of a second if anything could stop this. Such a silly thing to wonder, because she'd been just as intractable when she and Gabe had bonded. She might as well have been yapping away in Latin . . . and the idea of physical restraint—considering the men's fitness level and monumental drive to see their respective deals done—was even more laughable. Michael and John together wouldn't be able to do much here, although she was glad they were on their way.

Simon offered a final comment at the door: "We'll be gone for a month or two, and everything's going to be fine—we'll come back. Make sure to tell everyone I said so, Kate, especially Sylvia's folks."

Kate shrugged. Like she had a say? "Whatever." She waved them off.

Simon turned to his brother. "Aiden, bro, cover for me." Aiden tipped his head in acknowledgement without looking away from Maya. Then Simon and Sylvia were gone.

Michael and John arrived minutes later, heaving and sweating from the effort to come in time, which they hadn't. "Simon and Sylvia already left," Kate informed them tonelessly. Then, with a nod toward Aiden and Maya, she said, "You can see for yourselves how those two are doing."

John carefully approached Aiden.

Michael sighed and rubbed his eyes before addressing Kate. "We're won't catch Simon and Sylvia, I think. And we might be too late for Maya, too." He studied the couple in question.

"There was *nothing* I could do!" Kate insisted. "It was like watching the fuse burn down on a bomb three feet away and I was tied up and gagged."

Michael smiled kindly. "I know."

John put a hand on Aiden's shoulder, which Aiden shrugged off. "Get lost," he warned without taking his attention off Maya.

"No." John's voice was hard. "We can't have two sisters disappearing on the same night, Aiden."

"Fine. We'll stay here."

"And that amounts to the same thing, doesn't it? Come on, Aiden. You know I'm not the one you're fighting."

Aiden shut his eyes, after which Maya also closed hers. Kate saw the concentration between them break. John went to Maya, placed a hand on her arm and said, "You will forget Aiden's visit today and the exchange you just shared." Kate felt his instructions press heavily on all of them, as if he'd wrapped everyone in shackles.

Aiden looked furious.

"I can't seem to completely erase her memory of you," John told him, which earned him a small, acid smile.

"Way too late for that. This is not our first encounter."

Still John was able to lead Maya to the door with minimal resistance. She kept looking over her shoulder at Aiden, who held his face rigidly away from her. "I'm taking her home," John announced. "We'll figure out Sylvia and Simon later."

Aiden stormed out moments later, leaving Kate and Michael in a bitter pall of lingering frustration. Kate wrinkled her nose. "You know you can't trust them to stay away, don't you?"

"Simon and Aiden are good guys," Michael asserted. "They'll do what's right."

"You're all good guys, but what you think is right and what they decide might differ." She stretched then, truly inhaling for the first time in what felt like hours. She gathered her sleeping infant and his paraphernalia. Michael took Henry's carrier while Kate locked the door behind them.

CHAPTER TWENTY-ONE

Gabe exited the water still irritated over the mission Xanthe and his mother had assigned to him. He thought he should be past the point where his parents could dispatch him to do their bidding . . . and maybe he could have fought harder to stay put. But he wouldn't have felt right leaving them without help. He supposed he'd rather be here than participate in the ridiculous hand-wringing back home over Simon and Sylvia's sudden walkabout, which couldn't be more inconsequential in his opinion.

And then maybe he was a little excited to work on his cloaking, sneak up on someone as strong as Duncan without his knowledge.

So he'd come ashore to play detective and find Duncan Fleming, who could be anywhere, although he was likely somewhere along the eastern seaboard. Which was 1,300 *miles* long.

Sure. Why not? Gabe thought humorlessly. "Try to be back in a week," had been Xanthe's absurd directive. Ha.

He headed south on a whim, stopping in Roanoke to feel out his surroundings and formulate a skeleton plan. Something told him to go inland, an idea he resisted. Sirens didn't stray from the ocean, at least not for any length of time, and he doubted Duncan would have set up house more than a half hour from shore. So he ignored his initial impulse and walked south, smiling politely at those he passed. He cloaked just enough to avoid drawing a crowd, grateful for this facility. How would Duncan have managed among so many?

He for sure hadn't proceeded unnoticed as Gabe did. He would have pulled people in to feed his emotional appetite, wouldn't have been able to stop himself. Gabe stilled occasionally to feel out those around him, trolling blindly for some evidence one of his kind had recently called here. He lamented how difficult this was to do out of the water, first of all to concentrate on so many people at once; and then to resist them, to avoid the intuitive interchange his inquiries caused him to want. The vigilance necessary to control his solicitation drained him, and he tired quickly.

But he did feel something. A trace here and there of longing, of despair over intimacy coveted and lost, and of unattributed desires recently awakened. Again Gabe felt the urge to go inland. Which was one too many times to discount at this point.

He walked west, away from the water.

He tried to think of his sojourn as he would going to class, which took him out of the ocean the better part of each day. He would not return to Kate and Henry this evening, however, would likely be away an entire week. And his studies engrossed him when he was on campus and surrounded by a horde of hungry humans; he would not have his academic diversions this time, was following others' curiosity to track down Duncan, not his own.

He reminded himself he was here for his people and especially his parents, although the thought gave him little comfort. He had a heavy course load at school and a new wife and baby back home. He did not want this extra responsibility no matter how noble . . . yet here he was. He'd just have to find that bastard viceroy, hopefully confirm he was a non-factor for his mother's regime and return home. He made for the river.

When he reached the next city, he stopped outside a bar to rest and take a pulse on the crowd just as he had on the coast. He straightened when he realized he was, in fact, on the right trail; because the impressions he intuited were distinctive, definitely evidence of one of his kind. And while he could have assigned responsibility to any number of sirens who passed in coastal areas, he was too far ashore here. At least too far for emotionally secure sirens to hang around.

Duncan? This far in? He ducked inside the bar.

"Coffee, please," Gabe told the bartender. The man filled a mug and set it in front of him before returning his attention to the television mounted on an overhead brace. Gabe followed the antics on the screen . . . and set his cup down so hard it spilled. A journalist reported out of Raleigh, something to do with political controversy over a commercial real estate development. In the background, the camera showed two men in conversation, one of them shaking his head in response to a question.

It was Duncan Fleming.

"Excuse me," Gabe called to the bartender. "Does your river to the north connect with Raleigh?"

"Yessir. It doesn't run downtown though." Gabe pulled a five from his wallet and left it by his cup. "Thanks for the joe," he called as he left the bar. He headed for the river.

Duncan left Isabel to her own devices during the day as he went about his "integration" work with Julian. The emotional demands he made of her when they were together left her too exhausted to do much when she was alone, though, so he didn't fret over any attempts she might make to overthrow him. She certainly didn't have the energy to brave the human world unassisted, meaning she wouldn't likely run off. She spent a lot of time in her hotel room, and thank God for television.

Duncan had realized an additional benefit to Isabel's company other than the role she would play on his video series. As focused as he'd been on his political aspirations, he hadn't noticed the full extent of his emotional deprivation. He was unhappier than he'd realized outside the company of other sirens, and Isabel filled that void, strengthened him in a way humans—with their chaotic, over-bright and primarily self-interested offerings—could not. He found himself less lonely and his plans easier to execute given the relatively stable sustenance she provided.

His program—his whole life—was finally coming together. And without meaningful compromise to the folks back home, although not because he was opposed to a coup. He just couldn't figure out how to pull one off. For one, Carmen's genetics solidified her claim to the throne and he could do nothing about that. She also enjoyed universal—albeit in his opinion unwarranted—popularity, something he'd never been given despite his much more meaningful accomplishments. But no, as pissed off as he was to concede his dreams of a siren kingship, his fiefdom here on land served him better, comprised as it was of all the wealth and admiration he'd worked so hard to garner at the palace but would never apparently receive.

He wasn't going in without insurance this time, however. Never again would he hope playing by the rules would bring success, especially not when, with a little foresight and planning, he could carve out the life he coveted. He'd already implemented bold plans to protect himself from interfering siren higher-ups, and he'd ensured any attempts to curtail his power here would jeopardize the secrecy of every siren on the planet.

But he wasn't building the means to take over Shaddox. More a guillotine to cut off the head of anyone who tried to stop him here in Raleigh.

His royal ambitions to return to the palace as king had died hard, with Julian wielding the axe severing the last of his hopes. A real-time exposé—the one he would have used as leverage to extort the position he wanted out of Carmen's hands—wouldn't work after all, even though he'd manipulated like the devil to get Julian to deliver. But nothing could overcome Julian's arguments on how tricky the technology would be to coordinate, how impossible the personnel requirements. When he estimated how much additional time and cash such a scheme entailed—and without a guarantee it would work—Duncan capitulated.

He still wanted collateral, however, something significant to hold over Xanthe's head so she'd stay out of his way, and he guessed a raw video internet feed would do the trick. He couldn't wait to see the reaction of the folks back home.

Julian couldn't determine the full extent of Duncan's plans.

He knew him to be a deposed king who wished to regain power without causing harm to anyone, including the incompetent usurper who stole his crown, a woman named Carmen Blake. On this issue, Julian respected and admired Duncan for his clever, humanitarian approach to conflict resolution.

But after weeks of having his senses either stymied or misdirected, he no longer trusted his perceptions. And while he made no judgment concerning Duncan's demand for secrecy—or even over the man's frequent unreasonableness—he now suspected his employer was not as he'd represented himself.

Isabel was the biggest instigator of his doubts, although Julian didn't believe she'd deliberately undermined his loyalty. But the interplay between her and Duncan . . . well, it tarnished Duncan's leadership appeal. Even if Isabel was the problem in their marriage, Duncan had been appallingly inconsiderate of her. And when he became aggravated, the man was downright cruel. No matter what Isabel intended, she didn't deserve that.

Which begged the question: why would Isabel tolerate such treatment? She was stunning and smart and obviously brave to have come here alone. She was also more than a little charming. Julian thought Duncan was crazy to disparage her and crazier still to show his distaste. The man owed people more courtesy in general, but her most of all.

He thought back on an interaction he'd had with Duncan before Isabel had shown up. They'd been on a park bench feeding pigeons, with Duncan half-informing him in the way he usually did of next steps and how he wanted Julian's help. He wanted to get a Taser, and he wanted Julian to research his options. How did they work, and how specifically did they affect the neurological system? What were the different voltages available? What were the merits of one model over another?

Julian didn't know the answers off hand, but his past flirtation with violent video games had provided him with peripheral knowledge of stun guns. He promised to look into the issue and get back to him. For the first time since he'd begun their association, Julian wondered why Duncan needed such information.

CHAPTER TWENTY-TWO

Simon reluctantly left Sylvia alone while he went to negotiate—which might mean coerce—passage on a southbound ship. They could have traveled by water instead . . . and he'd briefly considered bringing her in this fashion. But he thought it was a lot to ask of her since she didn't yet know what he was, and the seas were so rough and forbidding in the Drake Passage. He could have kept her stable physically but he worried the shock of everything at once—seeing him in his siren form, a swim in roiling, freezing waters where full-size ships regularly sank to the ocean floor—well, he just wasn't sure it would make for prudent courtship.

"*Sylvia, honey,*" he imagined saying. "*Wanna watch me turn into a fish while we swim to Antarctica?*" Even controlling for heart rate and body temperature, he couldn't put her through it.

As he'd done several times already, he reviewed the series of decisions leading up to the one before him now. In his message to Carmen and Xanthe after they'd left, he'd explained he was taking her to the Antarctica camp because he wanted time alone with her, i.e., without their meddling or attempts to lure him back to Griffins Bay, and so he could engage her on his own terms. He told them he was, as usual, unwilling to tolerate the scrutiny accompanying one of Carmen's traditional matchmaking events. Carmen argued when she wrote back how these 'meet-and-greets' served a valuable purpose, one she predicted Simon would regret having foregone.

"When we're together, we support a mutual understanding with our human guests, which makes our revelations less of a shock and acceptance feel normal to them," Carmen had written in her reply. Thankfully she didn't insist they turn around, though. She also promised to support his bond in any way she could if he decided he wanted help.

Simon had begun to see her logic, although he refrained from such a confession to either her or Xanthe. The main reason he snuck off, after all, was because those two had prohibited their affair. He responded to Carmen's email with the request that someone reassure Sylvia's family she was safe and happy, which she was. He also promised to return with both of them intact. Best he could do for now.

He couldn't accept Carmen's offer to facilitate, wouldn't risk any attempts to separate them.

He never heard from Xanthe, which meant she was too angry with him to engage. He didn't care, wasn't going to change his mind and take Sylvia back at this point. He was also reasonably certain he'd be re-accepted into the fold again and forgiven as long as he showed up all bonded and stable. Maybe? He'd have to figure it out later. Right now, they needed a ship.

Left on her own for the first time since they'd embarked on this adventure south, Sylvia surveyed the view from the balcony of their hotel room with growing unease. They were somewhere in the very southern-most region of South America, well past the warm, tropical climes she associated with the continent. This village was a stopping place, their last stay-over before departing for their final destination, which Simon hadn't shared with her.

And without the influence of her companion, her surroundings started to really bother her.

Simon had suggested she rest while he arranged for passage on a boat for the next leg. He'd been unwilling to leave her, had procrastinated nearly an hour past the time he'd announced he'd be *right* back.

"I'll be away thirty, maybe forty minutes," he repeated for the umpteenth time. He worried she'd have a hard time without him, which had perplexed her before he'd left.

"I'll be fine. I promise. Run your errands. I'll hang out and read."

Soon after he was gone, his distress made sense to her. She tried to get into her book, but as her calm dissipated so did her ability to sit still. She got up and paced their suite, eventually feeling too confined to remain indoors. She walked to the balcony, leaned her forearms on the railing . . . and as she looked out on the town, her restlessness morphed into actual anxiety.

She was clear-headed for once, not floating in the dreamy, fuzzy consciousness she'd enjoyed since leaving Griffins Bay four days earlier. But this place, her departure from home . . . this was not a dream, she realized. For what felt like the first time, she considered her situation objectively. And she reflected on her lack of wisdom, how where she was and what she was doing reeked of idiocy, was possibly even dangerous. She graduated by slow degrees from concern over what she'd done to full-on alarm.

She tried to reason her way out of her dread. She'd known this whole time they were running away together toward some fabulous adventure. And all along she'd thought the whole proposition was perfect and marvelous . . . so nothing had changed, nothing warranted her newfound apprehension.

But. This couldn't possibly be a good idea.

She tried analyzing their departure from every angle to persuade herself she would have made a different choice. Had she been too rash? Probably, but she couldn't muster the necessary dishonesty to convince herself she would have walked away. She wouldn't have made any other decision than the one she did, which was to grab Simon's hand and run.

She took a deep breath. Okay. Time for a straightforward look at her circumstances, starting with, um, where on earth was she? Argentina? She tried to remember what language they spoke in Argentina. Spanish? Portuguese? She should know but she didn't. Wherever she was, the place was morose, remote and charmless with absolutely nothing to offer her by way of encouragement. When they'd arrived that afternoon, she'd been amused by how uniformly spiritless the people seemed, had even commented after several apathetic interactions on how the natives all seemed drugged. Simon had laughed with her.

This place was not at all her fantasy of a romantic getaway, and the lack of warmth here—human and otherwise—felt so contrary to their intentions as to call the entire premise into question. Had Simon misrepresented himself? She'd been stupid, so careless to leave without more information.

She panicked and searched their room for her purse. She hadn't brought one.

Oh, this was bad. She pivoted and ran out the door.

Once in the street, she searched for a public building of some kind, a library—anything. She didn't have a credit card, cash or identification, so she had to find a phone where she could place a collect call to the States. She didn't even know what she would say . . . so best not to call her parents. Maybe Maya or Solange? She decided Kate was her best choice.

But first things first. She looked for a flag, any suggestion of a government office and oh, what she wouldn't give to see Old Glory at the front of something like an embassy. She saw no such thing. Moreover, no one around her cared she was sweating and agitated and maybe hyperventilating. The whole town looked like one giant experiment in listlessness, from the storefronts in need of paint to the lack of traffic; even the children were odd, like they were genetically deprived of the energy and curiosity characterizing kids everywhere else in the world.

In a way she was glad for the bizarreness of her surroundings, because it helped sharpen her decisions. This, whatever this was, was wrong. And everything she saw and felt supported this conclusion.

Her foolish, headlong rush to romance—during which she had not taken two seconds to consider any of the implications . . . she shook her head, castigating herself again for her lack of intelligence. And here all this time she'd believed herself to be such a practical girl. Apparently not. She turned toward the waterfront, hoping to glimpse something helpful. Like a boat headed north she could stow away on.

The thought of sneaking off without a note to Simon bothered her, though. He'd been good to her—was warm, kind and solicitous, every bit the doting suitor. He was the one who'd suggested they take a little time to get to know each other before rushing to physical intimacy, a gesture which had at the time removed what she'd believed was her last reservation. Outside of his presence, however, her concerns mounted by the second. Sylvia began to jog.

She reviewed the events and decisions that had brought her to this point. Their last encounter at the bakery had been pure, sweet magic; and when Simon had taken her hand and looked in her eyes, she'd never felt so certain of anyone in her life. He'd shown confidence when they were leaving and therefore so had she. Also, he was as lost for her as she was for him. She knew this without a doubt.

Well, she *thought* she could count on him . . .

No, Simon was a good man. But her burgeoning panic had exposed too many scary holes in her logic, and she had to consider the possibility Simon might mean well, but he might also be crazy. Case in point: who did this sort of thing, asked a woman he barely knew to travel in secret to someplace foreign and isolated? Considered from this perspective, her decisions were even more strange and wrong. Her conviction Simon was the one for her didn't hold up under such cold, stark light, at least not today and not in this town.

She spied an old pay phone outside a gas station and dashed across the street. She struggled to understand the instructions adhered to the face of the device, pieced together "110" and "internacional" and pressed the numbers. She also mumbled a prayer she would reach an English-speaking operator. A ringing sound indicated her call was going through. She bent her free hand over the top of the phone box and leaned her forehead on it, feeling some relief. She would get help.

A hand on her shoulder startled her. "Sylvia."

She spun around to find Simon standing there and backed away as far as the phone cord allowed, a move which looked to cause him pain. "Sylvia. What happened? What's wrong?" His chest heaved and sweat poured off of him as if he'd just stepped from the shower, although she guessed he'd been running. He swiped his sleeve across his face.

"Hola," she heard from the receiver. She twisted away again so she couldn't see him. "Hello?" she said frantically. "I need to place a collect call to the United States. Will you please help me?"

Simon's eyes filled with tears. This was what he'd been afraid of when he left her, suspected she would second-guess herself and start to worry. She was well down that road, was terrified from all he could see and intuit. He reached over her, depressed the hookswitch and said, "Sylvia. Look at me." She stared at the phone as if she could will her connection back to life and gripped the receiver.

"Hello? Are you still there? You have to help me!"

Simon moved to stand in front of her and ducked to catch her gaze. "Please," he insisted, his voice hitching.

When she raised her eyes at last, her expression was heavy with accusation. "What is going on, Simon?"

He cringed at the recrimination in her voice, unable to deny he deserved it. Because he *had* acted according to all the fears she broadcast. He'd influenced her, sweet-talked her in the space of about fifteen minutes into leaving her job, family and friends; and she was, in fact, stuck in a foreign country where she couldn't get home on her own. "I'm sorry," he attempted, "but it's going to be okay. I promise." Sylvia started to cry.

Simon's regret gave way to full-blown remorse. He'd trusted his instincts concerning their compatibility, was sure of their potential bond and had believed matters such as telling her what he was and taking her to the south end of the planet were peripheral. Back at the bakery, he thought he'd come sufficiently clean with her to forestall any significant problems before their actual bonding.

Perhaps not.

She had intuitively recognized him as her "sea monster" when he went to her, and he'd revealed via a flood of emotions she was right as well as the impact of their interactions all these weeks on him. She'd accepted him without censure then and been relieved to know she hadn't imagined the craving between them. She was glad to pin her lovesickness to a bona fide reason. He'd fronted his pitch with genuine devotion so she would have no doubts he cherished her, although he didn't disclose just how much of a "sea monster" he was. Until now she'd believed he was just a guy who really liked to swim. But they'd declared their mutual longing honestly, he thought; he'd allowed her to feel the intensity of his belief in what they could be to each other, and he'd believed this display was good enough. They could take the next steps as they came.

When he first held her wrist and registered where she was in her cycle before leaving, he'd also known they had time to pace things out. They'd have nearly three weeks before they would be overwhelmed by the desire to bond fully. So he'd thought of her human traditions, how he could maybe give her a chance to acclimate to the idea of a lifelong commitment.

He'd thought he was being careful.

His little jaunt this morning had been successful in that he'd secured their passage to Antarctica. He'd negotiated without much effort, although to speed things along he had influenced the captain to accept them without delving into who they were and why they traveled. He'd hurried back to their hotel, anxious because he'd been separated from Sylvia, and because he wasn't sure how she'd fare on her own for the first time. Up to this point in their trip he'd stayed by her, touching her and directing her attention toward the wonderful future before them.

He knew he had a problem as soon as he found her gone, and he applied all of his senses to ascertain where she'd fled. He tasted trace elements of her panic and distrust in the air, and was pretty sure she'd fled to find help, to run from him. When he picked up more of her anxiety on the street he tracked her, eventually sprinting out of worry. If she found someone to listen to her, she might disappear. Had anyone in the street cared to pay him any attention then, they would have seen him move with too much strength and speed for a human. But he did not slow.

When he found her she was undone from fear, and when he felt her anguish he became equally distraught.

He couldn't answer her questions like this, not with them both shaken and unstable. He probably shouldn't tell her everything just yet anyway, not when she could still distract herself with thoughts of escape. Instead, he let his feelings reach into her, let his care and concern enfold her until she was unable to maintain her conviction they'd been wrong to come. Eventually she allowed him to draw her into him.

He buried his face in her hair. "I'm sorry," he said simply. She remained stiff in his arms but didn't fight him.

"I'm stupid," she said, her voice quavering. She looked down at the pavement rather than at him. "I don't know you, and I . . ." she gestured weakly at their surroundings, "I'm here. I don't know why I thought this would be okay." He tightened his embrace, and although she kept her hands flattened against his chest like she might push him away, she rested her forehead against him.

Simon swayed with her until he felt her relax. "We are here to be together," he told her after a while. She kept her face hidden but offered a couple of small nods. Simon rocked her and stroked her hair.

After several minutes, when he felt she was mostly calm, he took her hand and retraced their path to the hotel. Although she was no longer hysterical, her compliance now had a wary edge to it, a distrust Simon knew would take time to erase. He tucked her into his side and let her feel his concern—and belief in what they were together—as they walked.

By the time they reached the hotel lobby, her anxiety had been replaced by exhaustion. She sagged against him, and he willed her to give into it until he felt her feet drag. Then he secured her waist with one arm and tucked his other arm behind her knees to lift her off the floor, eliciting the first faint smiles he'd seen in this place from the people around them.

He brooded on the way to their room, still wrestling with the fear he'd had when he found her gone just a short while ago. When he'd tucked her under the sheets, he remained on the edge of the bed with his arms braced on either side of her. This whole endeavor had become tricky, and he didn't know how to avoid a repeat performance of that afternoon without telling her everything. Which he was reluctant to do while there was still a chance she could leave.

He rose to pace. In two days they would be ensconced and protected from outside influence. In a week, they would no more be able to stop their bonding than beam themselves to Pluto. He could avoid trouble for that long, couldn't he? He would simply remain by her side every second until then.

He walked back to the bed and lay down carefully so as not to wake her. He slid a hand beneath one of hers to hold it as he watched her sleep, and he felt his adoration swell with every breath she took. The drama surrounding their recent separation dissipated. He thought instead about how committed they would soon be and the joy they would soon share. *Everything's going to be okay*, he told himself. Relaxing at last, he, too, allowed himself to sleep.

CHAPTER TWENTY-THREE

Maya felt marginally better after her phone conversation with Kate, one of the few she'd allowed herself since embarking on her covert post-grad plans. She and Kate used to talk several times a week, but Maya had curtailed this habit, citing her athletic commitments and a wicked, final-semester class schedule. Which was a valid excuse in light of the MCAT prep course she'd layered over her college courses, something Kate didn't know about. But. Kate had backed off, must have guessed Maya needed to keep a few secrets because she'd mostly let her be.

And it wasn't as if Kate hadn't withheld; she'd stonewalled Maya's inquiries a dozen times following her kidnapping ordeal. Maya felt better about her own retreat from this perspective, like she wasn't the one responsible.

She'd been careful about calling home lately, too, had felt the need to protect herself from all the unwanted scrutiny she was under from her folks since she hadn't procured a "real" job yet. She hadn't mentioned her medical school ambitions to her parents, either, so like Kate, they didn't know about all of Maya's existential ruminations concerning Stuart and her future. Maya liked this situation just fine.

During their talk Kate had unknowingly shed light on the recent show of respect from Jeremy and Alicia, though. Up until last week, her parents had taken any and every opportunity to butt in, offering nonstop, really annoying career advice until Maya simply quit taking her mother's calls and praise heaven for caller ID. Maya thought Alicia had gotten the message when even her emails—providing job contacts in the roofing industry or to sell jewelry—came to a halt. She figured her parents were pretty worried to suggest absolutely anything that hinted of employment, which made Maya surly. Really? They didn't think she had it in her to take care of herself? She'd refused to engage in defensive argumentation, knowing she would cause an all-out fight. Maybe they'd realized she could find her own way. And that she needed to.

Kate had just disabused her of this notion. Enlightenment was not the cause of Alicia and Jeremy's sudden discretion after all; Sylvia was, the dog. She'd run off with her new beau, the one she'd recently told Maya she didn't have. And apparently they'd trotted out the door of SeaCakes for an extended leave without so much as a text to family or her business partners. She hadn't cancelled her mail or the paper, either, and had left a dirty cup in her sink, all of which made her disappearance a pretty big concern to their folks. Which was just fine with Maya, who believed Kate when she assured her Simon and Sylvia were off on some perfectly wonderful adventure.

Thank goodness someone in this family had it in her to follow her heart and damn the consequences.

Maya frowned, remembering how their older sister, Solange, had actually done the same thing half way through college. Their parents had stood by her without questioning every step she took, and why was that? Maya huffed, feeling irritated again. How come she got to be the only daughter they grilled and messed with?

Well, they would soon see she could look after herself just fine. She sat down to her computer and began reading up on the medical programs she was considering. She'd contacted a few advisors last spring, specifically at Emory and Mount Sinai. After talking to them, she'd filled out applications to each.

At first she'd been lukewarm to Mount Sinai and idea of living in New York, un-enamored with the thought of several months in the deep freeze they called winter up there. But she applied because it was a good school, and because of Stuart. They'd kept in touch, and when his schedule permitted, he flew down to see her. They always had mad, passionate fun together; and they always crammed a lot into their weekends in terms of plays and restaurants and various to-dos. Stuart was entertaining and social, and an easygoing counterpoint to the voice in her head, which was too close to that of her parents. Stuart didn't press her about her choices and abilities moving forward, although he had offered to put her in touch with someone at Mount Sinai.

Maya wondered why they were still dating, however. Not that he didn't look good on paper—because did he ever. She did too, though. It was the feeling she was something of a side project for Stuart, not integrated into his life like law school or his family were. She was the only one of his friends who had not attended an Ivy League university, although Stuart teased her she was forgiven because she was such a kick-ass athlete who had made good at the most prestigious program in the country for her sport.

And he was beautiful, so handsome. She remembered the first time he'd approached her at an after-game party, one where Maya's team had won and she'd been the top scorer. He'd been star struck, gazing at her in the same way those impoverished inner city girls she visited did, kids who thought Maya was really somebody. She found his admiration sweet, and then as he pursued her seriously, she'd been flattered enough to hope for more.

But now she was unconvinced. She'd been around Jeremy and Alicia—and Gabe and Kate—for too long, recognized a meaningful, uncontrived relationship when she saw one and her gig with Stu didn't measure up. Nonetheless she'd stayed with him, figuring everyone started out further apart than they finished. A few years of life together had a way of knitting people up, she reasoned.

Her fall into more permanent uneasiness had been when she tried to talk to Stuart about what she wanted to do after Penn State. She'd shared how she was at loose ends after her senior volleyball season ended, how the center around which she'd ordered her life since she was a child just dropped away. She confessed feeling a bit like someone had died, how she might never do anything interesting ever again. Stuart had frowned, possibly with disapproval, although she wasn't sure. Regardless, he'd said nothing supportive until she mentioned her interest in medical school, at which point he'd encouraged her. He also started to visit more often.

"You should come to New York," he advised on one of their dates, "check out Mount Sinai." Based on his initial distance when she'd first exposed her self-doubt that spring, she'd almost decided to be done with him. However badly she hoped to someday find a man she could love who would love her back, she wasn't going to force herself on someone who didn't. Plus, she cared for Stuart, who in his way had been a good companion to her. Consequently their experiment-in-limbo wasn't what she wanted for him, either. She believed they both should be with someone impossible to stay away from, not just fun when they made the time.

Her run-ins with Aiden played a bigger role in her dissatisfaction than she cared to admit. The sharp, raw emotions she felt in Aiden's presence bore no similarity to her entertainments with Stuart, nor did they refer to the pretty sit-com romances she enjoyed on television. In the moment before she left SeaCakes with John last time, she couldn't recall her own feelings . . . but she sure remembered Aiden's. He'd been about to give himself to her, and he wasn't cloaked in flowers or little dancing puppies. She pictured their exchange with him on the verge of reaching into his own chest to rip out his beating, bloody heart in offering, his expression one of defeat when he said, "Here, take it. I don't want it anymore."

Although this analogy was figurative, had he succeeded in whatever effort had been underway that afternoon, she would have followed him anywhere, just flat out caved. "Because I have no defense against . . . whatever that is," she murmured to herself. She rubbed her forehead with her fingertips. Now safely ensconced in her apartment and away from the threat of Aiden's overwhelming intimacy, she thought Stuart didn't look so bad by contrast. Nothing cataclysmic was just that—not cataclysmic. The more she thought about Stuart in those terms, the better she liked him.

She'd never believed she was the kind of woman to back away from uncomfortable truths, but the alternative terrified her, made her feel crazy. She remembered again the image of Aiden staring at her like an angel of death and the cliff he would pull her off of if she let him.

So. What would be so wrong with med school in New York and more time with Stuart?

Nothing, she decided. Nothing at all. She picked up her phone and called her contact at Mount Sinai. After a short discussion, she thanked him and promised to be in his office at the appointed time next Thursday. She texted Stuart, too, updating him on her plans. "I'm going to need an apt—not NY expensive, not NY tiny tho. Know a good real estate agent?" After hesitating, she also texted Kate: "Probly movin' to New York City and out of touch for a bit will call."

She then took out her coaching schedule to figure out the roster for her next game, grateful to be tackling things she understood. She didn't believe Aiden would ever fit into that category.

CHAPTER TWENTY-FOUR

Duncan's company exhausted and depressed her. And at any given hour, Isabel had to steel herself against leaving for that reason alone. She stayed not for further proof Duncan was up to no good—she knew with certainty he was—but because she felt obligated to do what she could to contain the threat he posed to family and friends. She wanted to remain in Raleigh until she could discover the details of whatever madness he plotted so she would have this information to take back to Carmen.

In what she considered the biggest paradox of her marriage, her complicity in this situation would allow her to undo whatever wrong Duncan would attempt, just as her complicity at Shaddox had supported his slide into selfishness. She hadn't quite understood what he was doing when they first talked after her arrival, but she soon figured it out. Duncan's reliance on primitive human hypnosis worked on her because at first she'd badly wanted for them to negotiate their relationship amiably, so she'd been open to him.

She felt so foolish over her initial naiveté back at Shaddox. Starting from the time she'd departed the palace, she'd continued to misunderstand both the depth of Duncan's depravity and her own ability to cope with it. Sometime during her first week in Raleigh, she found a registration form in Duncan's apartment for the hypnosis course he'd taken, which she immediately connected to their conversations. And that ridiculous cigarette he waved around.

Unfortunately, by giving him an initial entree into her psyche she'd allowed him to build a pathway of influence, which made her susceptible to his efforts thereafter, although she wanted to believe her own desire to act with integrity was at least as important as Duncan's facility. The problem, in her opinion, was her respect for siren society's principles of good behavior, which worked great if you could trust those you interacted with to conduct themselves likewise. She'd played fair, worked to diffuse potential conflict, and by now had lost any ability she'd ever had to engage in sustained acrimony.

Her long association with Duncan also sealed her fate concerning his manipulative forays into her subconscious, since she was literally unable to resist these requests from her one-time mate.

To her chagrin, he now accessed a conduit into her head whether she wanted him to or not, which he did often and without compunction. It wasn't a carte blanche ability to overtake her—she was too strong for such tactics to completely work—but she experienced a softening of her individual resolve, and a compulsive urge to follow whatever instructions he gave her regardless of her better judgment.

The most difficult component of these interactions had become overcoming the desire to quit, to flee Duncan's suffocating demands and deny him the control he sought—over her, over Carmen and Xanthe, over anyone she might interact with. She didn't know if he understood how much of herself she could still direct, which was not enough but not nothing, either; and she believed she'd lulled him into a false sense of security she could use to her advantage, which gave her courage to continue. Because during her hypnosis sessions Duncan was unguarded in his thoughts, at his most excited to seize power, and consequently he revealed more than he likely intended. She hoped by staying involved and later managing a covert escape, she could report home with all the details related to Duncan's sick undertakings. She believed herself responsible for keeping him contained before he harmed anyone.

Gabe made it to Raleigh by noon and found Duncan within two hours. His expedience annoyed him; he hadn't expected to be successful at all, much less find his target—who was two hundred miles *inland* by the way—in six hours. He would lie to Xanthe when he got back, ineffectively since she would see through him in about a second and a half. But he'd say it took him days and the mission was arduous.

He found Duncan walking the banks of the river Gabe had used as a travel route. A slovenly associate attended him, a man who appeared to be human. *Well. Of course he's human*, Gabe thought. He wasn't likely to come across a congregation of sirens this far from the sea. Gabe stepped behind a tree and assumed his cloak—his first attempt to appear as a dog—then followed the duo as closely as he dared.

Duncan's companion's name was Julian, and he was arguing in favor of a video of Duncan, which Duncan maintained wouldn't work. "You see, I'm only persuasive in person," Duncan stated. Julian did not see, insisted Duncan was the most charming and engaging person available for the shoot. Duncan shook his head. "You can still promote me using a spokesperson, but my 'charm,' as you call it, won't translate unless it's in person."

Julian continued to try to change his mind until Duncan raised his hand. "It grieves me to tell you yet again your idea won't work, but I'm unwilling to fight any longer. I'll consider it. What other questions do you have for me?"

Julian smiled as if he'd been given a free car. "The same ones, Mr. Fleming. I would be more effective if I understood what we're actually doing."

To his surprise, Gabe intuited Duncan's emotional response as if they were in the water together. He had no idea why he could read the man so clearly—maybe because Duncan felt so strongly? But he could tell Julian had asked these questions before: who was Duncan, really, what did he hope to accomplish, what were the peripheral components of his plan he'd not yet explained, and why would he withhold information from his biggest supporter?

In Duncan's opinion, Julian's curiosity had festered and fed on itself so much he appeared off-balance, not just to him but to everyone. Julian's comical list of hypotheses—Duncan was an alien, a time traveler, an escaped government experiment—posed a very unfunny risk to Duncan's advancement efforts. For one, Duncan had enough trouble passing for normal and didn't need his most public representative spouting conspiracy theories or similarly bizarre ideas that would repulse those he sought to influence.

Finally—and this insight inspired Gabe's first feelings of empathy for the human—Julian was as yet too insecure, too needy for recognition from others to be a trustworthy confidante. Duncan believed his truths in their entirety would provide Julian with social currency too valuable not to spend, and therein lay the threat Julian could undermine his schemes.

Which, Gabe learned, were whacko. He couldn't catch every detail because Duncan wasn't thinking about them all; but he apprehended enough to understand this reconnaissance mission was warranted. Duncan, if left alone, would pose a big, big problem for his mother's regime. Anger spread like a corrosive acid within him.

At which point Duncan abruptly faced in Gabe's direction. He was looking for another siren, Gabe understood . . . and Gabe hoped his cloak would hold. He resolved to better contain his emotional output in Duncan's presence.

An eerie stillness like the portentous calm before a tornado settled between them as Duncan's gaze landed directly on him. He made himself stay calm, sat on the periphery of the walking path and stared at a squirrel in the tree above him. Again Gabe was grateful to catch the minutiae of Duncan's thoughts as if they were touching or in the water, even if he found his ability to hear him so clearly confusing. Duncan registered him as a nondescript dog, a terrier mix reminiscent of a mutt he'd seen in North Carolina.

Oops. Gabe wished he'd been more imaginative in his selection of a cover.

It looks like the Blakes' pet . . . what was his name? Soley. That's it, Duncan mused.

But he realized Soley couldn't be here, of course. Griffins Bay was hours away, and the dog wouldn't be here alone. Duncan applied his senses more assiduously to catch the presence of another siren. Finding none, he looked away and returned to his conversation with Julian.

He intended to shore him up, to reveal just enough of his intentions to temporarily satisfy.

Gabe was certain he'd escaped recognition, but he couldn't see how. And the close knowledge he had of the older siren's thoughts continued to unnerve him. When Duncan clasped Julian's arm to impart private information, a jolt went through Gabe as if he'd been touched instead of Julian.

Gabe searched his memory for a similar experience but he could not ascribe his supersensory performance to anything he knew. He'd never actually met Duncan, which created the possibility that Duncan's nature was the primary factor here. Whatever the cause, Gabe had a direct line into Duncan's head and Duncan remained unaware he was under surveillance, which was extraordinary. As Duncan looked around, Gabe took the extra precaution of disappearing. The former viceroy shared more of his intentions with Julian.

Which led Gabe to conclude Duncan was legitimately psycho. As intuitive as Gabe was, he would never have known how unstable Duncan was without the access he had via this ultra-conductive cloak he'd somehow achieved. He felt Duncan's insecurity like the thrum of a whirring motor, central to who he was and a literal cyclone absorbing nearly all of the man's better inclinations. He also sensed the subliminal disconnect taking place in Duncan's mind between what he wanted and what was good and fair, a struggle so familiar to Duncan he no longer recognized the friction in the decisions he made, no longer felt remorse for causing harm.

Interesting given how he still differentiated between right and wrong, at least in theory, Gabe noted. Which caused him to conclude Duncan had been a better man at some point. At present, however, he cared only for the pursuit adulation, as well as release from the fear of not being good enough. The civility he exhibited had little substance; it was in place to convince others of integrity he didn't have, so they would be lulled in to helping him get what he wanted.

Right now, he wanted incontrovertible evidence of siren existence he could display to humans. It was some sort of film project, one Duncan knew could be contained and one Julian would see as a purely creative effort, not a documentary. Duncan would threaten Carmen with permanent exposure to ward off any efforts she or Xanthe might take to bully Duncan out of his bid for power here. According to his convoluted reasoning, this stand would give him the influence he craved over their monarchy because Carmen would be at his mercy. He would at last have the recognition, the deference, he deserved. Duncan figured Carmen would bargain just to keep Shaddox Island hidden. He knew he could hold all sorts of sway over her if he involved individual members of her family or court in his efforts.

Gabe felt a swell of anger every bit as intense as the one he'd experienced when Kate had been taken. He'd been counseled many times now against his 'penchant for retribution,' had taken multiple lectures on how antithetical violence was to siren nature. But his first inclination was to drop his cloak and tackle the moron threatening his mother. He didn't much care if the effort fell outside Xanthe's definition of civilized behavior, and wasn't that reminiscent of his fight with Peter last year.

He rested his hand on the hunting knife he kept tethered to his waist, on the verge of taking care of this problem right here, right now.

Something stayed him. In the instant before he drew his knife, he experienced a sharp internal reprimand, as if he were a little boy and his father commanded him not to be disobedient. Which felt bizarre. He was an adult and pretty sure his dad would feel as strongly as he did about the schmuck he wanted to off.

But the directive was absolute, and his interest in rebelling against it became nonexistent. His killing rage disappeared.

He decided instead to take what he'd learned back to his parents and Xanthe. In a flash of insight he understood how involving his community in the problem would teach them something valuable about human influence on their kind and their own capacity for deviance. It would also be a lesson in strength for the new ruler, and he was not to deprive her of learning it. He removed his hand from the hilt of his knife.

Duncan released Julian's arm, then praised him for his good work and asked him to return to his desk and order supplies. Julian trotted off.

For several seconds, Duncan watched his employee retreat. A smile of satisfaction stretched across his face, and Gabe once again wanted to kill him. As Gabe faded into the woods, he felt Duncan's curiosity reach out as he looked for the dog he'd seen earlier. When he didn't see Soley, Duncan started back toward his offices.

CHAPTER TWENTY-FIVE

"The Drake Passage is a 500-mile wide stretch of ocean that extends between the southern tip of South America and the polar desert that caps the bottom of the Earth," Simon had read on a placard placed by the docks. He'd known the Passage as a notoriously brutal stretch of sea that could toss ships on 20-foot waves and roll them to 35 degrees on either side. And he knew it as an infamous graveyard for sailors and travelers from earlier centuries, something he did not mention to his intended.

In this place where the Atlantic and Pacific Oceans met and shook hands, voyagers received an up-close demonstration on how little hospitality Mother Nature cared to offer human visitors here, and how easily she might annihilate even the most seaworthy of vessels. Which was why Simon had booked passage on a Finnish-made ice breaker shaped like a bathtub. They were in for a rolling ride, one he suspected would terrify Sylvia; but the crew was experienced, and the ship's design, which would bounce them like a bath toy, also made it sturdy enough to go through almost anything. And stay afloat.

Since swimming was not a good option, he'd selected the alternative with the highest likelihood of survivability, and wasn't he smart.

"She is calm today, non?" The French captain posed this question to Simon on the first day of their trip. He was a grizzled former naval officer of middle years, with deep-set iron eyes and teeth stained from heavy tobacco use. Sylvia found him unappealing because he stood too close to them and lingered despite having little to say. With this—perhaps his tenth approach—he officially achieved in Simon's mind the distinction of being the only human whose company he did not welcome. "I've spent my life at sea tu sais," the captain told them.

Simon was worried over Sylvia's seasickness at the moment. He could control her nausea when he concentrated, and he swallowed the urge to take her away from an interaction neither of them desired. Instead, he faked a smile as if he wanted nothing more than to stay and tolerate their overbearing host. He kept one arm around Sylvia's waist while she looked out the portal window. She'd told him a view outside might stabilize her stomach. She didn't bother to turn and greet their interloper. "Captain Benet," Simon said politely.

Antoine Benet had paid particular attention to Simon since they'd boarded, and Simon chafed under his constant scrutiny, as well as his attempts at friendship. He knew the captain found him enigmatic . . . but the man studied him like he wanted a look inside, maybe with a scalpel.

Simon's attempts at evasion mostly failed, because here Benet was yet again, too solicitous and intense as usual. Simon squirmed under the man's regard like he was a too-warm coat. Tomorrow, thankfully, they would reach land. Simon hoped to never see him again.

Benet nodded toward Sylvia. "Not so calm if one is not used to her, I see. She is better?"

Sylvia stood in front of him and did not see him shake his head. "She's hanging in there," Simon said to encourage her.

Sylvia was aware of the captain but not what he said. In her mind he was—along with Simon—one of the blessed, someone who thought nothing of the gravity defying tilts and sways wreaking havoc with her insides. Regardless, she couldn't be bothered to lift her head and greet him. Every roll to her felt like imminent death, and given the wretched seasickness she suffered, she prayed for a swift end.

A loud crash on the upper deck interrupted their non-conversation as the three of them were thrown to the floor. As soon as they could, both men leapt to their feet and turned their heads toward the direction of the impact. They started to make their way down the corridor toward its source. "I'll be right back, Sylvia," Simon promised over his shoulder. She pressed herself up with help from a wall. "Stay inside, okay?" and he was gone.

Sylvia's knees buckled. Without Simon's stabilizing influence, visions of the Titanic ran like a 3-D movie in her head. The possibility of sinking into the frigid, roiling ocean took away the last of her strength, and she dropped again to all fours.

She breathed and tried to convince herself the crash could have been nothing, even if it felt like a meteor had blasted into them. She calmed a little, but could not suppress the suspicion they were all going to die. She managed to stop shaking enough to stand, and when she was confident she had control of her stomach and bladder, she thought about getting back to their cabin. She peered down the hallway where Simon had gone.

A new anguish blossomed in her chest.

She started to feel as she had when he'd left her at their hotel in Argentina, when she'd decided her fast-talking boyfriend and her own foolishness had led her down the garden path and landed her in a pit of quicksand. When they'd returned that afternoon after her failed attempt to call the United States Simon had said very little, but he'd stayed with her and in so doing reassured her more effectively than promises ever could have. Eventually she reclaimed her confidence and rekindled the excitement that had made running away with him an imperative.

And in the hours following, Simon had exhibited such sincere worry over her well-being she could no longer doubt his reliability. In fact she believed her anxiety had disquieted him as much as it had her . . . and she grew ashamed for her lack of trust. Back at their hotel, he'd held her and whispered assurances she should not be troubled, told her he felt so fortunate to be with her and everything would work out in the end, she'd see. She'd believed him. Her initial anticipation and enthusiasm had returned.

Now, in the aftermath of their unspecified collision, her panic did not cause her to search for recriminations against Simon; instead, she felt desolate outside his presence and wanted him back. Combined with her unsteadiness—she literally could not keep her feet under her and she'd been tossing up her cookies for the better part of the past 24 hours—she was desperate to find him. She lurched toward the upper deck.

Simon broadcast his influence to the crew so he could insinuate himself into the group and help with the crisis at hand. They accepted him easily. The captain further facilitated his inclusion by draping an arm around his shoulders and then talking openly of the potential problems they faced, even asking Simon what he would do in his shoes. A rogue wave had slammed the ship with a sizable chunk of ice, much of which landed on the aft deck and had either jammed or taken out a propeller, no one knew. But the ship's steering was affected, and the crew discussed how to fix the problem. They debated a return to the South American shore for repairs.

The captain watched Simon too intently, until Simon, having gleaned enough information, turned to him. He stared at the captain with open annoyance.

"Fix her," Benet said, looking meaningfully into Simon's eyes. He then turned on his heel and announced he would be on the bridge.

From the way the ship moved, Simon believed a propeller was jammed. He decided to overlook the captain's strange behavior, at least until after he could 'fix her', as the man instructed.

He found the blockage within seconds of diving under and behind the ship. He'd grabbed an axe on his way in . . . and his instincts proved correct. He studied the problem briefly before taking a measured swing, then recoiled to swing again, using all his strength to dislodge the chunk of ice that jammed the propeller. After three blows, he succeeded. He jettisoned away from the turning blades as they re-engaged. He stayed until he saw the ship stabilize.

Sylvia. He turned his face upwards as he felt her presence above and heard her anguished thoughts. Oh no. She'd followed him.

Sylvia had known exactly where to look for Simon although she didn't know why; she'd simply closed her eyes and felt her way along the corridor until she reached the portal leading out to the rear deck. She attached herself to the harness anchored outside the door and grasped the tethers as she tried to see past the sleeting, violent blasts of seawater assailing her.

She saw him leap over the side of the ship into the icy waters, and she screamed after him, the wind and the roar of the water muffling her voice. Her feet carried her forward as she frantically searched the waves, the gusts so strong she had to crawl after only a few feet. She strained against the harness toward the spot he'd disappeared.

No. Please, God. She clawed her way forward, wild with despair as she scanned the water for him, knowing the futility of her effort but driven to make it nonetheless. The wind played cruelly with her attempts to direct herself, and the splashing water conspired to make sure she gained no footing, could only scoot on her belly. She slid along the perimeter of what her harness allowed and stubbornly studied what she could see of the ocean. She began to feel the effects of hypothermia taking hold.

She knew she should get back to shelter, understood she accomplished nothing with her search; but she had to stay. She refused to accept what reason told her. She felt he was nearby. She would not believe he was gone.

Simon bolted to the water's surface and launched himself, tail and all, onto the ship's rear deck. He converted quickly out of his siren form to reach Sylvia's side.

She was insane with worry and minutes from freezing to death in the chill deluge of seawater drafting over her again and again. He was so angry she would risk herself like this, as if she could do anything to save him even if he had washed overboard. He chided her even as he clasped her in his arms and kissed her face, berating her for her foolishness when he could take perfectly good care of himself . . .

He closed his eyes as he realized she still didn't know what he was, and in reminding himself of this fact, frustration with his situation overrode his anger. While he was pleased she no longer thought of running from him, her trust—her *blind* trust which had now put her in mortal danger—meant something more than it did eight days ago.

It meant he had to reveal himself to her.

Eventually, finally, she stopped quaking, and his temper flared again over how close she'd come to death. Taking a guess—and he was pretty accurate with these kinds of things—she wouldn't have survived another ten minutes without him. His muscles stiffened in denial, as if he was preparing physically to fight death off. But he forced himself to relax, and then renewed his resolve to share everything with her. He couldn't stand any more of these secrecy problems.

As he had done each day since leaving North Carolina, he wrapped a hand around her wrist and cradled their joined hands against his heart. They still had a little time, but he would tell her everything now. "I'm so sorry, Sylvia. I'm here," he told her. "Everything's okay. I'm sorry."

Within moments, she'd recovered enough to castigate him. "Jumping in like that was unforgivable, Simon." She squeezed her eyes shut. "You were so irresponsible and *stupid* . . . how could you even . . . ?" She became too angry to speak.

Simon's words rushed out of him. "I have some things to tell you, but let's get inside, first."

CHAPTER TWENTY-SIX

Back in their cabin, Simon stripped Sylvia out of her frozen clothes and soon had them wrapped skin-to-skin in a heavy wool blanket in their bunk. Sylvia shivered violently. Simon cursed.

He pulled the berth's curtains closed to block out light and other stimulus. "No distractions for you. I'm going to tell you everything. Even though you're livid. But I need to tell you I wasn't in danger. You, however, were."

Sylvia protested. "I know it seems like I'm okay since we're all cozied up, but I'm so mad at you I could spit." She paused to grit her chattering teeth. "Don't even think about trying to make love to me."

Simon laughed in spite of their situation. "Don't be mad," he begged. "It wasn't what you thought." He took her hands and clutched them behind his back so they were chest to chest. She finally stopped shivering. He stared in her eyes and she relaxed by slow degrees against him until he said, "And it's best if we wait another few days to make love."

Her retort was venomous. "I mean it, Simon. I do not think much of you right now." She tried to push him away.

"No—stay by me," Simon whispered. "Just until you warm up." He leaned down to kiss her.

She planted her face against his chest to avoid him, which made her feel absurd, since her arguments were now muffled. "You can't just gloss over what happened. I mean, it's one thing for me to trust you when we're both in, say, *America* where I have access to a phone and my ID. It's another to haul us to the ends of the earth where I'm completely reliant on you, and then watch you fling yourself into a kagillion gallons of ice water." She started to cry. "I mean seriously, Simon. What was I supposed to think?"

He tipped her chin up. "I was never in danger," he promised.

"Sure you weren't." She shook her head, but as she inhaled to scold him again . . . she stopped. She could feel his conflicting emotions as if they were her own—his anger over her near demise consistent with her outrage over his apparent suicide attempt, their mutual relief over the other's return to safety, their mutual belief the secrecy between them had become intolerable.

She wanted to argue with him, but she realized she would not make him feel more regret than he already did. He was sincere in his apology and, although she didn't see how he could possibly have a sane explanation, she decided to let him try and give her one. "Tell me, then." The corners of his mouth lifted.

"Give us both another minute to quiet down," he said as he stroked her hair. Her anger completely softened.

In the shaded enclosure of their bunk, the rest of the world bled away, and Sylvia's perceptions narrowed to exclude everything unnecessary, everything external. She became aware only of Simon and the movement of their ship, which for once felt soothing and gentle, like a cradle. She felt content for the first time since they'd boarded.

Her thoughts and feelings melted deliciously, as if she were entering into what promised to be a satisfying, luxurious sleep. As she stretched, she gained the impression she and Simon were no longer stationary on a mattress but floating alongside one another in weightless suspension. She recalled her imaginary encounters in Griffins Bay, the ones where she would remember vividly experiences she'd never had, such as swimming with whales or the view of an expanse of ocean as seen from an ice floe. She pictured these scenes again, reveling in the freedom and joy they suggested. She reached hungrily for other images like them.

She sensed but no longer saw Simon beside her now. She felt his presence as an invitation, and he was her conduit to the pictures she saw. She felt a seal graze her back and the nudge of a dolphin wanting to play. But although delightful, these creatures were diversions from what she really sought, so she did not follow when they beckoned. She searched instead for a particular creature, the one that had captivated her when she first had these dreams.

She saw it finally, a ghost image at first, the silvery green tail of her sea monster. It floated around her like a veil, undulating and graceful, until it seemed she swam behind it, chasing it. The tail was all she could see, and it enthralled her.

She thrilled to this particular experience because her fish stayed by her instead of disappearing as it usually did. Also, they were in the water together, something it never allowed. Although it let her get close, it remained out of her reach, leading her deeper and further away from their dark bunk and their sea-tossed ship. She followed. Her dream took on greater clarity.

When she was fully immersed in their imaginary swim, her marine companion stopped and let her approach, its magnificent fluke waving mere inches before her, begging her touch. She laid her palm on the base of the tail fin . . . and felt an immediate pleasure so compelling she reached with her other hand, as well, so she touched the smooth, brilliant scales with both palms. The contact delivered even more pleasure, as well as reassurance. She understood this creature adored her, wanted only happiness for her.

Her sea monster—for she recognized him as such now and welcomed the recognition—vibrated with an untamed energy that left her yearning for a final revelation he had yet to provide. She felt his emotions as her own now, and they were violent and raw and wonderful, no longer dreamlike. Everything in him called her to release all she felt—her hopes and desires, her fears and frustrations. She was given promises in return: she would be cherished and protected from every trouble because he would be there to fight everything, even sadness. *A foolish promise*, she thought. But she didn't hesitate to answer him.

Yes, I'll follow you. Yes, I'll stay by you. Yes, I'll love you and be your lover.

A man's arms pulled her now, drawing her up the body of her fish, her hands skating over the iridescent scales in a reverent caress as she progressed. The caudal fin feathered her legs as she ascended and her hands spanned the widening form. She paused at the transition between scales and skin, delighting in the textures. She savored the transition . . . because she was on the verge of a fantastic discovery, the biggest secret her fish had kept from her, and neither of them would ever be the same after she knew.

She floated and trusted in their devotion, that they would care for and protect one another. Her companion drew her upward.

When their torsos were even and her palms rested at last on the planes of his abdomen, then chest, she looked into the face of her beloved. It was Simon, and she was unsurprised. He gazed at her more tenderly than anyone ever had, and her return smile was radiant.

His eyes still held a question, though. She saw his worry, that she would turn away, and she shook her head.

Simon.

Yes, Sylvia.

It was you, by the shore back home. You're a mermaid.

Yes, Sylvia.

She wound her arms around him and pressed herself against him. "I will stay by you always," she whispered. Simon wrapped her tightly in his embrace and bent his cheek to her hair.

Yes, Sylvia. Please. Always.

CHAPTER TWENTY-SEVEN

Gabe followed his urge to find Duncan's residence and headed toward downtown Raleigh. He continued to be amazed by his hyper-sharp perceptions in this place, and reviewed his recent experience in the park for clues as to why he had been able to cloak so masterfully. And why he'd been able to plug in so well to Duncan's exchange with his underling at a distance. He could catch not just the gist of Duncan's plans, but his doubts and motivations, too, as well as all the nuances of feeling and response Gabe had never before been able to access from another siren.

Duncan hadn't even known he was there!

He had some mad skills going on and no explanation as to why.

He arrived at Duncan's building to find Isabel sitting on the front steps, which gave him an idea. Oddly the notion felt more like a suggestion, a little like the command he'd received in the park not to kill the former viceroy, although he also wanted to experiment with his sharper abilities. He sensed he had an opportunity to learn something here, something he could uncover better if Isabel didn't see him. And so he disappeared.

She didn't notice him, which again demonstrated a level of cloaking sophistication Gabe hadn't had last year. He was able to move all around without her becoming aware . . . which prompted him to try the next thing: reaching into her with his intuition.

Still no recognition. Gabe exulted in his success, actually laughed, and she remained oblivious.

He extended himself further yet with the rationale he inflicted no harm. He decided to appear as another siren, one she knew, just to see if he could pull it off. Last fall, when he'd infiltrated the palace to rescue Kate, he'd done so as Charles Gavin. But he'd been lucky. He'd avoided Peter both during his interview and his early days on the job, and he hadn't completely masked his appearance, just skewed his emotional projections. He'd succeeded with everyone who didn't know him, but presumed he would have been discovered if Peter had been around.

He felt infinitely competent now.

He considered appearing as his father but that seemed wrong for reasons he couldn't articulate. His next option felt like spitting in the face of fate, but was also the most challenging cloak he could imagine and therefore enticing to him. He acted on it as soon as the idea entered his mind.

His transformation rippled through him in a shimmer of warmth, the feeling not unlike when he changed from biped to siren. And he felt a surge of power unlike any he'd experienced before. He stepped forward . . . and even before Isabel spoke, he knew he'd succeeded.

Her eyes widened incredulously. "Peter Loughlin?"

Gabe bent his head back and laughed—over the idea to cloak as his grandfather in the first place, and because he was convincing to someone who had been a member of Peter's inner circle at the palace. He felt a thrill like he had as a young man first exercising his man's strength after boyhood, a joy he hadn't experienced in years.

But he dropped his cloak to appear as Gabe before he answered her, and his first impulse was to apologize. "No. I'm sorry, Isabel. It's Gabriel Blake, in case you don't remember. I've been practicing cloaks and thought I'd try our former prince." She looked so shaken he apologized again. "I'm really sorry if I startled you."

Gabe's hypersensitivity, which he first exercised not forty minutes earlier in Duncan's company, now felt permanent, and he coughed to hide his confusion—over seeing too much and knowing too much. Isabel studied him and forced him to meet her eyes.

She inspected him closely for several seconds. "You're upset," she concluded. "Why?" And then more sharply, "Actually, why are you here?"

Uh-oh. He hadn't thought about having to answer that last question, hadn't expected to run into another siren so far inland aside from Duncan. He responded to her first question instead.

"I'm agitated because as of about an hour ago I started feeling different. Like someone attached battery cables to me, powered me up, and I can all of a sudden do more than I ever could. I mean I can see more, know more, feel what others are feeling. And apparently," he waved a hand in Isabel's direction, "I can cloak better than I used to. A *lot* better."

Isabel assessed him shrewdly. "You began cloaking last year, when you thought your wife was dead. Am I correct?" Gabe nodded, and she continued. "We get stronger as we get older, you know. Our gifts can also become more refined. Maybe you've matured. Or rather your cloaking abilities have."

Gabe tilted his head. "I suppose that's plausible."

As with Duncan, Gabe realized he had more insight into her state of mind than was typical for him out of the water . . . and he was pretty sure she did not sense the level to which he read her thoughts and feelings. She was equally happy and unhappy to see him; glad because she felt isolated and anxious so far from home and seeing him felt like home. She craved the company her kind, was a little lost and desperate after her time away. She was unhappy because her bond with her husband was irretrievably broken. She knew Duncan was here with the intention to hurt them all, and she felt responsible for stopping him.

Gabe apprehended her more refined understanding of Duncan's metamorphosis from stable to destructive. She didn't have the word for what he was, but Gabe did: the guy was a sociopath. But she was focused on what she saw as her own contributions to the situation, was ashamed personally of what Duncan had become. She felt she'd facilitated his demise by being selfish, and she didn't want any witnesses to what she considered her failure, not until she had something to offer to set the situation to rights.

In what Gabe saw as a heartbreaking show of loyalty, she also worried about compromising her husband; even though she knew he no longer wanted her—was in fact careless of her well-being on every level—she believed she owed him her protection.

Gabe put his hand on her arm to comfort her, and through this connection, tried to convince her Duncan's deviance was not her fault. *The community will not blame you,* he promised. Aloud he told her, "You've done nothing wrong, Isabel."

She began to cry, nodding as if to convince herself he was right, and Gabe felt a niggling sense of purpose. He could do something he normally could not to help her right now. He also understood Isabel had no talent for guile and would inform Duncan when she next saw him how she'd run into Gabriel Blake, which would cause problems both for the community's efforts to capture him, and because Duncan might retaliate. Specifically against Isabel.

Gabe decided to make her forget their encounter and to convince her not to feel responsible for Duncan while he was at it. As early as yesterday, this undertaking would have felt ludicrously outside his abilities. But something had changed, and he knew—he *knew*—he could do it. He'd just cloaked as Peter Loughlin, for crying out loud, a ridiculously difficult effort he'd had no reason to attempt, much less accomplish. Oh yeah. He had his game down.

He'd reached into her before fully committing to do so, his new facility taking on a will of its own, and he made a shocking discovery.

Isabel had been tampered with. She didn't realize how much, but Duncan had planted suggestions so she would help him with some sort of extortion device, a scheme he'd created to threaten Carmen. He'd been ironing out logistics with that human back in the park, Julian.

Isabel didn't consciously recognize the details, but Gabe did: Duncan planned a show-the-world-we're-mermaids exposé. And Duncan was a lot sicker than any of them suspected.

The execution was crude and had likely worked because of Isabel's compromised emotional state. And because she still felt obligated to her husband, the big creep. Gabe followed the path Duncan had made, realizing he'd employed human hypnosis techniques, and holy cats as his wife would say. The man was really stooping.

In fact Gabe couldn't imagine such an artless effort working on any other siren he knew, certainly not his parents or Xanthe. He pitied Isabel her vulnerability, and impossibly felt even more distaste for the former viceroy.

Gabe continued to wade through Duncan's suggestions, cringing at the unsophisticated way they'd been planted, until he pieced together all of Duncan's tactics. Gabe then erased himself from Isabel's memory—"Peter's" appearance as well as his own—and he insisted she would not think of Duncan's sins as her own.

He should not have been able to do these things.

But. In keeping with his MO of deciding on the fly today, he also elected to bolster a select few of Duncan's commands, to give them more structural integrity in Isabel's mind so non-insane sirens could better predict Duncan's actions and see him coming, as it were. Isabel was protected for the moment; and the community could more easily take her ex out of commission as long as he thought he was still in charge.

Finally, Gabe told Isabel how strong she was. *No one I know would have tolerated all of Duncan's nonsense. You're going to be the reason we prevail against him, so thank you. You are very brave!*

His influence was faultless, and he left no trace of his presence when he retreated.

His triumphs prompted him to consider what else he might do. Perhaps he was competent enough to construct a series of cloaks at once, just as Peter had? If he could do it, he could orchestrate Duncan's capture from multiple vantage points.

Gabe no longer wanted to delay his return to Griffins Bay. He needed to warn everyone about Mr. Fleming's psychological issues and he needed to help Xanthe and his parents decide how to deal with their newest siren deviant.

CHAPTER TWENTY-EIGHT

Maya pored over her studies by the front window at SeaCakes, an activity made both possible and pleasant due to the slow afternoon. Two workers had come in a couple of hours ago to prep for the next day, pastries mostly, and Saturday mornings were busy so they doubled up on goodie-making. Maya had no training or interest in these tasks and so was free to tackle her schoolwork. She checked the clock on the wall. *Almost time to close.*

Dana had called her at school yesterday, frantic for help since Sylvia had gone MIA and created a massive personnel hole at the café. Would she mind scooting home for the weekend to help out for a few hours? Thanks to the arrival of their twin daughters, neither of the Fletchers could be at the business as Sylvia had been.

No one knew when Sylvia planned to return, but due to some mystical reasoning she didn't understand, Dana and Will had refrained from hiring her replacement. And this meant fire drills when it came to scheduling. Maya said she'd come.

Even though she had no more information than anyone else on Sylvia's whereabouts, she understood too well her sister's motivations. She'd felt exactly what Sylvia had, and she suspected she and Aiden would have played copycat if . . . if something else had been different. She knew nothing—not better judgment, not another person—could have stopped them; but she still felt guilty and weak for letting Sylvia go without any inquiry from her. Or even a goodbye.

Maybe she wished Aiden *had* been so hungry for a rendezvous with her he would have been just as incautious and she was jealous. She'd come home to do penance as much as to save SeaCakes from being understaffed.

She was exhausted by this time, though. She'd clocked in at five thirty that morning to prep and cover the front of the store while two other bakers worked on the food production end of things in the back. She'd barely caught her breath after the breakfast rush when the lunch crowd showed up . . . and although she'd wedged in a little study time, the sporadic appearance of customers and other interruptions that afternoon had made for a long day.

She felt rather than saw Aiden come in. The acidic thrill caused by his proximity was now distinctive, and she didn't even look up to verify what her electrified nervous system already told her.

He stopped as soon as he stepped through the door. "Maya? What are you doing here?"

He sounded angry at her, which offended her and made her angry, as well. So she kept her head down and pretended to read, although she couldn't have identified a single word on the page in front of her if he'd asked. She tried to sound disinterested. "I'm working, covering for my sister, Sylvia. The one your brother abducted. What are you doing here?"

He rubbed his face tiredly. "Maya, I come here every day." He took vindictive pleasure in her discomfort.

He knew how he affected her—could taste her feelings in the air like they were gun smoke—and he was glad he wasn't the only one fighting their attraction. She still hadn't looked at him, though, so he sat in the chair opposite her, a challenge to ignore him if she could. He was childish to force an interaction but he didn't care. If he'd known she was working, he wouldn't have come.

No, that wasn't true. He always hoped to see her when he came in. His daily visit was a petty exercise in self-abuse, a perverse need to revisit the crime scene where he'd sacrificed his own convictions for a siren ideal he neither respected nor believed in. Because what was one more siren-human hook-up in a town that had served up only four in the last twenty years? He skated on the under-edge of social acceptance these days, anyway . . . and he truly wondered why he'd complied with the directive to leave Maya alone in the first place.

Except he knew. If Simon hadn't relied on him—and if his own desire to bond hadn't competed with his brother's—he would have grabbed Maya's hand and run with her.

Anyhow. He was reasonably sure Maya was in Philadelphia whenever he dropped by. Still, his senses ranged forth as he approached with the hope maybe, just maybe he'd find her behind the counter. He could no more stop himself from seeking her out than he could quit breathing; nor could he stem his disappointment when she was absent. And then he made his standard, subsequent promise to himself not to return. His daily resolution to stay away from SeaCakes became a comical cycle of self-delusion and disappointment.

Even so he came each day because he wanted to be some place she'd been. Not an hour went by anymore when he didn't think about her or wonder what she was doing. Or wish they were together.

"Technically, Simon didn't abduct your sister," Aiden hedged. "She wanted to go along."

Maya looked sharply at him then and Aiden received her conflicted feelings as the contradictions they were. She believed her sister had gone willingly but wasn't thinking straight. She suspected Aiden and others knew more about the situation than they let on. She hoped their secrecy didn't hide anything sinister and thought Sylvia was probably happy wherever she was . . . but she wasn't sure. She thought about how she'd feel if she and Aiden had taken off instead of or in addition to Sylvia and Simon. She fought the pull she felt to him, wished she instead felt more attracted to someone named Stuart.

He glared at her. "Who the hell is Stuart?"

Maya looked horrified. "Please tell me I didn't say that out loud . . ." The bell over the door rang as another customer—two men actually—came in. Maya bolted away from him to attend them.

She recognized one of them. "Ethan?" she asked, and Aiden could tell she wasn't sure. His initial flare of jealousy faded; Maya didn't know the man she addressed, and she certainly didn't like him.

Ethan shifted uncomfortably. "Hi, Maya."

Her demeanor was decidedly cool, which Aiden liked. "We

haven't seen you in a while. You look," she eyed him critically, "different." Aiden smiled to himself. If this guy thought he could blow in here and charm his girl, Maya had just disabused him of the belief.

He still wanted to know why this Ethan had shown up, though. Aiden looked him over for the "different" Maya referenced. He didn't notice anything remarkable—the guy was nice-looking, Aiden supposed, and his clothes were colorful but in good taste. His most noticeable attribute was the sort of dewy happiness he put off; the man glowed like a bride, which helped Aiden relax further since this one's romantic tank seemed like it was full. He for sure wasn't here for his Maya. Ethan's next statement confirmed it . . . and provided new clarity.

"I know. I used to think maybe your sister and I . . ." He floundered before placing a hand on his companion's forearm. "This is my friend, Oliver. I was hoping to introduce him to Sylvia."

Ah. He used to flirt with Sylvia. And Maya thought he'd hurt her sister's feelings. Ethan came to explain himself, with Oliver as exhibit A.

Maya relaxed her stance and her expression softened. "You came to apologize? That makes you a stand-up guy after all, and I appreciate it. But don't worry; Sylvia left on her own romantic adventure a while back."

To his credit, Ethan looked genuinely happy. "But that's fabulous!" He glanced at Oliver. "I wanted to let her know I've, ah, had an epiphany of sorts, and I . . . well, I guess just wanted to stop by and see her, tell her I wish her well. I also wanted apologize to her. For how I acted while I figured myself out. It wasn't fair and I shouldn't have . . ."

Maya interrupted him with a hand on his arm. She regarded him kindly and told him, "You're off the hook, friend. Sylvia will be happy for you, I'm sure of it. Don't even worry." She grinned at Ethan's companion. "She's with her own Oliver." They all laughed, and Ethan pulled Maya into a rough hug.

Aiden used the opportunity to creep behind her since she was distracted enough by her drama with Ethan not to notice. He stopped a foot from her back, and when Ethan released her, ran a forefinger lightly from the base of her spine to the top of her neck.

He watched goose bumps form on her skin. "Who's Stuart?" he whispered insistently in her ear. Maya's breath caught.

I don't want to talk with Aiden about Stuart.

Yeah, sweetheart. I bet. Her dread was palpable, and good thing Maya didn't know about siren intuition. He snickered.

Ethan cleared his throat. "Anyway, we won't stay. But if you see Sylvia please tell her I stopped in." He blushed. "And I want her to know I'm sorry. I wish her well." Oliver beamed, proud as if Ethan had saved all the polar bears. When they turned to leave, Aiden accidentally caught them in his broadcast and they turned to watch him with Maya.

Which was a problem he'd address as soon as he sorted this Maya and Stuart thing out.

The whole of Aiden's focus was utterly wrapped up in the woman in front of him, his intent so strong he was sure she'd be unable to withhold the answers he wanted. Aiden felt her first concession to him and thrilled to it, felt how his heat suffused her and drew her closer. He placed his hands on her shoulders because he had to touch her. He leaned forward and inhaled. Mmm . . . longing for him, his favorite perfume. He could ask her anything.

He felt her further relax. She studied his face and he saw something of the diagnostician she would be kick in. *Something about his features reminds me of others I know, of Gabe and Michael and John and Carmen.* She took in his radiance and vitality, which made her think of a shark she'd seen once as it glided through a shaft of sunlight, so smooth and fascinating. She also recognized a peculiarity about his eyes, which she couldn't connect to anything familiar, a shape and keenness that appeared primitive to her.

An eerie beauty, she thought, and Aiden felt a dangerous joy she might come to the realization of what he was all on her own. If she did, he'd be off the hook with Xanthe and his aunt.

And he might be able to sneak in a claim on her after all. He said nothing but showed himself just a little, or rather didn't try as hard to seem completely human.

She noticed, and he saw that what he revealed were qualities that had drawn her attention before. Aiden sensed just how curious she'd been about him . . . and how unwilling she'd been to chase down her observations to the right conclusion.

But their subtle differences were now inches in front of her and unavoidable. As hoped, she began to speculate exactly how different he might be from her . . . and with his help several ideas occurred to her. *Aiden as a fish?* She marched up to the door of actual revelation and hesitated.

He encouraged her. *Think about it, Maya.*

She withdrew, which frustrated him, but at least he picked up more information on Stuart. He saw the conundrum she'd been in last spring, how her future had felt precarious to her. She'd been and still was hungry for direction, for a calling big enough to satisfy her desire for a meaningful life and fulfill her need to apply herself as seriously as she had to her athletic career.

She was unwilling to hypothesize about him—or consider him as a viable romantic partner despite their chemistry—because she was afraid. She wanted a future that felt better than the bag of questions he offered. And dammit, that's where that schmuck Stuart fit in; he looked like things she understood, like supercharged stability. Not like a glimpse of a beautiful predator darting through a shaft of sunlight.

He was screwed. And this realization caused him to release her.

That was all it took for her to pull away, just barely, but he saw her regain a little self-awareness. She thought she shouldn't be here and couldn't risk staying, not if her recent, painful efforts toward self-improvement were to bear fruit. So she did something she knew she'd be ashamed of later: brave, assertive Maya turned from him and fled out the door.

Ethan and Oliver stared after her nonplussed. "Are you going after her?" Oliver asked.

Aiden pressed his eyes with the heels of his hands. "No," he barked. "I want to. But I can't." He looked up suddenly as he had a new thought. "Ethan, you don't happen to know anyone named Stuart, do you? A guy Maya's been seeing?"

Ethan shook his head slowly, like he put himself in jeopardy by answering. "Sorry, dude." Aiden realized the effect of his frustration—he intimidated, looked like he might engage in physical violence. He considered explaining what they'd just seen and opened his mouth, but thought better of it and closed it. What would he say? He had nothing further to gain here.

So he tucked his hands in his pockets and eyed the floor, thoughts of the water helping him battle his desire to go follow Maya. He glanced at Ethan and Oliver, who were still waiting for him to say something.

He had to get out of there.

He walked to the door, tossed out a few nonverbal palliatives—*thanks for stopping by, I'll get a message to Sylvia, put the "closed" sign on before you leave*—and he hurried away. Once outside, he sprinted to the ocean.

CHAPTER TWENTY-NINE

"You're telling me my daughter is in Antarctica. Working as a meteorologist." Carmen—with Michael next to her—delivered the news to Alicia and Jeremy as breezily as if she reported what time it was. She'd been putting this confrontation off much longer than she should have—relying on other sirens and Kate to help preserve Sylvia's cover in Griffins Bay. Including the poor girl's job. Carmen should have come up with a better story . . . but honestly, she and Xanthe wrestled with larger issues these days. Duncan and the newest crop of miscreants and the deterioration of siren society as whole, for instance.

Jeremy faced his wife. "Did you ever in your life even once hear Sylvia talk about meteorology? Maybe stop in the middle of testing a recipe to turn on the weather report?" He glared at both Blakes. "Because I never did."

Alicia assessed Carmen before commenting. "No. I didn't. In fact I remember a recent conversation where she didn't know the difference between sleet and snow."

Carmen winced. "Well we heard she sure is into it now!" They still weren't buying it, though. And her eager nods and over-bright smile—Michael's too—didn't help their schtick one iota. Maybe they should have thought of something more plausible than Sylvia becoming an impromptu weather girl in Antarctica? But dang it, there *was* no good explanation for abandoning one's job and family to visit an ice cap. Carmen was out of ideas.

She fantasized instead about killing Simon Blake. If being queen meant she had any punitive authority at all, she would have that man's hide for this.

Alicia cleared her throat to reclaim her attention. "Carmen, you and I have known each other a long time, so I'm going to give it to you straight: that story is just plain stupid. What I can't figure out is why you'd try to get us to believe it."

Carmen gave Michael a speaking look. *Time to haze them. Since outrageous explanations apparently won't work.*

Michael clapped a hand on Jeremy's shoulder while Carmen took charge of Alicia.

They had to work hard to influence their friends these days, since repeated exposure—and in the last twenty years there'd been more than a few repeats—built up immunity to siren mental coercion. A couple of their recent attempts had outright failed, and Carmen mused over how to either fix the problem or confess, maybe take the Wilkeses with them to Shaddox sometime.

"We're like the flu vaccine," Carmen had lamented to Michael earlier that year. "All our friends have built up resistance to us."

This time they needed to succeed. Carmen couldn't afford to have Sylvia's parents launching an investigation that might lead them first to Simon Blake and then back to her and Michael . . .

So they put their backs into this one, and after too much time and way too much tension, Jeremy and Alicia caved.

Now that they thought back, they did remember how Sylvia had always harbored a secret passion for weather patterns. And she'd fantasized about a trip to Antarctica since she was twelve. She saw the offer to go there now as too good to pass up. Oh, and she'd met someone wonderful and couldn't wait to introduce him to them.

Voila. Another box checked off the royal to-do list, a list made more impossible thanks to one Simon Blake. Grrr.

Dana and Will proved trickier to sideline. They of all people knew Sylvia's drive and focus where SeaCakes was concerned, and they would not believe she'd stepped away due to a sudden interest in the

South Pole—with no warning and no indication as to when she might show up again. They also carried within them an innate understanding of the weirdness surrounding the Blakes, since the couple had been physically imprisoned on Shaddox last year for some impromptu, sub-conscious marriage counseling. They hadn't had the ongoing exposure Alicia and Jeremy had, but their experience had been intense enough to compromise Carmen's ability to haze them. But. If Sylvia did chase after a whim—and leave the business as thoughtlessly as appearances suggested—neither of the Fletchers were inclined to protect her interests in the cafe. They'd pieced together a rotating crew to fill in so far, but the effort was inefficient and annoying and wouldn't work long-term. Carmen and Michael had to compromise with this pair; they settled for convincing them to delay any big decisions—to not cut Sylvia out of her ownership contract or find a permanent replacement for her right away. Dana and Will reluctantly agreed to keep the status quo. For now.

Xanthe refused any assistance, withholding both compassion for the lovebirds as well as encouragement to Carmen to help them. "They made their bed, so to speak." She sniffed. "Simon's difficulties with Sylvia or her family or anything else in the deep blue sea are deserved and can't be punishing enough, in my opinion. He wants to go it alone? Let him clean up his own messes. You have more important problems to solve."

Carmen didn't entirely agree but she picked her battles with Xanthe. Sylvia's parents, for instance, were longtime family friends she felt bound to protect, particularly when the reason for their discomfort was siren-based; and Xanthe had no advice one way or the other on that front. "Do what you will," she told her dismissively.

"Time for a diplomatic trip to Antarctica?" Michael teased, knowing well how impossible the timing was to even consider such an excursion. But Carmen wasn't intimidated by the prospect.

"Right after we sneak up on Duncan in Raleigh," she quipped.

Worries over Duncan trumped all peripheral duties once Gabe had come home to report what he'd found. His story and analysis were alarming, to say the least. Carmen called a meeting at the Griffins Bay house to devise a response plan directly after Gabe briefed her.

Xanthe arrived last, irritable and really not herself. Conversation stopped and everyone cringed away from her when she passed.

Parker, who was terrified of the woman on a normal day, fled the room. Carmen hurried to her advisor to contain her. "Your eyes are flashing silver and you're glaring, friend." She decided not to bring up the more comical side effect to Xanthe's ire; the air around her crackled with electricity, making her hair stand on end. Still, Xanthe made no attempt to edit the sour energy she let off . . . and Carmen didn't dare laugh at her.

She supposed no one had ever seen Xanthe lose her temper, and so no one knew quite how to react. To add to the disturbing novelty of seeing her undone, her ill humor also threatened to destabilize the entire group, because if Xanthe was at the end of her rope . . . Carmen decided she'd have to come around somehow. She needed her to help solve their issues with Duncan Fleming.

Kate and Gabe went to Carmen's side, and Kate commented quietly, "She's *fuming*." Henry started to fuss, and she shifted him to her shoulder. "Maybe we should go. Or Henry and I should." Gabe gripped her arm. "No. Stay. Please," he begged.

Carmen agreed. "You should both be part of this. I'll sort Xanthe out."

She said this with more confidence than she felt. Xanthe *was* spoiling for a fight, and her frustration rippled across the room like thunder.

"What happens if she blows up, Mom?" Gabe asked. "I'm thinking apocalypse . . ." A quick scan of those gathered yielded similar thoughts. John envisioned mass, live evisceration. Carmen flinched. Xanthe's smile at John came out of a horror movie. The group inched further away from her.

Carmen only partially understood Xanthe's frame of mind these days, although she knew it was mostly due to her friend's professional frustrations. Xanthe had confided weeks ago she'd lost her gift for omniscience, could no longer summon at will the most necessary skill for her job. Carmen didn't think the loss was permanent; but she didn't welcome Xanthe's coping mechanisms much, since in her current state she jeopardized the cohesion needed to solve their problems with Duncan.

Fine. She was supposed to be queen here, so she would take charge. She faced the small assembly and addressed it. "Thanks for coming so quickly, everyone. You all know the gist of Gabe's findings: Duncan wanted the siren throne, and since he wasn't asked to rule here, he decided to establish his own fiefdom. Made up of humans. Which is not a problem in and of itself, although it's strange and I don't like it. The real issue is how he plans to protect himself. My understanding is he has the means to blackmail us, to coerce our cooperation so we'll grant him carte blanche to behave as he wants. Without disclosing what his plans entail or what impact they might have on our people.

"He threatens exposure, of course, which warrants some kind of security action on our part. Why don't you tell us what else you saw, Gabe?"

Gabe described what he'd found out during his eavesdropping session in the park and from his exchange with Isabel. Duncan intended to use her—Gabe described Duncan's crude hypnosis tactics to the fascination of all present—as the subject of a video demonstration and launch it via some online scheme Gabe hadn't been able to fully apprehend. But the feed itself would show Isabel transforming into a siren. He didn't know how much video Duncan already had.

There were gasps all around. Gabe continued.

"He knows a video clip won't convince people of the existence of mermaids. We can find someone who will explain it away as some nifty CAG project, a response Duncan expects. But he thinks a great clip would showcase his company's capabilities and maybe get him an audience with Hollywood filmmakers—and land multi-million-dollar creative projects from them. That's why he's using Isabel instead of just filming himself: he needs to seem like a regular business guy other business executives will engage with. Not establish himself as the freak he fears himself to be. And if he sends out enough of videos of Isabel, he figures he can make something stick." He paused to take in the looks of distaste and disbelief his listeners wore. "Infantile, isn't it? He's too shallow to pursue an exposé that would actually convince everyone. So he wants to intimidate Carmen with his derring-do, show just how willing he is to bring chaos and ruin to the community if we don't let him build his little kingdom. And of course he wants more commerce, more cash."

Xanthe gaped. "You think Duncan actually believes we'll be undone by a YouTube video?"

"I know, right? It's ridiculous," Gabe replied. "He kind of does, but that's not the point. He thinks—and this is to our advantage, I believe—he's destined for greatness. That his defection should mean we all live in fear of him because he's the only one with enough spine to lead. In his fantasy of how this drama spins out, Carmen will reveal her true colors and show everyone how weak and unqualified she is. He thinks she'll wring her hands and wonder what to do and run from conflict. That she'll do anything at all to avoid further instability, including backing down and agreeing to his demands."

Carmen inclined her head thoughtfully. "When he took himself away, he closed himself off. And the result of his insularity is this . . . truly awful decision-making." She frowned. "His threat is absurd. I mean, it's not even a threat."

"Exactly!" Gabe exclaimed. "He doesn't know anything other than his own thoughts at this point. For all these weeks, he's had this hope of being top dog with no one to offer him a dose of reality or maybe show him how unlikely his take on life is. He's like a mushroom—basically lives in the dark and eats the emotional equivalent of feces all day—and now he's come up with this wacky plan that makes sense to him and him alone. Weak as his ideas are, he's convinced of his own justifications. And he won't see beyond his own ambitions."

"He can't be trusted. That much is clear," Carmen commented. "I don't know that meeting him with force is the smartest approach, though." She looked at her advisor. "Xanthe? Any thoughts?"

To Carmen's relief, Xanthe weighed in with actual, level-headed advice. "He cannot be left at large," she stated.

"No. He can't," Gabe replied. "But I think it's good Duncan is so warped because it means we can stop him."

Xanthe studied him. "Do you have any thoughts as to how?"

"Yes!" Gabe replied. "Well . . . no," he amended. "I mean, I think so, but I'm not sure."

Xanthe raised her eyebrows. "Which is it?"

"I *may* have an approach . . ." Gabe looked at Kate. "You're not going to like it." He addressed the others. "I can jump him if I get close enough, which I can if I'm cloaking," he began. "You wouldn't believe how tight my cloaks have become. I could disappear, pretend I was something or someone else and catch everyone's thoughts as if I were in the water with them. And they *still* didn't know I was there. Anyway. I'll just need to know what to do with him once I have him. And it would be nice if someone could lure him here, maybe Mom?

Close to the sea if we can, so I don't have to transport him. Then I have backup if I need help. I'm sure as hell not carrying him from Raleigh."

Xanthe closed her eyes. "Fight him and hope you win? That's your plan?" she asked.

"Well, when you put it that way . . ." Gabe trailed off.

"I think it could work," Carmen said. "Duncan won't be expecting him, which keeps everyone involved safe. And if we can get him in the water with a security detail, we can read him together," she looked to Michael for verification, "which counts as a confession, does it not?"

"It does," Michael confirmed.

"Then I think Gabe's right about having me front the effort to lure him to the ocean. If he thinks he has a chance at me, he'll come. I'm sure of it."

Michael shook his head. "No. I'm not okay with putting you in jeopardy. He can't be trusted."

"I *hate* this idea," Kate blurted. Henry started to cry, which she responded to by patting his back and lowering her voice. "It's a gamble, Gabe. And Carmen, you're the Queen, making you possibly the last person on earth who should risk a physical confrontation."

Carmen's smiled tolerantly. "I won't be alone. So I won't be at risk. And since Gabe can cloak, he's the only one of us who *can* safely approach Duncan. Gabe's also the only siren around with hand-to-hand combat experience—Duncan doesn't have any, thank God. I think this is the most efficient way to catch him and protect everyone in the process." Michael looked away. "I don't like it." Kate's face fell, but she kept silent.

"Mom's right," Gabe insisted. "She's the one he wants to punish, so it makes sense to let him see her. If we can get him in the water, the rest will be a cinch." Henry by this time refused to be consoled, so Kate excused herself and headed upstairs. "Try to think of a plan that keeps you here," she pleaded quietly to Gabe before she left.

Gabe hugged her. "We'll talk when I come up."

"I wonder if more of us can learn to cloak," John mused. "If three or four of us could avoid detection, we could be even more prepared to nab him."

Gabe snorted. "There's no way that's going to happen. It's not like learning to swim or ride a bike. More like learning how to grow wings and fly. And anyway, we don't have enough time."

Michael eyed John thoughtfully. "I think John's onto something. If we can mask our presence even a little it would help." He eyed his son. "Or maybe you could set up a screen, Gabe. You know, make up a story like Peter did when he took Kate. Craft a bigger illusion."

Gabe fidgeted. "I really don't think . . . I mean, that would take a *lot* of skill."

"I have come to a conclusion," Xanthe announced, and Carmen felt a collective swell of relief spill out of everyone in the room, herself included. "You are on the right track, and I can be of greater use if I'm not privy to your plans. If I stay to hear details, someone could intuit them from me because my influence is too broadly felt among us. Meaning my broadcast would warn Duncan away." To Gabe she said, "Make your final decisions after I leave. You have my confidence—I believe in your approach."

She moved to the door. "My only mandate is to stay together. You must work closely with one another if we are to catch Duncan." Her stare at Gabe was piercing. "Under no circumstances are you to act alone. By yourself, you will not succeed."

Carmen caught her son's flare of anger but was grateful Xanthe had called him out specifically. Under Xanthe's scrutiny, Gabe revealed his own fantasy where Duncan was concerned, and he appeared to harbor hope he might engineer a private confrontation between them. If he could put an end to the man's behavior, he believed he could spare everyone a more dangerous encounter. Carmen hoped he would respect Xanthe's oversight.

"Fine."

"I'll have a tribunal ready for him when you bring him in," Xanthe said at the door. She paused to offer her friend a final encouragement. "I know you can do this, Carmen."

Carmen's return smile was warm. "We will do it together as you advise, Xanthe."

"And I'll be ready for you all at Shaddox." She left.

In bed that night, Gabe reviewed what went on at the gathering after Kate and Henry went upstairs. "Xanthe took off right after you did and then we hashed out logistics. A few of us are going to have to study up on Internet programming and distribution, which kind of blows." Gabe grimaced. "We have to, though, since that's how Duncan's letting his crazy play out."

"So what did you decide to do?" Kate asked. "And why do you think Duncan's love for tech shows he's crazy? I guess I don't see why wireless communicating is such a big deal to you people."

"I'll tell you what I can about our super-secret mission to capture Freak-Show Fleming in a minute—but I guarantee he's a few bricks shy—and his obsession with wireless toys is a sure indicator."

"I don't see how you can avoid technology to the extent you already do," Kate commented. "It's 'crazy' useful, and the rest of the world literally runs on it."

"It's not the technology itself but what his interest in it demonstrates," Gabe countered. "The problem with remote communications is how it replaces actual interaction. And how many sirens do you think would give up touch, eye contact, and all the nuances of a truly personal encounter to *type* a message or guess at the emotion behind a response?" He shook his head. "None, and that's why we know Duncan's off his meds. Seriously—it's like preferring cyanide to water when you're thirsty." He studied Kate's face. "You guys deprive yourselves, too, with all your devices. I mean check out the number of people you see hanging out together at a café sometime, exchanging texts on their phones instead of talking to each other."

Kate wrinkled her nose. "I guess I see your point."

"Exactly. So you see how, for us, that kind of thing doesn't work so well."

"I get it. Techno-media promotes social retardation. Agreed. And you have my blessing to be low-tech forever except in cases of emergency. But I really want to hear about the meeting with Xanthe and the plan for Duncan."

"Okay, so Xanthe doesn't know everything, for one," Gabe said. "She left early and pretty much told us to handle it. This is what we decided . . ."

CHAPTER THIRTY

If Simon was a natural when it came to friendly abduction, at least he was also a talented survivalist, a nice perk if one was to hang out with him in hostile terrain. And by that, Sylvia meant a place with no vegetation, paralyzing cold and no grocery store. At the "camp" he took her to they had a cozy, windproof shelter filled with warmth and light and all the physical comforts. He was pleased by her reaction when she first saw it. "I've been here before and liked it," he reported. "But I know it's not the Four Seasons."

It might as well have been, in Sylvia's opinion. Simon had arranged for everything—he'd put Aiden and his former excavation team on super-secret stocking and delivery detail—and had specifically thought of her when ordering supplies. She guessed she might be the first person on the ice cap to have a stash of European butter and pastry flour for making croissants. He'd even brought dehydrated apples, as well as cognac to rehydrate them. "In case you want to make apple fritters?" he ventured hopefully.

On the practical side, they had three generators at their disposal; space-age, will-not-fail winter wear; and high-tech water and waste systems that made her proud to be among a race of creatures who could contrive such things. Simon understood every small piece of information required to maintain them on this desolate continent, and his assurance gave Sylvia confidence they would live to tell about all this.

Her favorite feature of their hideaway was a domed solarium, situated as a semi-independent pod attached to the main living quarters, and the experience it offered convinced her there was no better place on earth Simon could have chosen for their tryst.

It said something about his sensibilities he had planned this particular excursion, especially given how far removed it was. Before their arrival, even with Simon's encouragement, Sylvia had doubted the location would have any romantic integrity, had maybe even felt a little sorry for herself. They would share no barefoot walks on the beach, no candlelit dinners beneath swaying palms, no carefree tropical atmosphere to complement their sensual explorations. Shortly after settling in, however, she understood Antarctica's unique appeal and loved Simon all the more for knowing it. And for taking the not inconsiderable trouble necessary to make this place their lovers' destination.

She would not have understood in advance how uniquely nature had formed this ethereal haven; or predicted the effect of its quiet, otherworldly beauty on her frame of mind. A uniformity of color—the grays, blues and whites of their surroundings, animals included—was so different from the palette that served as the backdrop to her reality back home. It made time feel like an altogether different dimension, one where past, present and future blurred. And certainly didn't matter.

But the real magic of the place revealed itself at night. Lying side by side on the floor of the solarium, she and Simon stared overhead and fell into a meditation enabled by the enveloping sky. Starting in the late afternoon, the dense darkness of night began its heavy press downward, seeping through the transparent dome until there was no division between inside and out. As the light from the sun disappeared, starlight took its place, emanating from a hundred million brilliant pinpoints that seemed close enough to touch. At these times, she felt suspended, floating in a beneficent and glittering canopy that spoke to them of heaven. As harsh as the elements actually were, the couple felt included in a gentler, freer world, one concerned only with the elemental.

And they loved each other.

Simon's revelation in the bunk on the ship resolved itself in the sweetest physical union Sylvia had ever known. And frankly, the news he was a siren came as a relief. For one, she'd known intuitively Simon and her sea monster in Griffins Bay were related so their being one and the same was not so great a shock. She also felt better about Simon's dip in the Drake Passage, since his mythical provenance made such things un-life-threatening.

And how lovely to be able to attach her confusion to something outside her own musings. She finally felt sane.

Following her understanding and their promises to each other, he apologized for keeping his secret, although he had honestly thought he was acting in her best interests. Sylvia dismissed his regret without censure, partly because she didn't want to bother just then. She was too engaged by his closeness, his physical presence finally real to her, the familiar flow of emotional intimacy he offered not just something she made up because she wanted it. In the dim light of their enclosure she felt free at last of all her doubt, was sure of herself for the first time since embarking on this trek. She gave herself to their mutual desire without reservation, exploring every detail of him with her hands, leaning into him to encourage him to touch her more, touch her everywhere. Simon indulged her.

He also made a half-hearted attempt to explain another component of their togetherness, something about how his kind bonded. He maintained they would feel greater urgency in a few more days but she didn't listen. The future—two hours, two days or two years from now—did not matter more than this moment, ripe with anticipation and heavy with an ache they'd nursed ever since their beach encounters in North Carolina. With his assurance she wouldn't get pregnant—she simply believed him—Sylvia surrendered to her longing and would not be distracted by practicalities, not that Simon fought so hard to interrupt them. He abandoned himself to their intent just as she did.

They were steadier afterwards, able to talk and touch with less tension; and a sort of unhurried, abiding enjoyment characterized their interactions from that point forward. Sylvia had never felt so content.

The next two days progressed with a wonderful lack of direction as they ate and slept and made love according to no schedule, acting on their desires as they felt them. Their seclusion—the absolute certainty of privacy—also lent their seduction a decadence they wouldn't have enjoyed in any other setting, since they were accountable to no one and nothing other than their own pleasure. Certainly no visitors would be stopping by, and calls were not possible. Sylvia sighed theatrically and with ill-concealed glee, "I guess this is all we can do." Simon laughed.

"I feel a little guilty," Sylvia confessed later. "Not enough to put my clothes on and go home, but like we're stealing." She frowned. "And like we'll be in big trouble when we go back." They were stretched out on the floor of the solarium, sleepy and lazy after hours of talking and lovemaking. Sylvia's head rested on Simon's arm while his fingers traced circles on her shoulder.

"I know, love," he said with more than a little apology in his voice. He shifted to face her. "We *are* stealing this time. But there was no other way for us." His expression hardened. "Xanthe won't be happy with me, but you won't be blamed for what I did."

"Who's Xanthe, and why would she care?"

Simon tucked a stray lock of hair behind Sylvia's ear. "Xanthe's a leader in our community. Sort of a state advisor. She—along with Carmen, Gabe's mother—told me to stay away from you. They warned Aiden away from Maya, too."

Sylvia hadn't given much thought to the sideshow Simon's brother and her sister had provided back at SeaCakes—her own melodrama had simply been too engrossing—but she thought of them now, remembering dimly the couple's rapt, desperate focus on each other. "Aiden and Maya . . . they were starting to bond just like us, right?"

"Yes," Simon said bitterly. "He'll be on a choker leash now since you and I snuck off."

"Why would what we did matter to them?"

"Because . . . well, because of your sister Solange. And Luke," Simon responded, watching her closely.

Sylvia's brother-in-law sprang to mind, and she remembered his face through the lens of what she now understood to be the physical markers associated with mermaids. She gasped when she realized how close she'd been to Simon's world all this time. "Luke Hokeman is a mermaid?"

"Siren," Simon corrected automatically. "And yes, your parents have now forked over two of their daughters to the cause. There's no way Xanthe and Carmen will approve of Aiden and Maya as a couple now."

Sylvia became philosophical. "That's too bad, because Maya's current guy is a dud." She brightened. "Maybe she'll dump him for Aiden. Your government can't stop *her* from making a play for *him*. Can they?"

Simon was glum. "Actually, they can. They would haze her so she forgot most of it, and Aiden . . . he could be exiled and that would be *really* bad. Like permanent-suffering-for-life kind of bad, since sirens can't do 'alone.' They'd maybe send him here. Again."

"Again? You were exiled here?"

"We both were. Us and a bunch of other guys. Who do you think built this place? Xanthe made up this labor program for wayward sirens, and anyone who doesn't fall in line gets recruited."

Sylvia was appalled. "You and Aiden were sent to the South Pole as punishment?"

"Not by ourselves, but yes. And not punishment, per se, since we all opted to come just to get away from the nagging. It was kind of our own voluntary penal colony."

Sylvia's eyes searched his. "You were a siren criminal."

Simon pulled her against him and nuzzled her neck. "Oh yeah," he said huskily.

Several seconds passed before her follow-up question occurred to her. "How?"

"Mmm?"

"What did you do wrong?" She felt Simon smile against her skin.

"I don't think I should tell you. You might run away." She pushed against him weakly, but he didn't budge. "Nothing you'd consider serious," he soothed. "Some of us can't decide on a vocation. All of us are suspicious of marriage. That kind of thing."

"That's really all? You didn't want to march in the band and you got sent to Antarctica? I can't believe that."

"I promise that's all it was. But I understand why we were considered a problem. Siren society is pretty regimented, and if you don't want what everyone else does, you destabilize the collective. Also, our dissatisfaction was no passing thing—I've been a skeptic for over a decade. Aiden has, too. So rather than stay and depress everybody— ourselves included—a bunch of us offered to work on an outpost."

Sylvia softened. "Well. You were hardly felons, then. I mean, jeeze. If humans got in trouble for that kind of thing, we'd *all* be locked up." She studied his profile. "And so I guess we really are different. Or our societies are."

Simon levered himself over her. "I'm more interested in what we have in common now . . ."

Sylvia wrapped herself around him and arched into his kiss. "Oh, yes. We should definitely work on our common interests . . ."

The next day, Simon's attempt on the boat to tell her about siren bonding habits came back to her. His suggestion—that they'd be even more inseparable when she ovulated—had sounded too improbable, so she hadn't paid it any attention. As soon as he touched her that afternoon, however, she recalled his warning and gained a firsthand understanding of its implications.

He returned from fishing, something she told him she'd like very much to see sometime, dropped his catch on the ice out front and marched toward her without pause. He took her in his arms before she could say hello.

"Wha . . . ?" she gasped when they broke for air.

He didn't explain. Instead he stared into her eyes and secured one of her hands against his chest, positioning his fingertips under her wrist.

Sylvia registered their desire—both of theirs—with a swift intake of breath. "Sweet heaven."

Each pulse was like a low-level sonic boom resonating in tiny bursts of vibration throughout her body. Chills skittered over the surface of her skin like an effervescent tide and a sound like the surf roared dully in her ears.

And the emotional affinity she associated with Simon deepened. She wouldn't have thought this possible.

Simon called forth her thoughts and feelings as he usually did, and in return flooded her with his own—again, nothing new. But this exchange included more, was a true synthesis of both of their responses. Their closeness felt magnified, the mandate to connect overpowering.

She would tell him later the next three days felt like a marathon race, the heretofore tranquil progression of their lovemaking obliterated by urgent, frantic coupling punctuated by sporadic, unsatisfying rest. Exhausted and plastered with sweat at the end of day two, Sylvia begged as lightly as she could for a reprieve.

"Simon, I think every single nerve I have is raw. I don't know how much more of this I can take." She laughed shakily.

"I know, my poor darling," he crooned, smoothing her hair with his hands. "My sweet, lovely Sylvia . . . I'm so sorry . . . I'll make it better . . ." He rolled onto his back and pulled her with him, taking her weight while massaging her back and buttocks, whispering soft endearments and helpless apologies in her ear. But within moments his body began arching against hers in a sinuous rhythm, demanding entry once again. Sylvia let her knees fall beside his hips to accept him. "I'm sorry, I'm so sorry," Simon said, eyes tightly shut as he bucked beneath her. She braced her hands above his shoulders and angled her torso away for leverage, her breath coming out of her in a way that almost sounded like sobs.

"I know it's not your fault. And I feel it, too." And in another few moments she decided constant pleasure warranted further exertion on her part, after all.

Eventually, thankfully, their compulsion lightened enough for them to resume their twilight stargazing sessions. Ensconced in the solarium two nights later, Sylvia stretched beside her lover to relieve the tension in her muscles. Simon ran his hand up her hip and across her stomach as she did, the pressure of his fingers hot against her skin. She swatted him away.

"Oh, no you don't, mister," she chided. "We're taking a break and that's final." At his pout, she scooted away several feet and glared. "I mean it. If I have to barricade myself in the bathroom, I will."

Simon scoffed and inched forward until they were chest to chest, holding her while she squirmed. "Won't work. I brought a box cutter, which is all it would take to get me in." He nuzzled her neck and hair. Sylvia sighed and let her head fall back.

"How much longer?" she asked. She was resigned to their need even as she responded with more enthusiasm than she thought possible given her exhaustion.

"Soon, angel," Simon told her. And at least he handled her gently. "Soon."

CHAPTER THIRTY-ONE

Duncan returned from New York—a harried trip Julian had arranged under an impossible deadline—victorious. As hoped, he'd persuaded a handful of network representatives to support him, which entailed accepting a video file from Julian in the next day or so; and then disseminating the thing broadly as and when instructed. He'd suggested a lack of personal attention to his project was a career-breaker, and unless these titans wanted to be shamed in front of their peers and looking for new jobs, they should refrain from passing his material down to their nobody underlings.

"Meaning once we have the clip, we're ready to launch," Duncan had told him, beaming.

The announcement should have felt like success to Julian . . . but his confidence in the whole endeavor had been tanking for a while now. Ever since Isabel had shown up, in fact.

His issue was not with Duncan's motivations—he still believed Duncan had a right to storm his stolen castle—but with the man's appalling rudeness, which was particularly evident in front of his wife. Now Julian's conscience rode him every second he spent working on Duncan's behalf without understanding why, and he wondered if could ever talk himself back onto the wagon of well-being.

The proposition, as he saw it, was either support Duncan—which felt like oppressing Isabel . . . and maybe aiding something sinister—and thrive; or sacrifice his newfound success and personal growth on the chance the cause—or the man—he supported was corrupt. And probably leave Isabel no better off anyway. He knew what he should do, but he wasn't willing to give up his self-actualization progress, even though he felt kind of petty.

He'd just come too far to go back. Or this is what he told himself. Since meeting Duncan he'd cut junk food and soda from his diet, maintained an aggressive training program at the local gym, and lost 50 pounds. He also started showing up for a life he'd previously found too depressing to face. Desperation to keep improving had pushed him forward one professional opportunity, one 15-hour workday, one grueling workout session at a time. He'd been given control of Duncan's entire office and felt competent for the first time maybe ever. Even better, beautiful women now talked to him and while he still felt tongue-tied, he didn't choke and run like a perpetual loser. For this reason alone he owed Duncan Fleming blind devotion, he thought.

He couldn't quite convince himself all was well, however.

Without fail now, everything about Duncan disturbed him. The man's quasi-aloofness and wicked powers of engagement no longer fascinated; instead, Julian found the behaviors troubling. And something about Duncan's endeavors now felt so wrong, like a beautifully prepared meal that had sat on the counter for two days and might not be safe to eat. He couldn't imagine why his convictions concerning Duncan had ever made sense.

He constantly had to rationalize, to look for plausible, non-threatening excuses why the arbitrary, disconcerting and strident nature of Duncan's directives to him and his staff were *not* abusive. Case in point, the three a.m. voice mail Julian had received that very morning about how Fleming Communications would decline in stature unless they appeared more professional, so would Julian please conduct a quick inventory check on their office supplies? He should pay particular attention to document clips and ink cartridges.

How was a guy to take that kind of request? Like an acceptable falter from a stressed-out monarch? Julian couldn't get there.

He had to wonder if Duncan deliberately wanted to undermine his own leadership, because his bizarre antics would make sense then. But maybe he was unaware? Which made Julian wonder if he should warn his boss he appeared to be losing it.

As he continued to obsess, he eventually remembered how of the two of them, he was the weaker link, and pretty much in all ways. He recalled his own less-than-pure motivations for first getting involved with Duncan, looked honestly at what had predisposed him to his employer during those early encounters in the park. He acknowledged how even now his support for Duncan was predicated on the wanton, shaky hope he could change his dull existence, maybe transform into someone witty and attractive whose company women would seek.

He had not been taken in by Duncan's innate greatness or generosity of spirit.

Try though he might, however, he couldn't assume all the blame for his unease. As Duncan's tantrums escalated, Julian grew ever more doubtful, ultimately over the underlying validity of Duncan's leadership claims, because he certainly didn't come off as strong and capable. Julian wondered if he'd been manipulated into his servile role, although again he'd been complicit in placing himself in it.

He also knew he would continue to buckle under as asked. What other option was there? He could hardly cry victim after begging to sign on and committing himself body and soul to Duncan's vision.

Isabel, by contrast, had not signed on for Duncan's takeover, and her mistreatment chafed Julian's already irritated loyalties concerning his boss. Then there was that debacle with the video promotion, which had made Duncan appear ugly for the first time since Julian's acquaintance with him, his ubiquitous charm undetectable.

When Duncan had tried to convince him he couldn't cut it in front of a camera, Julian should have listened. Despite a rock star cast of media trainers, make-up artists and lighting technicians, Duncan's on-air performance was a bust. In fact, it was a disaster. Watching the recording immediately after, the staff was without exception horrified . . . and Julian feared, genuinely feared, he was seeing the real man.

If Julian hadn't been present for the filming, he would have wondered if the image on the monitor was really Duncan. The man had none—absolutely *none*—of the engaging traits on screen he had in person, something everyone saw as the session progressed. Julian thought maybe if Duncan could just get into it more, this impression would prove untrue.

Nope.

The concerned, hopeful frowns the crew wore changed to looks of disbelief when faced with the digital replay, because no one had ever seen anything so off-putting. "He looks bloodless. And parasitic," one of them commented. Another woman teared up. "It's *depressing*. Makes me think there's no hope in the world and excuse me while I go call my mother."

"Get rid of it," Julian decided abruptly. "Erase it right now. That clip is never to leave this room."

Duncan was pleased with the outcome, to Julian's surprise. "I'm glad," he stated smugly. "I was sick of arguing with everyone about why broadcast was a bad idea, and now everyone knows. Now you know: it doesn't reflect my true nature." He said he hoped he'd closed the door to any future conversations on the subject so they could instead focus on tactics to advance his outreach, not hinder it.

Julian's discomfort worsened. While he wrestled with his misgivings—and blamed Duncan for them—still he couldn't contemplate stopping. Like he'd had some electronic torture device surgically implanted, and whenever he thought seriously of walking away, he felt an internal resistance akin to being zapped. Self-interest flooded him in the wake of such incidents until he abandoned his insurrectionist musings in favor of a new pair of trainers or handmade shirt.

He was also reminded of his need for Duncan's protection from the evil queen they were about to insult.

But he no longer trusted his employer as he once did, could not summon the blind loyalty that had landed him the chief position on Duncan's cheer squad. Thankfully Duncan didn't seem to notice Julian's diminishing faith, or maybe he didn't know to attach this circumstance to his own oddities. If he were to guess, Julian would say Duncan attributed his hesitancy to his myriad insecurities, the very ones Julian suspected had made him such a susceptible recruit. Whatever the reasons, Julian was grateful not to be called out. He kept his head down and continued to follow orders as if he was up for all this.

Today Duncan had thrown Julian a lifeline at long last, telling him all would soon be revealed. "Swing by the Brenlow and pick Isabel up, then come over for dinner. You'll know everything by the end of the night."

So Julian arrived to collect Isabel feeling hopeful. The ideal outcome—Duncan's moral compass had righted itself and his integrity would shine brightly once again—was unlikely, he knew. But if Duncan was even close, he might be happy enough.

His confidence evaporated as soon as he saw Isabel at the curb.

She didn't respond to his greeting when she got in, sat stiffly in the passenger seat and spent the trip to Duncan's distracted and silent. Julian's spirits tanked. He thought of running, just getting both of them as far away as possible and maybe saving themselves from the tragedy he felt looming over them like a leaden, suffocating fog. He glanced at Isabel frequently, wishing for some demonstration of the vitality she was capable of, wanting to know she would come out of all this all right. She offered nothing. Julian parked the car and they called Duncan from the lobby.

Duncan welcomed them grandly at the door and immediately began to gesture with his cigarette in strange, expansive movements as he spoke. He talked about nothing in particular—the meal he'd prepared for them, the storm brewing off the coast and the rain it would bring the next day. The provenance of a sculpture he'd purchased, and did Julian think it would look better in the opposite corner instead?

By the time they were seated at the table, Isabel's liveliness had further declined. Duncan stated how pleased he was she'd "succumbed as quickly as she had this time," as if this should make sense to Julian. "She opens so much more quickly now. I think she's finally trained— you know, the pathways for my suggestions are finally uncluttered." Duncan's smile was smug, his consideration of Julian too direct. Julian felt a simmering unease like the precursor to panic. Uh-oh—best not to show too much of that.

"Aw. You appear to have a . . . what do you people call it? A crush. How charming." He clapped Julian on the shoulder. "Let's move to the living room, shall we?"

Under Duncan's hand, Julian felt he was being drained of all his gumption. And as if all he'd hidden these past weeks, including his troubling inability to maintain enthusiasm for his boss, was now drawn out of him whole like a kidney stone, and here was Duncan inspecting it and calling it for what it was. Julian also felt compelled—truly, he couldn't resist the compulsion—to concentrate on the unpleasant, possibly dangerous repercussions of his vaguely romantic feelings for Isabel. Julian's concern for the woman in the room evaporated . . . and he at last felt the clinical detachment from her he'd craved since she'd first shown up.

Duncan released him with a satisfied nod. Julian reconsidered Isabel, expecting to feel nothing for her, and possibly relief over his unburdening. Isabel's return stare was kindly, almost pitying in its comprehension. He felt his stomach shrivel. If possible, he was now more disheartened. Isabel returned her attention to Duncan.

At least Duncan no longer focused on him at all. Watching the strange interplay between the two, he had the feeling Isabel's emotional output was more powerful than his and Duncan's, to the point where her essence filled the room. Perhaps she was giving him cover? He was ashamed of his earlier selfishness.

Soon, however, given Isabel's glazed, semi-conscious stare at the wall, Julian didn't know what he could do for her. Duncan apparently thought everything was fine; the man looked like he was holding court—jovial, beaming, as though Isabel's oppression was cause to celebrate.

Julian drew himself up. "Duncan, is she okay?"

"Never better," Duncan assured him, grinning disarmingly. Julian frowned, undisarmed, and Duncan turned toward Isabel. He took a seat at the end of the couch where she lounged, lifting her legs so her feet rested in his lap.

"I'd like you to work the camera if you would, Julian." Duncan indicated a tripod ten feet away. "She might move around a little, so make sure you have clear sight lines and don't focus too tightly. You'll want to see all of her." He removed Isabel's shoes and smoothed her skirt above her knees. He pressed the Taser Julian had ordered for him to her side and she arched off his lap. Duncan lifted her skirt higher.

If this was what it looked like—a porn flick?—Julian wanted no part of it. In an instant he was so furious he wanted to strangle Duncan—for getting his hopes up he had any integrity, for his unconscionable treatment of those around him, especially Isabel, for his blithe assumption Julian wouldn't hesitate to participate in something this sleazy and pathetic. Julian clenched his hands and stepped forward to attack.

Isabel stopped him, or at least distracted him enough to hesitate in his approach. She shimmered and lengthened—and then something really funky started happening to her legs. His anger morphed into fascination. Duncan continued to whisper to Isabel and stroke her soothingly, all the while watching Julian. He smirked at Julian's grunt of surprise.

She was a fish. A seven-foot long, opal-y fish, with the upper body of a woman and a tail that extended across Duncan's knees and over the arm of the couch. Her wide, translucent fluke brushed the floor to and fro . . . and Julian could picture the movement in the water, lost himself in the idea of a swim with such a creature.

"Huh." He could think of nothing else to say.

"Shall we try this again?" Duncan inquired. "This time with you behind the camera?"

Julian ignored him. The man was river slime, and whatever he was trying to accomplish with this recording . . . well, if it involved putting a Taser to Isabel and a great big pile of lies and evasion, then Julian was done second guessing himself. Whatever Duncan had going on was wrong, period. Julian wanted out.

For the span of about a half a second, he noted how he didn't disbelieve what he'd just witnessed. Moreover he knew to attach the definition of what he saw to Duncan as well as Isabel. A brief inspection of their physical similarities—even excluding the tail—was all it took to know he was the only person in this room who was not a mermaid.

Regardless, Julian prepared himself to suck up better than he ever had to Duncan Fleming. He straightened and remembered exactly his level of admiration for the man when they'd first met, then pretended as much adoration as he could toward his morally compromised, truly inhuman employer.

"You're amazing," Julian told him. "Splendid in every way."

Duncan appeared mollified. "Your emotional broadcast is inconsistent, which makes sense given what you've just seen. And what you say is true: I am doing something extraordinary here. And I'm going to be great."

"This record you want—of what she is and what I'm guessing you are, too—this is the video clip you want to show the world?"

"Why yes! I'm impressed you worked that all out already."

"What will you do once it's broadcast?" Julian asked as politely as he was able.

"He means to use it as collateral," Isabel interjected. "He wants to be left unchallenged, to hold power here in Raleigh since he wasn't permitted to rule back home. If he threatens to out us, he believes he can force our government's compliance."

"So you see, I don't wish for violence," Duncan hurried to say. "It's the most harmless way to protect myself, to build an organization here worthy of leading." Julian found his smile ghastly. "With you at my side, of course."

Julian pivoted toward the camera in the hopes he could hide his horror. And disappointment. "Brilliant," he said, and he hoped his weak flattery would save them. Then he thought of a truth he could say with feeling: "Truly, you deserve every single thing you get from this. And didn't you say you had a bottle of Champagne chilling? We should celebrate."

"Yes, indeed!" Duncan replied. "I'll fetch it from the kitchen. Would you mind grabbing the flutes from the sideboard?"

The home was spacious and Julian stood tensely as Duncan took forever to traverse the room. The second he was out of sight, Julian removed the memory card from the camera. Then he seized Isabel's hand and pulled her toward the door. "We're leaving!" he hissed, and to his surprise, she stood and scanned the room alertly.

"Wait," she whispered and then walked to a large aquarium at the back of the room. She placed both palms against it and breathed deeply. After several seconds she pushed herself away. "That will buy us a few minutes. Let's go."

CHAPTER THIRTY-TWO

Kate shouldered the phone against her ear. She held her invitation in one hand and clutched the edge of the table with her other, tapping her foot while she waited for Maya to pick up.

But she didn't answer, smart girl. At the sound of the beep, Kate let loose. "Maya." She sputtered, pausing to collect herself before continuing. "I'm holding an invitation to your *wedding* in my hand—your wedding! So I'm calling to ask: what the *hell* is going on? I didn't even know you and . . ." she checked the name on the card, "*Stuart* were serious. Is this a joke? It has to be a joke. Call me!" She put the phone down shakily and tried not to cry, a battle she quickly lost.

Gabe had been humming calmly to Henry on the other side of the room, but Kate felt his disapproval. "You think I should have handled that better?" She swatted at her tears. She spoke before he could answer. "It's just that I'm so hurt," she whispered. "How could she not talk to me about this? I find out through the *mail?* I mean, I know we haven't talked since she moved to New York . . . but why didn't I know she'd found the love of her life?"

"Because I don't think she has, honey," Gabe answered.

Kate stared hard at her husband. "Why do you think that?"

"She was conflicted when Henry was born, like she wanted to crawl out of her own skin, you know? I touched her back when she was holding the munchkin to see what I could figure out. She's happy for us but jealous and that makes her feel like a schmuck. She was watching us, stewing about Stuart and wondering what it would be like to have children with him. She's afraid she'll never find someone who loves her like Jeremy loves her mom, or I love you. She hasn't known what to do with herself since volleyball ended. She feels stuck."

"Huh." Kate was stunned. Of course Gabe was right—Kate saw it immediately now. And here she was, selfishly thinking of how betrayed she felt when Maya was probably the one hurting. If Maya truly loved this man, Kate *would* have heard about it.

She recalled their most recent bantering session, where she'd told Maya how high on life she was and how marriage might just solve every last one of the world's problems. She cringed at her insensitivity.

Maya wasn't getting married to offend anyone. She was reaching for happiness, and the way she revealed her decision—a formal announcement in the mail—demonstrated how unsure she really was.

Which pretty much made Kate the worst friend in the history of friendships. If she hadn't been so wrapped up in her own life she would have realized this wasn't about her. And if she hadn't flown off the handle and dialed in anger, her friend might feel like she could turn to her. "Ahhh," Kate groaned. "I wish I hadn't left that message." She also wished she could talk with Sylvia, who'd been incommunicado for too long now in Kate's opinion, something she understood well enough but regretted in light of Maya's news. Then again, Sylvia would be pregnant when she and Simon turned up, something Maya maybe didn't need to know.

She saw sympathy in Gabe's small smile. "Someone probably should ask her a few probing questions about what she's doing. Maybe you could talk to Solange?"

Kate called Maya again, who still didn't pick up. "Hey. It's me. I'm sorry I lost it a minute ago. It was just the shock. I'm really happy for you . . . if this is what you want. And I love you. So call me."

Aside from her first, angry voicemail, Kate tried hard to portray herself as supportive of Maya's wedding plans when they finally connected. Maya knew better, but she did not explain herself in spite of her friend's gently probing questions.

She didn't blame Kate for her reaction, especially since the proposal had been somewhat of a surprise to her, too. And when she mused about her relationship with Stuart leading up to it, the progression only made sense in retrospect, an understanding she alone would have. No, she didn't blame anyone who wondered at the suddenness of it all.

Maya had established herself in New York and following a strong showing on her MCAT was enrolled at Mount Sinai Medical School. Stuart had been thrilled for her, or rather her accomplishment. His vagueness—over her, them, and anything to do with their future—disappeared, and their once playful relationship became serious. Maya was unsettled by the turn-about although she was mostly flattered.

"I feel like a different person in your company," she'd reported a couple of weeks after her move. They were in her new apartment. Stuart sat on a couch with his feet up, and she studied the view out the window.

Stuart half-listened as he rifled through the play list on his phone. "What do you mean?"

"Like you see me differently than you used to when I lived in Philly," she supplied tentatively.

"Hmm. And that's a bad thing?"

"No . . ." Maya equivocated before trying again. "It's just different. I mean, we used to hang and have fun, and never thought much about where we would end up long-term, and now we seem serious. And it's all about cocktail parties and brunch with your family and going to the theater." Stuart set his music player down and rested his hands on his thighs, giving her his full attention for what felt like the first time in weeks.

"I was under the impression you moved to be closer to me, and that getting serious was the point."

Maya felt guilty. "I did move to be closer to you. And you have lovely friends and a nice family—everything is very nice, really. It's just such a change from what we used to be."

Stuart's expression was inscrutable. "Isn't that how it's supposed to go? Would you rather go back to Philadelphia, with no plans for your future, so long as we hook up once a month?"

This conversation had taken a painful turn and Maya didn't know how or why. But she sensed an ugly secret lurking within her, one that would hurt his feelings or more probably make him angry with her if she showed it. She also found herself wading into a self-examination she didn't care to undergo. *Then I'd best get this over with.*

"Stuart," she began carefully, "I've been feeling out of sorts, what with the move and getting into medical school and all. These are big changes for me, and I'm walking into this blind. I was really worried not too long ago about what I was going to do with the rest of my life. So I just marched in this direction and I don't have a solid feel it's the best thing. I'm just, I don't know, ruminating." She strained to think of the right words, ones that would spare his feelings. Or maybe hers. "I'm sorry if I made it sound like I don't want this. That's not it."

His glare made her feel vulnerable and ashamed. "You sound like you're having second thoughts about coming. Are you?"

Well. Maya's second thoughts had happened in Philadelphia, she believed, before she'd made the decision to move here, not after she had committed herself and brought everything she owned to New York. After all those months of anxiety over what she wanted to be when she grew up, the prospect of completing a rigorous course of study that would absorb and validate her, combined with Stuart wanting her near . . . well, it had been too tempting to resist. She could too easily look ahead, say in ten years, and picture herself happy, ensconced in a sports medicine practice somewhere, with a stimulating life that included a house of her own and playing ball on a league or maybe coaching kids.

And she pictured herself married to Stuart—handsome, smart, funny Stuart, with his society family and old money and sure station in life. Stuart, who never had to question where he would go to school or what he would do after graduation. Of course he wouldn't understand where Maya was coming from. Stuart had always known his place in the world and had a right, in fact, to be annoyed with her indecisiveness. His confidence was one of the things she loved about him.

He deserved better treatment than she was giving him at the moment. So she linked her arms around his neck and relaxed into the type of Southern flirtation she knew Stuart found charming. "Don't listen to me, sugar. I'm just a little turned around, and all I need is for you to maybe turn with me a little. Tell me you want me here."

Stuart pulled her flush against him, but his words were hard. "I want you here. I don't think I could have been more clear."

Maya kissed him, but she had to work to get him to relax into her. Eventually, she took his hand and led him to the bedroom . . . and his smile told her the storm had passed. It was better this way, she thought, better not to bother him with worries that only had to do with her. She resolved to keep her petty musings to herself in the future.

Simon walked into the living room where Sylvia sat by the stove with her book. He'd just used the satellite phone to contact Aiden, which he'd done only twice since their arrival, a function of what Sylvia saw as Simon's carefulness to reach out. "I'm more confident we'll be welcomed into the fold now, but I'm sure no one's happy with me," he'd told her. "And everyone's watching Aiden. So. Best not to involve him any more than I have to."

He put the phone back in its cubby and plopped down in the chair opposite her. "Who's Ethan?" he asked.

She put her book in her lap. "No one important," she countered warily. "Why?"

Simon's smile was smug. "Apparently, he's gay."

Sylvia examined Simon's expression. "Okaaaay. Who told you anything about Ethan, and why do you think he's gay?"

"I just heard from Aiden. He went to SeaCakes a while back to see . . . well, to get something to eat, let's say. This guy, Ethan, came in looking for you while he was there, and he had his new boyfriend with him. Who is he?"

Sylvia braced her hands on her knees and stared at Simon's feet. What to say? "I went to culinary school with him, and we, well, kind of . . . flirted, I guess." For *two freakin' years*. "I used to think we'd maybe date someday. I guess not."

"Not," Simon agreed. "Aiden said he came in to apologize to you, for stringing you along."

"He *said* that?"

"No," Simon said, still smirking. "Of course not. Aiden picked up on it, and on a few other details the guy didn't intend to share. Would you like to know more?"

Sylvia wondered if Simon had all his facts straight. "So," she said skeptically, "he brought his boyfriend to my bakery so we could all talk things out?"

Simon laughed. "He came in to introduce 'Oliver,' with whom he'd recently discovered some things about himself, and to tell you he was sorry he hadn't been more forthcoming with you. Those weren't his words. Aiden said he felt pretty bad over how he'd behaved, that he hoped he hadn't hurt you. But no summit—he was going for more of a quick apology, like, 'I'm sorry it took me so long to figure things out.'

"Aiden said his admission was one he didn't wanted to make to himself, much less the perfect woman—that's you, by the way—who he'd hoped would entice him into another way of life. His parents are upset. He thinks the world of you. He's sorry he made you wonder about him."

Sylvia leaned back. "You know, it makes sense. I just didn't want to see it. And in a way it's a relief. I mean, nice to hear the problem wasn't that I didn't appeal, you know?" She studied her hands. "And I'm glad he's found someone. Really. I hope he's happy."

"Good. But there's more." He reported on a former head of his government out to strong-arm and ultimately disgrace the new siren queen—Gabe Blake's mom, in fact. "Duncan's launched a potentially devastating campaign against us—his own people—and he wants Carmen to answer for it, basically. Everyone back home is gearing up to capture him, which Aiden thinks is the primary reason no one's been sent after us. So I guess there's a small upside."

Simon cleared his throat. "Also, it seems Maya's engaged."

"*What*?!" Sylvia vaulted to her feet. "To whom? And it better not be that corpse, Stuart . . ."

"She's engaged to Stuart," he replied flatly.

"Simon. That's a problem."

"I agree. Aiden actually figured that out when he saw her. Trust me—he's taking this worse than you are."

"How I'm taking it is not the problem. Maya and Solange and me . . . we're close, Simon. She wouldn't make a decision like this and let me find out about it from someone else. There's something wrong. We have to go back."

Simon gazed around their little haven. "I know," he said dispiritedly. "I should help contain the viceroy, and I really need to relieve some pressure on my brother. But I hate for this to be over."

Sylvia was instantly contrite. As concerned as she was for Maya, going back meant opening themselves up to realities she'd rather avoid as well. "Yeah. Home might well end up being harsher than Antarctica. And isn't that a paradox." She searched Simon's face. "But our honeymoon doesn't have to completely end, does it?"

Simon went to her and drew her to her feet. He wove his fingers through hers and lifted their clasped hands to brush his lips across her knuckles. He smiled. "It'll be all right, angel. Let's go see what everyone else in the world is up to. Just remember, whatever comes our way, we're in it together from here on out, okay?"

She pressed her cheek to the back of his hand. "Always."

CHAPTER THIRTY-THREE

Duncan returned from the kitchen with chilled Champagne and strawberries and paused at the door in confusion. No one else was there.

He'd have to worry about that in a minute, though, because his aquarium was shouting at him.

Well, not shouting, but calling to him, and goodness how he missed the ocean. He set the wine and strawberries on his sideboard and drifted forward to inspect.

The tank was beautiful, of course—he'd designed it himself, and his aesthetic was, after all, uniquely informed. The installers had been awestruck when he first activated the light, casting what felt like serenity not just within the tank but throughout room. One of the workers joked, "It's like Valium."

To Duncan the tank and the response humans had to it represented not only the superior beauty of his ocean-bound home, but also his personal transcendence of the pedestrian, unsophisticated realm he now inhabited. His godlike status here—so easily attained—gratified him, although his success was laced with disappointment. Since this was not Shaddox. And because of the insidious voice in his head whispering anyone could have accomplished here what he had.

Which was why he'd come so far ashore, so he *was* the only siren around and didn't have to worry over how he'd fare in a competition against, say, one of the Blakes, for whom human socialization was such a cinch. Best not to think of that, though. He leaned against his aquarium and pressed his face to the glass.

It was like he swam in his siren form within the tank and the sea creatures within were his familiars once again. He could feel the rush of displacement as they passed him, felt the delicious resistance the water made against him when he moved. Ah. When had he last transformed? He wished again for the life he'd chased in his old world, where he would never be without this particular pleasure.

The sound of the filter hummed within him like a song, and for several blissful moments Duncan was a child again. He closed his eyes and gave himself to a particular memory that beckoned.

He was nine, and he floated near his family's home in the mid-Atlantic, almost asleep. One of his aunts sang to him as he dozed. The sea sparkled under bright sunshine. He was surrounded by people who loved him, and he was happy.

He opened his eyes in a state of meditation and wished again he could be so immersed and free.

But he remembered he couldn't be because he had something to take care of. He'd been finishing an important task tonight . . . what was it? As he refocused on the environment outside his aquarium, he regained awareness of his intentions that evening. As well as his aloneness, which wasn't right. Hadn't he just been talking with Isabel? And Julian.

The events of the evening came back to him like a barrage of daggers, and his reverie lost its influence. *Where are they?* He scanned around him with every sense he had.

They weren't here, weren't likely even in the building. His gaze lit on the camera, noting the open port where the memory card had been removed. He'd wanted video of himself with Isabel when she transformed—hence one of his motivations to invite Julian this evening, to man the camera so no one who saw it would question his involvement; but he 'd filmed clips of Isabel transforming alone as a trial. These recordings would have to do.

But he'd been betrayed.

Anger boiled within him like lava, until he was more furious than he'd ever been in his life, to the point that he—polished, composed Duncan Fleming—craved their deaths. Was it beneath him to chase after them, to hunt them down? He would do it regardless, and Isabel would forfeit her life when he found her. He rubbed his chest in acknowledgement of the danger he would cause himself with his untried style of execution. He vowed to inflict it anyway.

First he would ensure their defection had immediate repercussions. Petty of him, perhaps, but he was too enraged to check himself. Also he could safely assume they were on their way to the ocean and he wanted to exact retribution at his leisure, which meant launching the videos— which would be unedited, but oh, well—before any efforts could be made to stop him. At least he had other footage he could use.

Yes. If he did it now, he would pre-empt any interruptions Julian and Isabel might cause, and he would cement his campaign once and for all. He went to his desk and retrieved the supplemental drive he'd tucked away, attached it to his desktop and began downloading. With nothing to do but watch the screen, he fretted over the solo nature of this launch—he would have preferred the oversight of his talented but apparently faithless techie. Julian was altogether familiar with the protocol he intended to follow if not the reasons behind it. As Duncan accessed the delivery database and synced it to email, he stopped once to wring his hands. He had to make a conscious effort to control his breathing. He was nearly too undone—with excitement? Remorse?—to reassure himself.

He reviewed his motivations: he was here to secure a worthy life, which would include a continuous throng of adoring humans and all the emotional sustenance he needed. So even if he had to do everything on his own for the moment, wasn't he fortunate to be so prepared? He mopped sweat from his brow one final time before pressing "Send." His hands shook.

Julian—the pre-independent Julian who knew better than to challenge Duncan's happiness—would have been impressed, would have appreciated how quickly Duncan had understood and applied the tutorials he'd suffered through. Duncan worked methodically, executing with perfect accuracy the program Julian had designed. Ten minutes later, his computer pinged with the final notification.

Download complete.

He leaned back in his chair and felt the coiled muscles in his neck and shoulders unwind. For the first time since walking into his empty living room, he was confident he would prevail in spite of his tattletale wife and loyalty-challenged aide-de-camp. He even appreciated the immediacy, how he'd been forced to act now rather than next week, because the frustrating part of this effort—the waiting—was over. The future he wanted was imminent.

And he was now free to chase down his traitorous sidekicks without worry. In the unlikely event he was captured or waylaid, he had leverage.

Yes, siren officials would do well to respect his modest demands, in exchange for his promise to refrain from future publicity campaigns. Who knew—if he tried often enough, he might actually convince a throng of humans to scour the water for his kind, really make life difficult for Carmen and her regime.

He grabbed his cell phone and headed downstairs.

Outside his building, a trail of panic hit his senses like a two-ton whale. Isabel and Julian were afraid of him, as they should be. He followed them with barely contained excitement and only vague shame over his eagerness for retribution. He spent the early minutes of his pursuit negotiating with himself, to confirm that his desire for revenge was morally defensible. It must be, or he wouldn't feel so motivated . . . He knew he was justified in wanting to confront his betrayers—no need to deliberate that point—but he truly hungered to inflict damage, was picturing the life leaving Isabel's eyes and relishing the prospect of killing her while Julian watched. He would catch up with them in a few hours at most, so Isabel's little trick with the fish tank hardly mattered. Her pathetic ruse to buy time wouldn't save her.

Naturally the trail led toward the coast. He knew the pair meant to hide behind the siren justice system, but he would catch them before they even got close. Xanthe and the rest of her government remained so terribly compromised in the aftermath of the Loughlin suicides, he rationalized; she wasn't the force she could be and the new regime was precisely that: new. And so laughably unprepared for the monarchy they couldn't possibly respond to him as they should, certainly not as he would if he ruled from Shaddox.

No, he was operating from a position of strength, from the standpoint of experience and also because his political maneuverings had teeth. He doubted Carmen & Company understood the first thing about political maneuverings.

He continued to pick up trace scents of fear where Isabel and Julian had passed, and this calmed him. Yet more evidence that he was behaving rationally, because they fled like cowards when, had their intentions been honorable, they would have talked with him, attempted to argue their side. They must know they were guilty because why else would they slink away like thieves?

Their cowardice was the deciding factor in his favor. He could be blameless, at least in his own mind. He lifted his face to the sky and continued eastward, reaching with his intuition to apprehend what more he could of Julian and Isabel's intentions. He resumed his hunt with a light, fast pace.

"I think that an old sailor who has traveled the whole world can determine by the movement of his ship which sea he is sailing."

– from *Story of a Shipwrecked Sailor*
by Gabriel Garcia Marquez

PART THREE

CHAPTER THIRTY-FOUR

As much as she could these days, Xanthe retreated to her sanctuary with as many others as she could gather in the hopes of mining some collective wisdom, since she'd become mostly unable to manufacture wisdom on her own anymore. She and her companions floated with their hands joined and brows furrowed in concentration, all focused on the goal of helping her overcome her recent lack of insight.

She didn't know to where her heretofore infallible abilities had disappeared, the ones that had elevated her to the leadership position she'd held for more than a century. Her former knack for analyzing a problem but fast—and just as quickly envisioning multiple ways to solve it—had died. Like she'd never had it.

Before attending the gathering to hear Gabe's findings on Duncan, she'd believed her failures were situational, thought she'd been stymied by the onslaught of human-like individuality blossoming within her community and the rash of sirens gone rogue. But then, toward the end of the discussion, when Gabe had suggested his ridiculous apprehension plan for Duncan, she'd experienced her talents like old times. She'd in fact had an epiphany of sorts, one that left her with the conviction she wasn't responsible for her loss of skill. She thought perhaps if she investigated this idea she could cure herself and alleviate her incompetence. As well as her frustration. She badly wanted her equilibrium back.

Her irritability, which had become tiresome to everyone, including herself, didn't help matters. Her impressive track record had carried her these past months, gave her some breathing room to try and fix what she hoped was an aberration, and at least no one was calling for her resignation or blatantly questioned her strangeness . . . but then her image was not what concerned her.

After Gabe's briefing, she felt—actually felt—interference within her, some influence designed to mess with her specifically, and the source was something she couldn't see or even define. At the time she'd briefly negotiated around the blockage and, once on the other side of it, saw it for what it was, an external tampering.

Not internal.

Not a failure of her own making.

How wonderful to see her shortcomings this way, and to believe she could eliminate them if she identified the source.

Her confidence in herself remained tentative, however. What or who could get into her head enough to scramble her thinking as well as her outreach? What or who *would*, and why?

Gabe's descriptions of his feats in Raleigh also disturbed her. He was a promising young siren and the fact he could cloak at all was impressive, but she did not believe he had the maturity to achieve the sophisticated outcomes he'd described, where he cloaked convincingly *as their former prince* to a member of the royal court; and intuited others' thoughts and feelings fluently—from a distance and on land. With both Duncan and Isabel, he'd tiptoed without notice into the minds of much older, acutely sensitive sirens.

These things were unheard of, and while she could believe Gabe had latent talents which might one day develop into something so extraordinary, she had a hard time believing he'd been able to pull it all off so recently in Raleigh.

As she ruminated, she drew strength from those gathered around her, and she calmed under the understanding this unique connection afforded. She felt almost as strong as she used to, when her quicksilver intelligence was a muscle that never failed her and the barrier inside her didn't exist.

For three divine minutes she had wriggled around that barrier at Gabe and Carmen's summit, meaning it was surmountable. What bothered her now was how personal the blockage felt, how it seemed deliberately targeted to her, too much to have been happenstance. Could Duncan have developed some new trick to contain her? She didn't think so. He wasn't capable. Also he was three hours away tending to his own psychosis, and he didn't have the capacity to reach her from such a distance. Still the containment felt unmistakably intentional; her experience, in this case, not her intuition, made her sure.

Which meant the effort required sentience, and the influence had to be some*one* not some*thing*. Humans were certainly out; and no one—absolutely no one from her world—had such capabilities. She thought again of Gabe's masterful reconnaissance effort inland and...

Well. Wasn't that a thought. Peter Loughlin could have performed as Gabe had; and had he been alive maybe, *maybe* he could have interfered with her abilities. But he was dead . . .

Xanthe thought back to the aftermath of Peter and Gabe's underwater confrontation, where even she was confused by the cacophony of grief emanating from the crowd. The violence of the event, so unprecedented and so shocking, had made the proceedings impossibly more surreal. And then afterwards, following Kenna's self-destruction and all the shame that caused . . . Xanthe remembered feeling a tiny prickling of awareness that something was not as it seemed. Nothing had been as it should, however, and so she had allowed herself to be distracted by the larger emergencies at play.

But she returned again and again in the following weeks to this intuitional warning she'd felt, which happened whenever she mused over all the motivations and consequences related to the Loughlin double suicide. She could not pinpoint the exact inconsistency, but her sense of incompletion—the feeling somewhere in that mess of events something was off—stayed with her.

Just as she had when Gabe first suggested Peter had kidnapped Kate, Xanthe disciplined herself to look at the situation as she should, not as she wanted to. Her companions helped her with this endeavor now, adding their support and confirmation to give her direction. She didn't think she would have continued without it, as evidenced by the fact that she previously hadn't.

After not much more time and with the backing of everyone around her, she saw the truth cleanly: someone had orchestrated her involvement, was possibly shadowing the others, too. That someone could only be Peter Loughlin.

Xanthe's consciousness returned in force, the pieces of this bizarre puzzle fitting together for the first time since the prince's demise. She saw with swift clarity a series of disjointed events that now cohered: Seneca's sudden return, Carmen's ascension to the throne, and Gabe's turbo-charged stealth and interrogation techniques.

She allowed herself a short, bitter laugh. And here she'd been worried about the manipulations of that artless sneak Duncan Fleming. What a joke. She had the feeling Duncan—and the rest of them for that matter—were about to get a real lesson in what it meant to be played.

Isabel's race toward Shaddox with her human companion drew sirens from miles around, although the couple proceeded alone for the first hour of the marine leg of their journey.

After escaping Raleigh the pair passed through Griffins Bay and kept right on going until they reached the Blake house, where they did not stop since Isabel said she could sense no one was home. Julian stumbled along wide-eyed, mumbling concerns about trespassing and did she know these people and what if they got caught? Isabel ignored him. They crossed the lawn to the back of the house like they belonged there, and then followed the stairs and half-walled walkway leading to the sea. Julian protested in earnest when he saw Isabel's intention, evidenced by her single-minded approach toward the terrifying, black expanse of water off the pier. He suspected the worst, and he was right. She flung him mid-scream into the ocean and dove after him.

She'd been mostly uncommunicative since leaving Raleigh. As soon as they exited Duncan's building after their escape, Julian began plying her with anxious questions, although he might as well have been silent given her lack of response or even acknowledgment. Isabel had hesitated only once, as if she might answer him, but she changed her mind and turned away, because why bother? She had gripped his upper arm like she might cinch it off and emitted an ear-splitting shriek that brought five cabs screeching to a halt at their curb.

"Just clue me in on the basics, Isabel," he pleaded as they drove east. "I mean obviously I'm an idiot for getting myself into this pickle so I understand why you wouldn't trust me, but I promise I'm going to see this thing through, make it as right as I can. Are you taking me to see the Queen? Is she . . . vindictive? Any chance she'll grant me a pass since Duncan is the bigger crackpot here? And I have to know: have you or any of your kind ever eaten anybody?"

Isabel closed her eyes briefly at this last question but still said nothing. "Can't you tell me anything at all?" Julian whined.

"You won't understand yet, because everything I tell you will be out of context," she replied. "Just *relax* for a little while longer. You aren't in danger."

Julian contained himself for less than a minute before his nerves once again got the better of him and he resumed his inquiry. "I'm not prying, truly I'm not, it's just that I did quite a lot to help Duncan make his little campaign possible, you know? Procured the necessary equipment and specced everything on the tech side, including the destination sites and protocols for delivery . . . can you maybe see why I might be unwilling to run into the folks he wanted to hang out to dry? I mean, won't they just skewer me with a marlin snout or something?"

"No," Isabel answered. She did not elaborate. Before he could begin pestering her again, she stopped him. "I'm not unsympathetic, Julian. But in light of the larger threat Duncan poses, your fears are ridiculous."

Julian thought about this for a minute before he conceded. "I suppose you're right." And Isabel seemed to be taking care not to kill him. After that terrifying catapult off the pier—the first several seconds of which he spent thrashing and begging to be set free—he calmed.

See, I won't let you drown, she told him after a while.

He began babbling once more, although to himself this time. *So... maybe I'll survive this? I mean, I'm not cold or air-deprived or uncomfortable; and Isabel doesn't seem like she'll eat me . . . even if she looks wild and fierce and terrifying.* She followed his train of logic while he reasoned through his experience, pleased when he realized nothing that would have normally troubled him—the dark, the running away from a madman, the possible encroachment of flesh-hungry sea beasts—upset him, because the second he felt any distress, it disappeared. *Is Isabel responsible? She must be. If she turns into a fish and exhibits other superhuman qualities, what was one more?* It was all good. He'd take compulsory bliss over panic attacks any day of the week.

And then came the really cute corollary to this progression for Isabel: Julian mooning over her. *Couldn't a guy just look at her forever? She's exquisite, so graceful and lovely and strong.* Her appeal was a powerful antidote to any remaining anxiety he nursed. What was there to fret about? He was swimming with an honest-to-God siren, one who was, for the moment, devoted to him. He loved her too, of course, because honestly, how could he not? She was worth every bit of his adoration.

Even if this was to be his last dance, he would go out like Ben-Hur or Rhett Butler, my dear. He would exit the world a romantic hero. And what a thrilling departure from his mole-ish, spiritless existence not six months ago. So he couldn't care about the repercussions of their underwater jaunt.

Which Isabel appreciated. Julian's earlier hysterics put her too much on edge, a risky proposition when she was trying not to drown him. Meaning his compliance was one less mortal complication to wrestle with today and she was grateful for the reprieve.

She was terribly proud to be managing so well, was especially relieved to learn she could swim with a human and not kill him when only a few short weeks ago she absolutely would have. She still felt his stunning pull and attending euphoria, but it didn't subsume her, didn't throw her into the mindless frenzy of need that would have left Julian dead and her horrified and ashamed. She wasn't sure where her new self-control came from, but she had a pretty good idea; oppressed as she'd been in Duncan's company, she suspected she'd developed internal armor as a way to cope, to protect herself against her husband's soul-numbing lack of consideration. She thought of it as an adaptation, one she hadn't anticipated but delighted in anyway. Looking back, she remembered times she didn't think she could survive her interplay with Duncan unless she put something of herself on reserve.

So perhaps she'd derived some benefit from this whole, awful experience; and now she could manage better as she made her way in the world of humans and solitude and bizarre siren subterfuge. Julian would appreciate this newfound competency, too, if he understood what she would have done to him six weeks ago when she didn't have it.

Best keep that information to myself, she thought. Julian was easily agitated, and his imagination didn't need any new fears to feed on. In fact, now that they'd made it most of the way to find help, maybe she could afford to answer his questions and put him at ease.

I'm taking you to see Xanthe, she announced. *She's sort of our secretary of state, and she's kind and fair, not at all vengeful. You're not in trouble—your sin was running into Duncan Fleming, although maybe you were too suggestible . . . but you were coerced. I'm bringing you home for your protection, not punishment.*

She glowered at him as she delivered her next piece of information. *And we don't eat people so you can quit picturing yourself on a spit.*

She knew Julian didn't care if he died, but not because he didn't think it wouldn't happen. She frowned at him. He smiled blandly back.

Other sirens straggled into their periphery, coalescing into a kind of formal escort as they intuited her purpose. All of them regarded Julian with wild, hungry expressions Isabel understood and he didn't. They sidled up against him and then swam quickly away in ever more disturbing forays, until Isabel hissed at them and insisted they stand down.

Julian remained unperturbed but Isabel explained anyway. *They are drawn to you because you are human, and because of the emotional intensity of our quest.* More and more joined them from the shadows until Isabel knew they made a quite a display. She scanned their immediate environment: they now numbered more than thirty . . . and Duncan Fleming was nowhere near. Good.

Where's everyone going? Julian's inquiry was offhanded, his curiosity detached. She disliked him for this, would have preferred him to have more internal fortitude than concede control of his existence to her. She could have manipulated him regardless, but Julian was literally no match for her complexity and vitality . . . and she realized he'd just answered a question she hadn't known she was asking herself.

We're taking you to Shaddox, she told him soothingly, as if he were a child.

He stared dreamily at his surroundings before returning his gaze to her. *I don't know where that is, but I don't care. Take me where you will.*

And I will, dear Julian. She would deliver him safely and then abandon him to take his life's path without her. He was not the man for her, and she wouldn't pretend to want him in a way she didn't.

She would seek fulfillment elsewhere.

CHAPTER THIRTY-FIVE

Parker slammed the door to her room, leaned against it and ignored Seneca's call from downstairs to please come back and talk. She didn't need yet another explanation as to why she would be left at home while Seneca went on a secret—and probably dangerous—mission to capture a criminal siren. Someone named Duncan Fleming.

"It's for your own safety, love," Seneca had scolded her gently. Parker glared in response. "And what about your safety? What if you don't come back?"

Their plan was sketchy, Seneca conceded, but she was keen to play a key role in Duncan's capture. Kate's husband, Gabe, was orchestrating the mission; and he was the only one with full knowledge of the plan, which he was not sharing. His rationale for withholding info was to prevent their target from intuiting it before he could be detained, since Duncan would be able to read the intent of those around him and would run off to cause more trouble if he got spooked. Gabe, Parker was told, could completely mask his thoughts and feelings, could not be read by Duncan or anyone else.

But Gabe was keeping his mouth shut on how he meant this capture to go down.

To be fair Seneca had shared what she knew, which was precious little. This Duncan guy apparently wanted Carmen's head on a platter, and Seneca was to serve as some sort of diversion, meaning she would actually interact with this nutcase, although Parker was pretty sure the contingent traveling with her could protect her. Still, the endeavor seemed precarious. Worse, it felt risky for someone as transparent and guileless as Seneca . . . and Parker badly wanted to go along so she could look out for her.

Not that she had any right to deny her participation, but she stated her opposition to anyone who would listen, including Kate the previous afternoon.

"She's not like the rest of you," Parker had argued. "I don't think she has the social smarts you all do, and she'll get into trouble. I mean, if this guy tries to hurt her, she won't see it coming."

"And that's why she won't be alone, honey," Kate had soothed. "I'm not arguing your point, but I have complete confidence Gabe and Carmen will bring everyone home safely." She described Gabe's cloaking skills and suggested Parker's anxiety was unwarranted.

"None of you know her like I do," Parker had protested bitterly. She walked away feeling she might just as well have said nothing.

Her direct plea to Seneca—which quickly became a strident demand to stay out of it—was equally unsuccessful.

"Carmen needs my help, Parker. I'm going."

Parker ran to her room, not even bothering to hide how undone she was—stomping, crying, and ultimately slamming her door. After another minute, Seneca quit calling for her to return, which was just as well since she'd said all she was going to. No matter how many people told her—or how many times they patiently explained—she would continue to see the effort as a big fat disaster waiting to happen. Using Seneca as bait to lure a criminal into custody would *never* be a good idea, not because they weren't taking precautions, but because of who Seneca was.

She resolved not to sit idly by. She couldn't. She would find a way around her adoptive mother's orders to stay home like a good girl and then wouldn't everyone be surprised. It was to be her new response to an old problem, the same problem that had plagued her since she could remember: she didn't want to be left out. No, more than that, she didn't want to be less important than Carmen or other people, or to responsibilities that sounded noble when used as an excuse to walk away from her. And she *really* wouldn't beg to be Seneca's first priority.

Parker stared out the window as she contemplated how wonderful it would be to be "normal," to go through life like other kids who could take for granted their importance to the people around them. In the face of this particular despair, everyone's calmly reasoned arguments did not and would not matter.

She needed a distraction. She flopped on her bed, grabbed the remote for her television and pointed it at the screen.

The image that came up was so out of context she didn't understand it at first. It looked like a soft news story, following as it did on the heels of a fashion reporter's review of upcoming trends in footwear. The announcer's voice eventually registered, and then what she saw made sense. *"A series of video clips is taking the web by storm today, according to multiple sources."* The anchor's subsequent smile at the camera was deprecatory, like she apologized a little for her report. *"The broadcast shows a woman changing into a mermaid, and experts are baffled as to how the videographer managed to produce such a lifelike transformation. We'll go now to our correspondent in Los Angeles for commentary."*

Parker shouted for Seneca.

The scene changed to an interview with a man from "N'oeuf Graphics" out of Los Angeles. *"We do CAG—that's computer-aided graphics—for all the major film studios, and you can bet we have the best tech and people in the world to make our stuff convincing. I cannot—and neither can anyone else from my team—figure out how this was pulled off. To us the only explanation is they found some chick who can actually turn into a fish!"* He and the announcer chuckled.

Seneca had arrived in time to hear the end of it and watch the clip of a female siren transforming. Her breath hissed as she sucked it in. "That's Isabel Fleming." Parker stared at the screen in shock.

"Is that really . . . ?"

"It's real," Seneca confirmed. "I'm sure this means we'll be leaving sooner than we thought." She engaged her cell phone. "So we're out of time for you to come to terms with the fact that I'm going." Her attention shifted as her phone call was answered. "Carmen, turn on your television. I'm dropping Parker off with Kate, and then I'll be over."

Xanthe learned of the video release minutes after Carmen did. And thanks to the technology upgrades Duncan had made at Shaddox before he left, she could immediately pull it up for review.

Poor Isabel, she thought as she watched the forced transformation. That Taser . . . and then she was on land and lacking buoyancy. Their forms became so weighted their lungs compressed, which was why none of them much liked to change out of the water. Some of them couldn't, which Xanthe suspected led Duncan to use that vile electronic device. Xanthe hugged herself in sympathy as she observed Isabel's labored breathing.

She grew angry on Isabel's behalf and resolved Duncan would fail for his barbarity and because his threat would not be effective. Human perception could and would be managed, even if doing so on a broad scale would take some cleverness. But Xanthe knew Carmen, and she knew she and Michael and Gabe could figure this one out. She estimated they'd have Duncan under arrest within a week.

She marveled at the lengths Duncan had gone to negotiate power for himself, however; and how he genuinely thought he could blackmail the new regime, believed they would back down due to his shallow terrorism. Her people would never, never tolerate extortion, and Duncan's outrageous tactics had secured his own demise. How deluded could the man be? Perhaps, as Gabe had suggested, Duncan didn't see his fallibilities because he only listened to himself, only told himself what he wanted to believe.

Overall Xanthe was relieved to finally understand the scope and intent of Duncan's scheme. She knew he could and would be reined in and could see the threat he posed was inconvenient but not truly dangerous. She didn't even feel guilt over recusing herself from his containment or capture. Because—and Duncan would soon find out how wrong he'd been to underestimate the new regime—Carmen and her family would deal with him handily.

Nonetheless she dispatched an envoy to Griffins Bay to consult with Carmen. He was told to make her confidence in Carmen's judgment clear but decline to offer her personal involvement. Xanthe intended to let the Blakes have this win all to themselves and secure the confidence of the siren society they ruled.

And her blindness—that exterior restraint she wrestled with—

might sideline her anyhow, which meant she should pursue her more pressing—and for now private—preoccupation.

She had a ghost to hunt down, and Duncan Fleming had just conveniently provided her with a cover.

CHAPTER THIRTY-SIX

Kate and the rest of Maya's wedding entourage—namely Maya's mother and sisters—had run out of patience with her. None of them understood Maya's reluctance to receive them. And Maya's strategy for keeping them at bay—she pled exhaustion due to medical school and required outings with her fiancé's socialite family—no longer held up.

Her excuses were valid; she really was overscheduled, although she much preferred the demands of school to the parties and social outings she'd agreed to when she handed over planning for her very large, very public wedding ceremony. Stuart's mother and sisters had some mystical knowledge necessary to life in the societal stratosphere their family inhabited, as well as the stomach to tackle the mind-boggling minutiae that went with being drafted in. Maya was only too happy to step aside and let the experts have at it.

But after putting the Griffins Bay contingent off the last time, Alicia, Solange, Sylvia and Kate simply announced to her they were coming. They used her own evasion tactics—the citing of practical concerns—against her to ignore her request to wait yet again, just walked right over all her arguments.

"I'm your maid of honor, for crying out loud," Kate told her with unconcealed exasperation. "We all have to be fitted for our dresses, and I'm going to give you my opinion on the dang flowers whether you want it or not."

Maya didn't mention the budget for her flowers was something in the neighborhood of fifty thousand dollars for the ceremony alone, because she knew Kate would be as unable to grasp this concept as she was. Plus, these kinds of details embarrassed her, trained as she was in the social philosophies of her class, which could not condone the kinds of frivolous purchases her in-laws were making when there were starving children and homeless families wandering the streets.

No one brought up the real reason for Maya's reluctance to get together, which was the protection of her fragile assertion that she wanted all this nonsense.

She knew she should examine these feelings more closely just as surely as she knew she wouldn't. She was getting on with her life, by God; and even if the entire state of North Carolina felt they had a say in how she was going about it, they didn't. She was getting married. Period, end of discussion, no need to delve.

As out of place as she felt in Stuart's world, at least no one here wondered about her sudden change of heart where Stu was concerned or had to be shut out of her life so she could make herself go through with it. The simple answer was she was ready to claim some independence, which meant marrying a Yankee and putting down roots in New York City. Her former community was just going to have to learn to butt out and leave well enough alone.

In a dim corner of her brain, Maya knew her defensiveness had to do with her own doubts, not others'. And in those rare moments when she could honestly evaluate her decisions, she understood she would suffer more than anyone if her family and Kate completely backed away. She couldn't stand this idea, but neither could she allow the intrusion they seemed to think was their right. Kate's initial question—about why no one knew she and Stuart were serious until the wedding invites went out—was not unique. Her whole family had badgered her on the subject, not that it did them any good.

"Can you imagine any of us doing this to you?" Solange asked during one phone conversation. "Did you think about how Mama would feel?"

"Actually, I can imagine it. And I did think of Mama," Maya rejoined. "And I don't recall any long, drawn-out discussions with the folks when you married Luke. In fact, as I recall, you two dated for five whole minutes before throwing your decision out on the dinner table. I remember *exactly* how excited she was about your news." Solange's pause afterwards was pregnant, although all she said was, "I was so nuts about Luke, I didn't have a choice. You're all about rationale and timing." Which didn't sit well, even if it was true.

"Also, I kept Mama involved, as you'll remember. Seems like you're hoping none of us will show up until the wedding."

Maya's evasion sounded good she thought. "Well I'm sure none of you would be comfortable with how they do things here, what with their professional planners and personal assistants and over-the-top extravagance on every blessed detail under the sun. It'll be more of a floor show than a wedding." Solange's silence after that comment was eloquent. Maya hung up feeling, if possible, even more like she had something to prove.

Which was why keeping them away continued to feel like her best option.

All of them *were* in the wedding party, however, including Sylvia who had been MIA for the better part of the last half-year. She'd just returned home—pregnant, thank you—and had jumped right on the 'let's all get up in Maya's business' bandwagon. Sylvia was not, to Maya's mind, anyone to judge given the bizarre progression of her own romance. Apparently to their parents' way of thinking, ditching one's responsibilities for a tryst in Antarctica was less worrisome than attending medical school and marrying well on the North American continent. A girl couldn't get a break.

The byplay with Sylvia notwithstanding, her sisters and Kate were to form one quarter of her twelve-attendant spectacle, so when they told her they were on their way even Maya couldn't argue them down. Their dresses did have to be tailored. And once everyone arrived, she saw the situation differently.

Maya went straight to her mother, put her head on her shoulder and started to cry, a surprise to both of them. Alicia held her tight and whispered encouragements until she could hold herself together. Maya looked away when she wiped her eyes to avoid seeing any condemnation from Kate, Sylvia and Solange.

Alicia gripped her hands and forced her attention back to her. "Everything okay, honey?"

For once Maya didn't try to hide. "Yes. No. I don't know, Mama. I think so. It's just been a whole lot of running around to shop for things I don't care about with people I don't really know, and you would bust a gut laughing to hear how serious my mother-in-law is with the seating arrangements. I can't stand to even ask how many people are coming, 'cause I already know it's some ridiculously high number. And school is intense . . ." she stopped because it was either that or break down crying again. "I guess I don't allow myself to think about how it feels, but seeing you, I can't help it. And I'm homesick." She offered them all a tremulous smile. "I'm really, really glad you're all here."

Their expressions softened and Maya felt a whole lot better, at least for the first hour. Kate cornered her then.

She and Kate were shopping for shoes while Alicia and Maya's sisters were off perusing the wedding registry when Kate started in.

"You've lost weight. And you look tired."

Maya tried to brush her off. "If your wedding had royalty and doves and little, dancing ballerinas in it, you'd flip out too, Blake. Also, no one seems to remember I'm *in medical school*. It's not like I'm leading a balanced life here."

Her friend remained skeptical. "Appetite?" She stated her question like an accusation.

"You've got me there," Maya allowed. "But wait until you meet my in-laws. I didn't even know there was such a thing as a size zero but I'll be the only chick in the family who isn't one. I'm nervous every single time I take a bite of something." She rubbed her eyes. "I wish I could get their skinny hind ends on a volleyball court," she lamented. "They'd find out real quick what happens to girls who don't eat their pancakes."

"Sounds like I need to start sending you care packages."

Maya felt her eyes go round with hope. "Holy sweet heaven. Would you?"

"Heck yeah. I've got cookies in the freezer. I'll ship some when I get home."

"I'll love you forever. Longer than forever."

"Pfft. You'll love me regardless. We've been close since we were kids," she reminded her. "Which is why I must say I don't understand how it is that we never once had a deep, probing conversation about Stu. Like how ga-ga you are for him, or what a great kisser he is, or how you can't keep your hands off each other." Kate struggled to hide her hurt, and Maya felt like the biggest jerk on the planet. "I wouldn't judge you for marrying who you want, you know."

Kate would have no way of knowing about the angsty script she'd written herself on this very subject, but it leapt to the forefront of her mind like it was on automatic replay. She sighed unhappily, because as usual the comparisons she made between her romance and that of everyone she grew up with—Kate's especially—undid her. On her own, she rationalized her choices like a pro. But she couldn't bring herself to explain why she felt none of the starry-eyed giddiness Kate and her family expected from her.

"Just . . . don't harsh me out on this, okay? Who knows what I would have done if I'd met someone else at another time—like you did with Gabe, or my mom did with my dad. But we don't know what you'd do if you lived my life, either." She hated how defensive she felt and probably sounded. She deliberately softened her tone. "I've thought about this a lot, Kate. *A lot.*"

Kate's posture drooped. "I just want you to be happy, Maya. And I'm not seeing anything to convince me Stu's the right guy. I *know* it's none of my business . . . but if I don't say anything to you, who will?"

"Every other member of my family and half the neighbors back home," Maya retorted. She crossed her arms and looked away. Kate sighed, and after a long moment went to hug her.

"Okay, hon. I'm done being a buttinsky. From now on, I'm just here for the party." She punched Maya playfully on the shoulder. "Let's go meet these size zero in-laws and make mean-girl fun of them."

Maya indulged in the first true laugh she'd had in what felt like forever. She hooked an arm through Kate's and led her away. "You're one in a million, Blake. Wait until you see these chicks. You will be dazzled."

CHAPTER THIRTY-SEVEN

At one point, Duncan saw his approaching ruin with a sense of inevitability, like he watched a news report about a catastrophic train wreck that had already happened. He saw the train approaching the broken trestle over the canyon, knew he would plummet to his death in a crush of mechanics and steel. But he was helpless to stop his own hurtling momentum.

He was delayed from reaching the ocean for no reason he could understand. He'd made good time to Griffins Bay . . . and then somehow fallen asleep. He awoke in a ditch outside of town with no injuries and no memory as to how he got there. As he walked Main Street toward the Blake house, the digital date on the sign over the bank revealed he'd lost track of the last twenty hours, almost an entire day. Could he have slept that whole time? He searched his memory for clues as to what had happened, any clue at all, but no explanation popped up.

He didn't feel otherwise compromised, was energized and alert, in fact, so perhaps he'd been overcome by exhaustion and his body had simply taken the rest it needed. Which made sense the more he thought about it; he'd worked so hard for so long to carve out a life in Raleigh . . . and, well, that kind of stress had to have had an impact. He decided he could ignore the hole in his memory because he really felt well, lighthearted even.

And he was grateful to be moving at night again, since the darkness gave him cover to walk too quickly, and he didn't have to maintain a "normal" appearance in front of humans since there weren't any out.

He was so close to the water. He could feel the sea in the air, which lifted his spirits further. He would soon transform, something he missed more than anything. He closed the distance to the beach feverishly, anticipating the rush of water over his body and the suppleness and strength of his siren self.

He regretted the impact of an overnight delay since he was still keen for revenge, couldn't wait to hunt down his errant wife and punish her. But he had full confidence he could deal with her as he intended. By now they would have reached Shaddox and told their tale, which was not a setback since he'd deployed his insurance policy back in Raleigh. And then, too, he knew the palace—including how and where to get in and out of it—better than most.

He was almost there, having cut across the lawn of the Blake house on the outskirts of Griffins Bay. He spied the stairway to the pier . . .

A man stepped in front of him to block the path. He started, but then realized he knew him. "Michael Blake?"

"Duncan."

Of course, he should have realized someone might be in residence, although he'd assumed Carmen and Michael were installed at the palace. And he hadn't felt anyone's presence . . . but he'd been so absorbed in his thoughts.

He had traitors to catch and wasn't interested in a confrontation, though. He might not have a choice now, so he sized Michael up, and given the man's challenging posture—chest out, hands clenched into fists—decided his best defense was offense. He retreated a pace and stiffened into the officious stance of his former position as viceroy. "Step aside. I'm on my way to Shaddox." He waited for compliance if not deference. He didn't get it.

Michael had expected him, Duncan guessed, although he wondered about the extent to which Michael had been warned. Possibly not much, which would be ideal since he preferred a cleaner comeuppance for his bride—just him exacting vengeance with no witnesses other than Julian. Maybe Michael had just happened to be here?

The appearance of John Blake, fresh out of the water, killed that hope. Duncan surmised he'd been lurking off shore in case Michael failed to detain him on land. Which meant they knew more than he wanted them to, more than nothing. Duncan scanned for others.

"Everyone you want to see is here," Michael crooned. "Most of the new royal court, in fact. That should make you happy. You can argue your case directly to my wife." His smile was evil.

Duncan thought fast. An additional delay was apparently inevitable, but if Carmen was here . . . well, he relished the idea of seeing her reaction to his pet video project, envisioned her timid capitulation and the subsequent satisfaction he would feel. He looked from Michael to John. "You know you need to let me return to Raleigh if you hope to contain the damage, don't you?"

The blast of fury from Michael Blake came at him like an ice storm, and Duncan stumbled backwards. John literally hissed, which caused Duncan to retreat further. He sniffed. "I see where your son gets his aggression, Michael. I caution you both not to do anything unwise."

John was further away and consequently seemed a less immediate threat. But he growled which, combined with Michael's hostility, gave Duncan pause for the first time since embarking on this initiative. They should both know he was too high functioning, too emotionally evolved to stoop to actually fighting, shouldn't they? Surely they understood how capable and thorough he was, that his plan back home was absolutely perfect . . .

No, he was here to convince them of the threat he posed, nothing more. When they thought it through, knew how little he actually wanted from them—his freedom, essentially—they would calm down. They were sirens, after all. He relaxed his stance and nodded toward the house.

"I'll go if you promise to hear me out." He glanced at each of them reprovingly. "And when I have your assurance you won't attack."

"You're coming regardless," John drawled. Michael held up a hand to stay him. "No need to spook the guy, John." To Duncan he said, "You will be heard out. So let's go." He gripped Duncan by the upper arm.

Furious, Duncan shook him off. They thought to manhandle him?

They'd best know what they were dealing with, in that case. He concentrated on constricting Michael's arteries, smiling when the man pressed a fist to his chest. A sharp shove from John broke his focus. "Knock it off, Duncan." When Duncan's eyes narrowed on John, Michael stepped between them. "There are two of us, Duncan, so that trick won't work. And you don't want to jeopardize your chance at Carmen, do you?"

Duncan felt a pang of fear. They knew about his "trick," as they termed it? But Michael *had* reacted, so it worked . . . although not if he was interrupted, as it seemed he would be with both of them there. He shrugged. He'd made his point and he did, in fact, want to face Carmen. He sneered and started forwards. "By all means." He marched to the house before either of them could grab him.

With the exception of Xanthe, the gang was all there, looking much too composed, Duncan believed. Had they not seen the clip of Isabel changing? Did they not know?

Carmen gave him a pitying smile, although—and Duncan was relieved to feel it—she *was* nervous. "We've seen the video releases, Duncan. What was it you hoped to accomplish with them?" Gabe stood impassively at her side, looking more like her bodyguard than son.

So there were to be no niceties, then. Fine.

Duncan didn't hide his disdain when he leveled his gaze at the new siren queen. "I have no confidence in your ability to lead, Carmen. Not even I could help you perform as you should in your new office." He examined the faces of everyone else in the room. "Please remember I served the Loughlins for several decades," he focused on Carmen, "and that I performed the duties of your office—extremely well, I might add—before your *pedigree* came to light."

He paused to determine everyone's reaction, which ranged from unresponsive to - of all thing—*bored.* This wasn't going as expected, and he wondered if they misunderstood the import of his campaign, what he would do if they refused him.

They just weren't getting it. That had to be the problem. And where was Xanthe? This meeting should have required her attendance.

He was committed to this conversation, however, so he rallied to complete the interaction on his terms. He tried to sound conciliatory.

"I just want . . . I have no real desire to reveal ourselves to humans."

Michael regarded him like he was rotting seaweed. "Then why did you?"

"It can be contained . . ." Duncan began.

"We already know this," John interrupted, and again Duncan was appalled at the lack of concern this group exhibited. He glared at John.

". . . and the additional images I have can be withheld," he continued, "provided you agree to let me run things as I please in Raleigh."

The slam of the front door drew everyone's attention as a red-faced, panting human girl entered the room. Carmen stood in alarm. "Parker!" The girl looked at Carmen in confusion and then scanned the rest of the room. Her gaze rested on Duncan for several seconds and turned speculative. She advanced toward Carmen. "Stay right where you are!" Carmen commanded, and Duncan was pleased to see her so discomposed. Parker complied, taking a spot against a wall. "I'll stand over here, out of the way," she promised, and Carmen nodded at her once before returning her attention to Duncan.

"It's as we thought, then," she stated. Her expression hardened. "And the answer to your request is no." Gabe advanced on him.

Duncan was astonished. This was it? The new queen would risk the exposure of her people to thwart him? He looked around wildly, unwilling to believe his bid for sovereignty was truly at an end. "You obviously don't understand what you're saying, Carmen," he said nervously, putting a chair between himself and Gabe. It was a weak barrier, but he still thought to appeal to the queen's reason and wanted whatever time it would afford him. "We don't need to make this any uglier than it already is." He opened his mouth to speak and then choked on his words as his attention, as well as that of everyone else in the room, was pulled away.

A chilling stillness had pervaded the space, and everyone tensed as they searched for its source. There was a presence, one that felt like . . . but no, *it couldn't be*, Duncan thought. He looked to Gabe, who stared thoughtfully over Duncan's shoulder.

At that moment Duncan knew—*knew*—his plans were lost, that he would not be allowed to run a fiefdom in Raleigh, would not be allowed even to leave this meeting. A frustration greater than any he'd experienced ignited within him, burning through every civil inclination he'd ever had, including the desire to appear respectable in front of his former peers. If he could not have the power he craved, if he would be denied even the rule over some pathetic human outpost far from the ocean, he *would* have revenge. Revenge for the life taken from him first at Shaddox and now inland, for the supreme insult he'd suffered at the hands of the transition committee and the vagaries of genetic lineage that made him subservient to inexperienced imbeciles like the woman before him.

No, if he would be made to give up everything, then so would Carmen Blake.

Could he do it? Driven to accomplish at least this much before he was captured, he closed his eyes and concentrated on Carmen to place a killing grip on her heart and lungs. How many heartbeats would it take? The others were still distracted but he didn't have long.

He felt her heart stutter at his very first foray and he thrilled to the knowledge he now had: he would need mere seconds to end her. He was so angry, he didn't care that his own insides mirrored the mortal injuries he sought to inflict, that this effort might result in his death as well as hers. In another second, he restricted her breath. He intended it to be her last. He took a final, deep breath himself and dedicated all of his fury to their mutual destruction. Reaching into her to squeeze, he sensed the first small tears in the tissues of her heart, knew with certainty the damage he was causing by the sympathetic reaction of his own body. He opened his eyes to see Carmen's shape shimmering before him as she prepared for dissolution. He knew he responded in kind.

Two extraordinary things happened then. The human girl, Parker, dove forward and gripped Carmen's forearm; and Duncan's influence was broken the instant she made contact. "No," she said simply, looking directly at Duncan. He could not reestablish a connection, and he roared in aggravation.

As he looked on, Carmen herself changed into the form of someone else, someone he'd seen before but couldn't place, and he realized Carmen wasn't even here, had never intended to confront him herself. Which meant the woman before him had been cloaked to appear as the queen, cloaked by someone very, very good at it. Duncan swiveled his gaze toward Gabe, who nodded curtly in acknowledgment. Duncan's fury turned to panic.

He clutched at the first argument that came to mind. "You

promised you wouldn't attack me," he gasped. He eyed the doors, the stairs, the window at his back. How to escape?

"You attacked us, you moron," Gabe retorted. He disappeared and then immediately reappeared at Duncan's side, reaching for the man's arms to bind them. But in that instant, Duncan flew backwards as if he'd been thrown, crashing through the window behind him to land on the lawn, his legs and arms now bloodied by cuts.

Then began the most terrifying experience of Duncan's life.

For one, he was not acting under his own influence and could not by any means re-establish control over his own body.

Just before his dive onto the lawn—through double-paned glass and certain injury, something he would *never* have risked—he'd felt . . . well, like an alien had charged into his body and taken possession. This at a time when his veins were coursing with adrenaline, his muscles tensed to respond as he wished.

But given a choice between imprisonment—tantamount to death for his kind—and freedom, which gave him a slightly better chance, he'd thought to get away and briefly eyed the window behind him. It was his last self-directed act.

He really was flung backwards by a force outside himself. As he rolled to his feet and sped toward the sea, he functioned like a remote-controlled robot, his body ignoring the plea from his mind to stop, if nothing else to remove the painful shards of glass he wore from his injurious shove onto the lawn. Now each stride, each impact from his feet hitting the earth agonized.

Still he could not slow. His panic, his efforts to resist whatever drove him, had absolutely no influence on his actions. He sensed Gabe, Michael and John all giving chase . . . and he should not have been able to outrun all three of them.

He feared what his puppet master would do once they were alone.

By the time he made the pier, the only physical capability he retained was the ability to cry, because he was confused and afraid and because he knew he raced toward a fate he could not avoid. He hit the water and transformed without pleasure. John, Michael and Gabe followed several hundred yards but couldn't catch up. At some point, they must have turned back, because he no longer sensed them at all.

He felt abandoned and desolate. Was this how Isabel felt during his hypnosis sessions with her? He was powerless, humiliated, and extremely sorry.

I think it was worse for her, his controller commented, *since she was abused again and again in your company.*

That voice . . . Duncan knew it well.

The denial he'd called forth at the Blakes', when everyone there had recognized an unidentified presence in the room, crumpled as he acknowledged something he badly wished not to. The man they'd all believed dead materialized in front of him.

You've been a very bad boy, Duncan, Peter Loughlin admonished. *What were you thinking?* Then, before Duncan could answer, *Don't answer me. I've no interest in your excuses.*

CHAPTER THIRTY-EIGHT

She found him thanks to blind, dumb luck. Well, luck combined with a six-person search team, grassroots forensics, and a covert trip to New York.

Xanthe's investigative efforts to establish the existence and whereabouts of their former prince bore immediate fruit. Following her epiphany over her stunted professional performance of late, she employed, with great distaste, the internet to search for news items hinting of siren influence. If Peter were alive, he would have needed some kind of community around him to survive, and the natural choice would have been a human enclave close to the water. Also, Xanthe guessed he was too used to the discipline of work—and too reliant on it for his identity—to opt out of all professional activities. Her aides sifted through millions of bits of information for mention of something that fit.

Her hypothesis proved accurate. After three days, her team found a lead on a New York City woman's blog, "Bridge-It: My Journey to Sobriety." The thread began with Bridget the Blogger's endorsement of a new recovery program she'd just completed. She claimed her addiction was one hundred percent, unequivocally cured in two weeks, and the center where she'd stayed had lined her up with dozens of services she hadn't even been aware of to get her on her feet again. She now had a decent place to live, was enrolled in a professional training program, and had a healthy circle of healthy friends. Even better, none of this had cost her a dime! She didn't have an address or phone number, but she encouraged readers to hie themselves to 48th and MacGuire. "Ask around for a guy named Peter. No last name, just Peter. But you can't miss him, folks, because he's tall and blond and gorgeous, and he'll make you feel like anything is possible."

Xanthe took a day trip to New York City and made discreet inquiries at the periphery of the neighborhood Bridget suggested. She didn't want to get too close and risk running into the man himself . . . and she found she didn't need to. She immediately drew in a dozen people who bore the signs of his influence. Far too many of them, upon seeing her, asked if she was related to Peter.

"You look like you might know him," one admirer opined.

"How kind of you to say. Although you must *not* mention you saw me."

She left after twenty minutes, hazed the humans she interacted with to forget her, and hoped Peter would not sense anything amiss; or if he did sense her, ascribe blame to his own presence and appeal. She returned to Shaddox, grabbed a cell phone and headed to an atoll near Griffins Bay.

When the call came from Gabe outlining their confrontation with Duncan, she was ready. She believed she and Gabe shared an understanding concerning Peter, although she'd made no mention of her suspicions to anyone yet. Gabe reported on a presence in the room before Duncan fled, however, and how improbable Duncan's escape had been—the quickness of his movements despite injury, his ability to outrun all three of his pursuers, and the fact that his trail disappeared. Just like a cloaker's would.

"I think I know what's going on, Gabe. Give me a few hours and I'll get back to you."

In the water, Xanthe trolled a wide swath of ocean surrounding Carmen and Michael's pier. He might sense her if she got too near—after years of working together he would know her emotional signature cold—but the area was something of a hub for their kind, which she hoped would give her a little cover. *Many, many sirens swim here*, she reminded herself. Some traffic would be expected. And a sufficient amount would maybe confuse her output? She hoped.

She thought back on the fight Peter had lost to Gabe all those months ago, when she and everyone else witnessed Peter's death. Gabe had described afterwards exactly how he'd located their prince in the center pool, information Xanthe thought she might put to use in her current circumstances. At the time Gabe had hunted not for the vital emanation of a living being, but for the absence of vitality, a flatness in energy and lack of emotion. Xanthe employed this tactic now, wishing Peter was in the smaller body of water at Shaddox instead of the much larger, harder-to-search ocean.

Still, through triangulation she defined the area Peter was likely to be given the time he and Duncan had left shore. This kind of concentration was foreign and uncomfortable to her, drawn as she was to life and energy, not deadness and nothing. But she persisted.

Eventually she did sense, barely, the kind of stillness Gabe had described, and she followed this gossamer thread of suggestion until it gained substance. She knew then she was getting close.

For no reason she could explain, Peter dropped his cloak when she was thirty yards away. He looked directly at her, his expression savage and challenging. "Stay back, Xanthe." In an instant, she understood why.

The distance was for her own protection.

Duncan was with him and not doing well, his heart and lungs painfully compromised, his face a grimace of pain. His misery echoed within her own body, not as strongly as if she were close, but intensely enough to cause her form to shimmer. Peter, Xanthe could see, was poised to kill him, and she dared not approach unless she wanted to suffer the same fate. As it was, her heart and lungs constricted . . . and she withdrew to a safer distance.

Duncan's eyes rolled back, his body twisting in the convulsions that accompanied the end for all sirens. As she watched, her hands pressed against her chest for relief. Duncan arched a final time then burst into dissolution, all those tiny particles of matter and light.

The burning constriction in Xanthe's chest disappeared. Duncan Fleming was no more. Because Peter Loughlin had somehow executed him.

She felt no fear as Peter swam to her, only curiosity; as well as a riotous joy he was among the living. Peter had been a formidable leader in their community, talented and accomplished and almost omnisciently capable. With the exception of the very last stretch of his tenure at Shaddox, his existence among them had been a source of pride as well as a comfort in uncertain times. And his propensity for deviance aside, his erasure from the social fabric of siren life had left a gaping hole that no one—Duncan Fleming least of all—could fill.

Unwise as she might be, Xanthe could not care in this moment who he had kidnapped or killed. Everyone missed him. She missed him.

Peter acknowledged her reception while still wearing the terrifying expression of the executioner, although again, Xanthe did not fear for herself. He clasped her hands between them, and her heart filled with some mixture of gratitude, relief and affection for a lost friend.

His smile—as well as the warm, living grip he had on her hands—made her cry. He squeezed her hands once and looked as if he might embrace her but didn't. *It's good to be missed*, he said. *But no, you should not trust me.*

She felt the base truth of his statement, and while it tempered the sweetness of their reunion, she still could not fear him. But neither did she hesitate to question him on what he'd done and where he'd been. *How . . . why . . . ?* she began.

How did I not die? What have I been doing since Gabe challenged me and I dissolved? Let me tell you. They clasped forearms.

He extracted what she knew first, which she thought of as a dirty trick although he would not be deterred. *Ah-ah. I have questions of my own, and your story will be shorter than mine.* His inquiry was so deep, so thorough, she fidgeted; but she could not retreat, physically or otherwise. Without any effort on her part he saw everything she'd seen, from his confrontation with Gabe the previous year to her recent visit to his human community in New York, to his execution of Duncan Fleming five minutes earlier. *I'm sorry you felt that*, he commented off-handedly.

Then he reciprocated.

He truly had intended to let go of his life after the confrontation with Gabe. He'd anticipated accurately the consequences of Kate's abduction and could not foresee living through them. She felt how, as he sought his death, he regretted deeply the anguish he'd caused everyone—Kate, Gabe, their families, as well as the siren community. He hadn't understood until that moment how harmful his plans to achieve fulfillment had been. So his apologies were sincere.

In the very end, though, he couldn't overcome his will to live. In those final seconds, when he realized he would fail, he created an illusion only he could, one convincing to every single siren in attendance, including Xanthe. Since the palace guards were centrally gathered in the pool—and because Peter could cloak so well—he had escaped first to the periphery and then exited at leisure through one of the palace exit tunnels.

He'd spent several days alone combing the north Atlantic coast for caves and other suitable locations to camp out while he deliberated his future. The need for emotional nourishment eventually drove him to shore, landing him in New York City, whose teeming population and constant distractions allowed him to interact and behave as he pleased. He found compromised humans easiest to engage with, those struggling with drug or alcohol addiction, or poverty or abuse.

His particular affinity was for people abandoned by society.

For Peter, fixing their problems was a simple proposition. After rejuvenating his spirits in their adoration, he would reach into them and adjust their definitions of who they were and what they needed. He sent them back to their lives happy and self-sufficient, a one-man social services team who could rehabilitate dozens of disenfranchised humans inside of a month.

Minus the crushing professional demands of the siren monarchy, his days now permitted ample time at the library, which he used to research the psychological impacts and treatment options associated with the humans he healed.

I found this effort instructive given my own psychopathology, he reported.

No doubt, she replied uneasily.

After an exhaustive study of maladaptive human behaviors—and because he was apparently incapable of containing himself to a smaller stage—he infiltrated the bureaucracies of local and state offices dedicated to providing challenged populations with support services. *There were so many resources*, he commented. *You would think no one would have these problems, that the services in place could have alleviated all challenges to recovery.*

He decided people must not know about them. When he selectively engaged with humans in need again, he harvested their devotion as usual and then performed a more thorough rehabilitation, this time with the help of the Health & Human Services Department.

I never formed an organization, as the woman from the blog believed. I have no desire to be accountable to anyone other than myself in this.

He admitted that after a while he was unable to sustain himself solely in the company of humans. He'd pined for his own, which was why he'd returned to Griffins Bay from time to time to look in on the Blake family. He'd felt replenished even as an invisible bystander.

I worried when I first returned I would covet Kate, but I didn't. His studies in New York had informed him enough to resurrect at least this much mental health; he understood now his desire to take Kate had been about his craving for love, not her own attributes. When he observed her after his disappearance, he felt very little for her. She'd become indistinct in her appeal, no more or less attractive to him than any of the dozens of women he'd encountered and helped in the city.

You might laugh, but the sirens I stalk these days are Carmen and Gabe. He'd indulged his fascination with them for several weeks, eventually noticing enough physical similarities and other coincidences to raise his suspicions about a genetic tie. Months ago, he researched Carmen's background and then followed a hunch to the Midwest.

Will it shock you to learn I was the one to compel my ex-wife to find our daughter? Although Seneca didn't require much convincing. Especially after the sick plans of that shallow worm, Duncan Fleming came to light—and later via Gabe, his plans to sabotage her hold on power. But I hastened Carmen's ascension to the throne. He then engaged as necessary to protect Carmen, which included tailing Duncan as he made his bid for inland supremacy.

Gabe was a pleasure to work with on this front, I must say. Of course he could never have achieved those cloaks or in-reach with other sirens on his own, Peter admitted. *But he is very talented, and I've no doubt he could become so accomplished with instruction and practice.* He was terribly proud of the boy, couldn't have asked for a better grandson.

I'm certain he does not hold you in the same regard, Xanthe warned.

I expect not, Peter said easily. He resumed his narrative unconcerned.

As she suspected, Peter had been at the root of her professional problems, news that temporarily erased her happiness at finding him alive. He'd wanted to guide his family as he saw fit, which meant having fewer cooks in the kitchen, in his opinion. He also hadn't wanted to reveal himself. *I couldn't have avoided your detection, Xanthe. I consider it a failure you figured me out anyway. I was hoping you would take a leave of absence.*

Xanthe became angry enough to try and pull away, although he maintained his hold on her. *Please don't be mad. Aren't you glad to know you're as capable as you ever were?*

Your meddling made me an unfit advisor, Peter, not just in matters concerning your daughter. I was a wreck over this, unable to understand what had happened to me . . . and I cannot forgive you for taking away the most important piece of who I am. You almost caused me to retire!

Peter shrugged, unrepentant. *I knew you would recover. And before you castigate me further, allow me to finish my review.*

The gathering at Carmen and Michael's an hour ago had been intense given all the players involved, but Peter had operated in these situations before. The entrance of Seneca's orphan child, Parker, interrupted him, because her appearance was noteworthy on several levels. The girl was uniquely sensitive for a human, as intuitive as many sirens he knew. After very little hesitation she saw through his cloaking of Seneca as Carmen—Peter found this astonishing in and of itself—and then when he reached into the girl to learn how she'd done it, she perceived him.

No one, not even Gabe, noticed when he made this kind of covert inquiry.

But Parker felt his intrusion; and for the first time in his life Peter was pushed out of another's thoughts. In his shock, his cloak thinned to the point everyone noticed him, or at least sensed an anonymous presence. *Although I believe Gabe suspected me personally*, he confirmed.

By the time Peter could disappear again, Duncan had attacked Seneca and very nearly ended her life. This was the last offense Peter was willing to tolerate from the former viceroy.

I'd hoped to facilitate Duncan's containment via Carmen. I thought I'd just help with the set-up, and then let the new regime accomplish the rest. But this? Peter shook his head, and his grim smile frightened Xanthe for the first time. She'd forgotten, but this man's complexity was stunning, his capacity for deviance both demonstrated and visceral. He was a nuclear bomb to Duncan's firecracker. Fleming thought *he* could play the villain? The man was deluded, which gave Peter's personal execution of Duncan a kind of symmetry she appreciated.

He believed himself so clever. You could have given him lessons, Peter.

Quite. I'll take that as a compliment.

Peter imparted the rest of the story quickly. He made the decision to take care of Duncan on his own, caused the former viceroy's exit from the Blake house, and then killed him using the same method Duncan had attempted with Seneca. *Just so you know, he intended to kill Isabel and Julian in the same way.* Peter released her.

Why was Duncan delayed? Xanthe asked. *Isabel and Julian reached Shaddox last night. He was no more than an hour behind them.*

Peter rubbed the back of his neck and smiled. *Ah. Yes. Well, I wanted the new royal family to gain confidence, to decide how to deal with the most deviant siren since . . . well, since me. I intercepted Duncan outside Griffins Bay, gave him a day of rest, as it were, so Carmen and her crew could prepare their response. And they did very well. But as I said, I tired of Duncan's tyranny. And his pathetic definition of power.*

Feeling like herself for the first time in recent memory, Xanthe's former habits of steering and analysis reasserted themselves. And through the filter of professional obligation, she found Peter's story troublesome on several fronts, including the glaring fact that Peter was, by function of being alive, technically—since no trial had ever been held to divest him of the title—the reigning monarch. Would he re-assume power? Was his execution of Duncan legal? And these matters aside, should he be prosecuted for his earlier misdeeds?

He answered her without prompting. *These decisions are not yours, Xanthe, nor anyone's other than mine. In any case, you couldn't prosecute me if you tried. You couldn't catch me. No one can.*

But I'm going to make my re-introduction easy on you: I will not be defined as I once was. I will not accept my former title and if you require a formal abnegation, I'll give it. I will not be subjected to any of the expectations you or others have of me because of my past, not in light of my accomplishments, not in response to my crimes. I will not allow our society's hopes or demands control over me ever again, and I really don't care how the collective thinks of me. I will be involved as I choose, how I choose.

Xanthe probed his emanation for malice. *You will allow us no definitions, no way to relate to you?*

Peter shook his head. *If you have a role you want for me, I'll consider it. But make no mistake, Xanthe: I am not able to sublimate my self-interest. And I do not want and will not be beholden to duties that isolate and sicken me.*

If he would not agree to abide by any laws, he could not be trusted, which Xanthe recalled he'd acknowledged early on in this encounter. So . . . if he was too powerful to contain (and he was); if he could do as he pleased (and he could); if no one could impose consequences, where did this leave them? Where did it leave her? An entity like Peter at large, with no commitment from him to behave honorably, could prove disastrous.

And yet there was nothing she or anyone could do.

In spite of these frustrations, Xanthe remained in awe of his capabilities, what he could accomplish in the future if he engaged constructively. She was perhaps unwisely eager to welcome him into the fold in some capacity.

I am at a loss, she confessed.

Peter's smile was noncommittal. *I have no desire to distress you. But I will share in my family's life, and I will define the terms.*

Perhaps your need for your siren family will exert sufficient control over your actions. She eyed him speculatively.

Perhaps, he conceded.

Then we'll go back to Griffins Bay, talk with your family and reveal what you've just told me. She'd spoken decisively . . . but would he accept even this much oversight from her?

Apparently he would. *I agree.*

CHAPTER THIRTY-NINE

The beach hippies were leaving, and Jodi thought her heart might actually break.

For five days she'd watched a group of twenty of the most gorgeous, poorly dressed human beings she'd ever seen walk through Google's front door, disappearing into the inner sanctum as if they worked there. They didn't, because Jodi's job was to check, even though they would have needed employee pass cards to get into the main lobby and make it to her desk.

But they did get in, so maybe they were employees? Although Jodi would have remembered these people. Regardless, they approached her where she sat at reception and each day poofed some sort of fabulous mojo her way. So she let them pass and felt euphoric doing so.

She didn't know their names but didn't care. She would have given them anything, followed them anywhere.

They were supposed to flash her their identity cards. Instead they took her hand or caressed her hair and walked away, and they left delightful gifts behind. Flowers, a bracelet made of silver and sea glass, her favorite miel cappuccino from the corner café. This morning they'd left an entire cooler filled with sushi grade tuna. Yum.

Their endearments rang in her ears throughout the day and

sometimes made her cry, because every time she thought of them she was seized with longing. She had to steel herself to remain at her post when she wanted badly to find them in the back offices even if just to look at them.

Individually and together they appeared distinctive enough to cause a stir, a feat in this environment. Google headquarters was a polyglot visited by as diverse a population as one could find; from the more laid back, slovenly geniuses in tech to the polished internationals on the professional side. Her hippies, while beautiful, were appallingly ungroomed, looking great but like they got dressed at the last possible minute. Also, their attire, while nice enough for the beach or Sunday coffee indoors, was too casual even by California business standards. Didn't any of them own an iron? And was that *sand* trailing behind them?

No matter. She loved them, would have promptly given them the keys to her bungalow or Mercedes convertible, could have with little effort been persuaded to hand over her elderly parents to be eaten.

Their CEO even came out to wave them off each day, blowing kisses and clasping his hands to his heart in what should have been an embarrassing display of sentiment. It wasn't, because they all did it. Each morning a crowd gathered in the parking lot to greet them, responding with sighs and applause when they appeared.

Nothing definitive was said, but Jodi and everyone else knew today they would leave forever, would walk away never to be seen again, and Jodi was devastated. She stood when they began their sad march toward the exit late in the afternoon, the majority of Google's staff trailing behind them, spouting supplications. She stumbled from behind her desk to make entreaties of her own.

"I'll be your receptionist forever! You won't even need to pay me!" She wiped desperate tears from her cheeks. Shoot, everyone was crying at this point. "Please don't leave," she begged. "I'll . . . I'll . . . I don't know what I'll do, but I have to come with you." Her pleas were drowned out in the veritable sea of them floating around.

But no one accompanied them. With one final wave, they sped away too quickly for anyone to follow or even really see. Jodi and one of the interns collapsed in each other's arms and wept. The hippies, she knew, cried too. Their grief was a hollow echo within her, and she pictured them as she knew they were: they clutched one another, keened and pulled at their own hair on some nearby beach. They wanted to come back but couldn't.

Goodbye, beautiful friends! Goodbye, happiness!

The emergency council put Aiden in charge of one of five ops teams, all dispatched to hijack the more influential outlets governing internet and broadcast feeds throughout the country. The human interactions at Google had nearly derailed their effort.

"I know they're distracting," Aiden advised his team. "We have to plow ahead anyway." But all the talk about keeping your head in a throng of humans . . . well, this knowledge didn't prepare anyone for the actual experience, even Aiden, who thought he'd be all competent and calm thanks to his previous tangles with Maya.

They got the job done, albeit artlessly since they all had to stumble around lovesick and distracted. Then again the human emanations sustained them in a way, since the technical aspects of the work were so inhuman and distasteful. Actual interaction did temper the awfulness of all that remote communication effort.

And the pleasure and anticipation each day as they returned to their land-bound friends inspired them to finish.

Thank heaven everyone was out of the water, though.

At least they pulled themselves away more easily than the New York team; Aiden heard those human admirers plied their sirens with alcohol and then imprisoned them in one of the office suites to keep them from leaving, the little sneaks. That contingent was on lockdown until late in the evening, when a siren reconnaissance mission commandoed their way in and fished everyone out. He heard the human employees were all put on psych leave.

They'd fixed the problem, however; Duncan Fleming's videos were soundly discredited as well as disabled, and any future efforts to convince the world of real, live mermaids—from anyone—would pick up some funky code in transmission that would corrupt the downloads.

Xanthe was happy they'd succeeded, although the post-campaign effects of all that human congress were less welcome. Having tasted the elixir of human admiration, all heretofore content siren operatives became restless, and eager to execute virtually any other inland project to put them in contact with people. They wanted more of the same rush, they told her, as if they'd enjoyed sunshine for the first time and now were banished to live in a dark cave.

"Necessary as mass engagement was, it was also counterproductive it seems," Xanthe lamented to her friend and queen. "My idea of keeping the human world at arm's length isn't working very well."

Carmen sought to console her. "The world is a dynamic place," she contended. "Humans are reactive, less disciplined than we are. And I know it's hard for us to understand, but I think we're more adaptable than we've believed."

Xanthe straightened, prepared to argue, but Carmen put a hand on her arm. "Ah-ah," she admonished. "You don't get to carry this problem on your shoulders any longer my friend. We'll address this challenge together."

Xanthe's response was a heart-felt smile. She decided Carmen's display of self-assurance had just made their problems with Duncan worthwhile. "You show the wisdom of a true queen. You are no longer a regent in training, in my opinion, and I am at your service."

"Well and good, Xanthe. Happy to have your confidence. Don't wander too far away from me yet, though—we still need you. But you're right on one score: I'm in charge now, and I'm going to look after everything and everyone, including you." Xanthe relaxed—truly relaxed—for the first time since Peter and Kenna's demise at the palace.

"I'm ready, Carmen. I won't get in your way."

CHAPTER FORTY

Maya thought the only thing she'd remember from the spectacle of her wedding would be the mind-numbing extravagance, but she was wrong.

For weeks she'd been resigned to a soulless proceeding with no heart and no privacy; instead she got to experience a genuine celebration of love and commitment, one she believed would inspire a deeper relationship with her husband and bring them both joy when they had grandchildren.

She suspected she'd been shanghaied—along with her in-laws—and since the shift occurred after Kate appeared on the scene, Maya believed her friend was responsible for the change-up. Credit for the core elements of the event still went to Stuart's family—the church, the service, the reception, the press corps. But Kate assured her she'd "taken steps so my girl will outshine the ice sculpture." Maya should have maybe asked a few questions but was so disinvested by then she couldn't make herself care.

"I want your wedding to be about you, and I won't tolerate seeing you led around on a leash all day," Kate affirmed. "Which means I've enlisted a brigade of Blake cousins, and you're to do whatever they tell you, no questions. Got it?"

Blake cousins? Maya didn't remember the guest list having so many but they were *everywhere*. Four of them—complete strangers she couldn't have named even after they left her—showed up in her room before sunrise. As if they were invited and had keys . . . and they must have had some covert skills to breeze past security as they did. But she'd found their chatter hypnotic and pleasant, and as they spoke to her they unraveled the tightly wound ball of concern she'd nursed for months now over her life's choices. In their company she became optimistic, even a little euphoric.

They'd also brought doughnuts, meaning from the outset their agenda was superior to the one she expected from everyone else. She welcomed the intrusion, made no protests, asked no questions.

Guided by three more of the ubiquitous Blake contingent—seriously, they must have come to her house in a bus—Stuart's mother and aunts stumbled into her room then, and she suffered a moment of alarm. But they weren't the bringers of doom she feared, weren't actually capable of taking control any more than she herself was. The women were only fuzzily awake and confused, harmless as baby ducks. They did as they were told. Good.

Next in the progression of strangeness came a cadre of what looked like artist supplies in the rattiest, most ancient-looking ateliers ever to have existed. "Did you fish those cases out of a shipwreck?" she demanded. "'Cause seriously, dudes . . ." Her attendants ignored her and unpacked their things, carelessly toppling thousands of dollars' worth of make-up and creams to make space for things like Dead Sea salt, seaweed emulsions, and finely ground mother-of-pearl. They also set out jars of brushes and an array of oyster shells, which turned out to be mix-on-the-spot receptacles for gel-like, vibrantly colored extracts.

She and her mother-in-law and aunts then received the most thorough, gratifying spa treatments of their lives.

But the outcome justified everything, including everyone's loss of consciousness. After their final grooming responsibility—pastry consumption—they all wore sated expressions, a light flush, and filled-out faces with softened eyes.

"I have never looked more amazing," Stuart's mother declared after seeing herself in the mirror.

The groomsmen, when Maya saw them, looked like they'd been treated to a similar makeover session, which one Blake valet confirmed when he reported they'd gone for a "Rat-Pack-meets-corsair" effect. The tuxes were still crisp and tailored but their crew had added gem-colored waistcoats and messed with the men's conservative hairstyles. Stuart even received a pierced ear and some eyeliner, which one of her attendants justified by saying they "had to soften that stiff upper lip somehow."

Fed and polished and humored until she sparkled, Maya felt radiant walking down the aisle. And this luminous happiness she felt, the overflowing affection she accepted and gave off, created the wedding she'd fantasized about since she was a little girl, the grand cathedral and embarrassing number of attendants notwithstanding. *Thank you,* she mouthed to Kate as she approached the altar on Jeremy's arm. Kate beamed at her.

At the back of the church, Aiden watched the proceeding bitterly, and Maya's engineered happiness only blackened his already crap mood. He eyed the bride as she faced her groom—the wrong groom in his opinion—at the altar and toyed with the idea of kidnapping her.

If Simon could get away with it . . . ?

Simon's hand on his arm broke his reverie. "Aiden. I'm sorry, man." He leaked regret, which was the only distraction worthy enough to turn Aiden's gaze away from his girl up front. He searched Simon's expression for understanding, for any hint of permission to disregard legalities and go after what he wanted. He didn't receive it.

"That's rich, Simon."

"Yeah, I know I'm a bastard," Simon admitted. "I aced you out of a bond. But you can still find someone else." Simon's eyes settled on his wife in the bridesmaid's line-up. "I didn't have that choice."

Aiden's laugh was curt. "I'll have to take your word for it, brother. Because it's not like I'm in this for the laughs." Simon opened his mouth to respond, but Aiden cut him off. "And I don't have a choice, either."

Simon studied his brother intently . . . and Aiden saw the surprise bloom on his face. "My God. It's like you're already bonded with her."

"Yeah and isn't that great?" he retorted. "I get all of the compulsion, all the impulse, and none of the back-end satisfaction."

"I'll help," Simon resolved.

Aiden stared hard at his brother. "How?"

"Not sure, but . . ." Simon nodded toward the altar. "You know no one who knows her—*no one*—believes they'll make it."

Aiden grunted. "Small comfort. Like I should wait around for her marriage to fail, which may or may not happen in the next fifty years."

Simon seemed to deliberate, scanning the pews for someone particular. His eyes settled on their former regent. "I know someone we can talk to."

At the reception after dinner, Simon stuck by Sylvia, leaving Aiden to wander around until he could excuse himself without seeming rude. When siren facilitators commanded the dance floor—to the delight of human companions—those remaining talked in small groups, adopting bland smiles if anyone outside their circle stared too intently or sidled too close. Aiden took up with Xanthe, Gabe and Kate by the bar.

"I feel awful about shutting him out, but there wasn't any place for him at Shaddox," Xanthe lamented to him. "Isabel told me she wasn't ready for another relationship, and I agreed Julian didn't feel like the right mate for her. So we delivered him back to his human life—installed him in his former job and cleaned everyone's memories as thoroughly as possible, although I'm worried Duncan may have made too much of an impression on them for it to stick."

"I'm sure you did well enough," Gabe soothed. "Julian will be fine. Better than fine, I predict."

Aiden spied Simon along one of the back walls talking to Peter. When Peter looked up, he focused first on Gabe, then Kate. When he started their way, Aiden excused himself for the evening. "I'm not up for any more drama tonight, Xanthe. I'll see everyone around." Xanthe nodded his way without looking at him.

CHAPTER FORTY-ONE

Kate was nervous over the prospect of Peter's re-entry into their lives, but she wasn't as opposed as she might have been. His reappearance shocked her, of course—how his apparent suicide at Shaddox had been a ruse—and she'd questioned reality along with everyone else when he materialized at her in-laws' house with Xanthe following the Duncan debacle. Gabe was the only person whose jaw didn't drop, something Kate resolved to ask him about later.

Gabe's non-reaction aside, Peter's appearance in Griffins Bay galvanized all of them. No one knew what to make of him, particularly since he arrived with Xanthe, meaning his presence was presumably sanctioned. And then he'd sauntered in like there was no reason he shouldn't be there.

His explanation was equally unapologetic. "I've returned," he said curtly. "I wasn't able to die as I intended, and so I created the appearance of a dissolution when I knew I would live." He made eye contact with each person in the room, daring any present to comment. No one did.

His attention settled first on Carmen, and then on Gabe. "I facilitated the situation with Duncan, who I've done us the courtesy of killing this afternoon." Everyone recoiled. "I know Carmen is my daughter and Gabe is my grandson. I do not want my crown back. I intend to participate peripherally in all of your lives somehow . . . and that's all I'm prepared to say on that subject today." He addressed Kate.

"I already made my apologies to you, Kate, and they were and are still heartfelt. You needn't worry for yourself or anyone you love. I know now I projected my needs on you, gave you characteristics I wanted for my own companion. You are in no danger from me."

She looked away, too flummoxed to form a coherent response. Gabe tightened his arm around her and replied for both of them.

"She doesn't owe you forgiveness," he stated. "Nor do I, for that matter, although I'm curious."

Peter raised an eyebrow.

"Was it you? Were you with me in Raleigh, and again at the house with Duncan?"

Peter put his hands in his pockets and studied his feet. "I wish I could give you the answer you want—that it was all you—but I can't. I enhanced your cloaking abilities, and I sharpened your inquiries with Duncan and Isabel." He looked intently at Gabe then. "You have the native talent to do these things, Gabe. You could become as proficient as I am in time."

Gabe's expression went cold. "I do not want to be like you."

Peter shrugged. "I understand." He then met the wary stares of everyone in the room, in which Kate interpreted his unspoken argument. Peter was not here to make excuses for himself or justify his intentions. But he did care for everyone and missed them, which defrayed the worst of the tension in the room.

While she'd been uneasy, though, Gabe remained obstinate; he'd stated at the meeting following Duncan's demise he wanted nothing further to do with the man.

So she stiffened when Peter approached them at the wedding reception. Gabe stood tall and stepped partially in front of her.

"It was a beautiful ceremony, don't you think?" Peter said, sipping champagne as he surveyed the crowd. "Pity they're so ill suited."

For the first time since Maya revealed her marital intentions regarding Stuart, Kate defended her friend's choice of husband. She agreed with Peter . . . but she refused to share an opinion with the guy on any romantic front. "You never know," she argued. "They might make it. I mean, think of all the couples who start out young and poor and otherwise doomed who pull through."

"Mmm. Perhaps."

"I give them five years tops," Gabe said darkly.

Kate's exasperation got the better of her. "Guys. We *can't* be talking like this at their wedding."

"It is rude," Peter agreed. "But the event has inspired me." He faced Gabe. "I've made a decision concerning my role in the community, which is what I've wandered this way to share with you. I mean to train several of us to cloak and become accustomed to a higher level of aggression. I think we need protectors, defense specialists if you will. Given the trajectory of our world and that of humans, this need will only increase, I'm sure."

Gabe eyed him doubtfully. "I don't disagree, but I dislike the solution you propose. I don't think fostering aggression among us is a solid plan when we can't know what the back end of such training looks like."

"Point made," Peter allowed with a small smile. "But I can feel your own hunger for greater proficiency in this area, no?" He didn't wait for a reply. "At any rate, your cousins, Simon and Aiden, have already enlisted. I believe you should join us."

Gabe's response was mulish silence until Peter added hastily, "Not that you need to be a frontline operative—I understand you have your own calling to fulfill—but you should be prepared to lead such an effort for when you personally come into the crown. And of course you already have the fundamental skills. I think you'd find instruction empowering," Peter glanced at Kate. "I'm quite certain you'll also appreciate the security you'd gain. No one would be able to threaten your family again, Gabe."

"No one except you, you mean?"

Peter was impassive. "You won't know unless you try."

Kate sensed Gabe's interest, which he fought because it conflicted with his desire to keep away from Peter altogether. With a few reservations, though, she trusted Peter and said as much. "I think you should listen to him, honey." Peter's answering smile was creepy.

Gabe relented grudgingly. "I can't lie and say I'm not interested. And your logic has merit."

Peter straightened. "Excellent." He deposited his empty glass on the tray of a passing waiter. "I'm afraid I can't stay any longer, but I'll be in touch." He bowed and then pivoted away, stopping briefly to acknowledge his former wife, Seneca. Neither spoke . . . but Kate noticed no animosity, either. Seneca, followed by Parker, joined them after he'd gone and confirmed her analysis.

"If someone had told me I would feel so little for a former intimate, I wouldn't have believed them, but I am not bothered to see him, nor he me, I think. We did the best we could all those years ago . . . and I carry no resentment. We are both free." She addressed Gabe. "His talents are tremendous, you must know. I realize he's behaved appallingly, but I don't believe he's inclined to ongoing deviance. He could again be a valuable asset to our community."

Gabe snorted. "Yeah I saw how 'un-inclined' he was less than a year ago."

Parker interrupted with, "I want to help him." A cacophony of resistance bubbled forth from all three adults, from Kate's, "Honey I don't know that's wise . . ." and Gabe's "You don't know him, Parker," to Seneca's more abrupt, "Absolutely not."

Parker held up a hand. "I'm the only one who can stop him, remember?" She smiled smugly. "*I* resisted his cloak."

"*You* are too young to tangle with the likes of Peter Loughlin," Seneca asserted. "We'll talk about it later. As in when you're older, maybe thirty."

Kate and Gabe excused themselves to join Simon and Sylvia, who they hadn't talked with since the couple's return from Antarctica. After hugging, Sylvia asked Kate, "Enjoying yourself?" and made a face.

Kate grimaced. "I know. Our watery friends made the day beautiful. But."

"But," Sylvia agreed. "I know it's her choice, but I feel like I've let her sign herself up for eating sawdust while we feast."

"You're not letting her do anything," Simon disagreed. "She's a grown woman, and this is her path to walk."

"Maybe," Sylvia conceded. "I just wish things were different for them."

"I think we can look on the bright side here," Simon insisted. "I mean, marriages fail and people move on, right?" He looked way too confident.

Sylvia pivoted sharply Simon's way. "What are you planning?" she demanded. "And don't think I didn't see you and Aiden huddled together during the ceremony."

Simon lifted his chin toward the groom. "We're not planning

anything. I believe Stuart is going to muck things up all by his lonesome." He grinned at all of them. "And Maya will have a lot of support when that happens."

"I know it's awful to hope for, but I hope you're right Simon," Kate said.

"Me too," Sylvia rejoined glumly. "I shouldn't, because it's bad form to bet against your sister on her wedding day. But I don't have a good feeling about this one." Her expression softened. "But I agree she'll be okay if things don't work out."

The groom's father picked that moment to call everybody's attention to the head table with a series of taps on his champagne flute. When the room quieted, he began his address. "I'd like to welcome you all to the celebration of my son's wedding and thank each of you for spending this special day with us. I have a few thoughts to share, which if you'll excuse the use of a crutch . . ." The crowd laughed politely as he unfolded a piece of paper from his pocket. "My wife wisely suggested I rely on another's words," he said wryly, "so I'll start with a quote from Hemingway's, *The Old Man and the Sea*." Kate stifled a laugh as every siren present straightened in attention. Thad cleared his throat.

"*His choice had been to stay in the deep dark water far out beyond all snares and traps and treacheries. My choice was to go there to find him beyond all people. Beyond all people in the world.*'

"Strange words for a wedding, perhaps, but I think they speak to all of us who have sought what Hemingway's character did: a communion outside the familiar, one we must brave traps and treacheries to get to, and one that brings fulfillment nonexistent anywhere else.

"Marriage is this place of fulfillment for those who persevere to find the right partner. It has been so for my wife and me and many of our friends gathered today, and I expect it will be so for Stuart and Maya. As I watched my son court our new daughter-in-law, I saw in each of them everything they'll need for a vital, happy life: their warmth, their tenacity, their dedication both to their ideals and to each other . . . these are the strongest foundations on which a marriage can be built, and Stuart and Maya have a bounty." Thad looked his son in the eye before delivering his next line, "Needless to say, with a woman like Maya at your side, I'll be expecting great things of you, son." He paused to allow the laughter to settle and then raised his glass. "So please join me in congratulating Maya and Stuart for each catching their 'big fish.' May you find joy in every day you have together."

"Hear! Hear!"

Sylvia murmured to Kate, "Call me sappy, but I think the strongest foundation for marriage is love."

"Mmm," Kate agreed quietly. "His fish metaphor was pretty freakin' perfect though, don't you think?"

"Would be even more perfect if the groom were a different guy . . ."

". . . who we'll all meet at Maya's *next* wedding," Simon interjected brightly. He wrapped an arm around Sylvia's laughing form and announced, "I need to get out of here. Take a walk with me?"

"We could stand to take a breather ourselves," Gabe said while loosening his tie. He grabbed Kate's hand. "Let's all run away, baby."

The cool evening felt like magic to Kate. She let the dimness and silence absorb the more irritating effects of over-stimulation and the forced cheerfulness of a wedding she didn't believe in. She sensed a calm settling over their little group and smiled when Simon commented, "I'm glad we eloped."

"A small ceremony isn't so bad either, though," she offered.

Sylvia grimaced. "I know I suck, but do we have to go back in there?"

"We don't!" Gabe insisted. "We've eaten and danced and thrown the rice. I say we ditch!"

"Once again, you are my favorite life form on the planet," Kate crooned. To the others she said, "And he's right. We've done our duty."

Simon opened his arms. "Brethren, our freedom awaits! Let's cab it to the water."

From a window behind them, Carmen watched the couples pile into a taxi and smiled at their playfulness. Michael stepped behind her and she drew his arms around her. She relaxed against his chest as the kids drove off. "They're heading to the beach. Think they'll be discreet?"

"It's two in the morning. Discretion is optional, I say," Michael replied.

"I suppose you're right. I shouldn't worry."

"Worrying is a terrible habit. And since you've already fixed every last thing, it's unwarranted as well. You have prevailed, love."

Carmen flushed with satisfaction . . . and a little relief. "Good enough. No more worry until there's a need, right?"

"Until there's a need."

The End

Thank you for reading *Breakwater*, the second installment of the Mer Chronicles by Errin Stevens. If you enjoyed it, please share your enthusiasm with others, especially in the form of a review on your favorite social media platform(s).

For now, please enjoy the following preview of the third book in this series, *Outrush:*

PROLOGUE

Maya took a break from her laptop to stretch in her chair, using the activity as an excuse to check if the men following her were still across the street.

Yep. The Undertaker was behind the wheel of his car, reading a newspaper as usual; and Jethro was in the window of the café opposite hers, texting on his phone.

These weren't their real names – she didn't know the men assigned to watch her every move. But she'd needed to call them something, and one was a gaunt, cadaverous-looking guy she just knew was draining the blood of the dead in some dungeon-like, basement mortuary during his off hours. Every time she saw him, she pictured herself laid out before him on a cold, stone slab, a macabre smile on his face as he stood over her with a bouquet of axillary drain tubes. She shuddered and looked toward his companion.

Jethro was the Undertaker's opposite, seemed even less the detective, but at least she could convince herself he was harmless. He was just too fresh-faced and beefy and wholesome; and too cheerful compared to the stern-faced urbanites surrounding him. Her made-up story for him was he'd been waylaid en route to an ad audition – a toothpaste ad, she decided. "Pssst, buddy," rasped a Mafioso lurking in the shadows and waving a wad of cash. "Wanna spy on a rich girl?"

Maya was a little proud she'd won out over dental hygiene.

She sighed and rubbed her tired eyes. *Week twelve,* she thought, and almost three months since she'd noticed she was being followed or watched or whatever. Most people would have run, she supposed, and at first she'd wanted to, not that she'd done anything wrong. But being the subject of someone's surveillance mission was creepy, made her want to slink off even if she was innocent. The scientist in her had prevailed, however, meaning instead of acting to avoid scrutiny, she'd done the opposite. She'd maintained an even stricter schedule, leaving and returning to her apartment at the same times each day, running errands to the same places, even stopping for coffee at the Bean Machine each afternoon as she was doing now. If she found her regular table taken, she took her second regular table instead, and then moved if her first choice opened up.

This constancy, which she knew made her easier to track, also allowed her to verify she was being followed and by whom. Now, she easily recognized the cast of characters sent to attend her, no matter how careful the men were, which they weren't. Physical appearances aside, their quirks showed and showed big. The Undertaker, for example, tended to drum his fingers; and Jethro had a fondness for bubble gum, making him the only adult she'd ever seen who periodically sprouted small, pink balloons from his mouth.

But she'd trained them well during their tenure; like good little ducks following her mother duck lead, they'd fallen into the pattern she'd dictated, meaning they took up the same posts in the same places each time she took up hers, and wasn't that just a sad testament to their spying competence. There were four of them on rotation, assigned in pairs, Monday through Sunday. Porky and Popeye had the day off today, which she could predict at this point since it was Tuesday, and Tuesdays were Jethro and Undertaker days.

One thing for sure, these guys weren't the low-level paparazzi who occasionally dogged her socialite in-laws. They didn't have the look – no cameras, no lurking around in what appeared to be permanently slept-in clothing. Even their expressions were wrong, devoid of that mixture of desperation and defiance Maya considered a kind of trade calling card.

No, these men were paid babysitters looking for something other than media currency, which was the variable in this situation she couldn't, no matter how hard she racked her brain, figure out. What could they want? What had she done to warrant all this attention? She stared at her notebook screen again and pretended to take interest in her search…

…and then she felt an overwhelming sense of peace she sometimes, heaven knew not often enough, experienced like a gift, always when she was teetering on the edge of a nervous breakdown. Her last reprieve had been months ago. But here it was again out of nowhere, comforting her like an embrace from her mother, and oh, how lovely to feel so cared for and protected. Like everything was going to be okay. She understood just how tightly wound she must be if a fantasy encouragement could so undo her. She thought she'd been coping just fine with her disaster of a life and smashed-up emotions. Apparently not.

But for the moment, her feeling of well-being was complete, and better yet, intensifying.

Someone approached, and she opened her eyes, realizing only then that she'd had them closed. A man walked toward her table, no one she knew… but she instinctively identified him as the source of her comfort. When he reached her, she smiled at him as if they were old friends.

He stopped to rest a hand on her shoulder, a hand she clasped and held against her cheek.

Everything will get better. I'm going to help.

She heard the words as if he'd spoken them, and she was so grateful, she wanted to cry. She turned her face to press her forehead against his arm. *Thankyouthankyouthankyou pleasestaybyme,* she thought. The man looked out the window and frowned, and then gently disengaged his hand. After a stroke to her hair, he walked away.

Maya noticed the alarmed expressions of her watchers across the street but couldn't be induced to care at first. She was reveling in her break from anxiety, felt too light and free to give in to her usual moodiness and fear, even if it looked like a little fear might be warranted. Jethro spoke grimly into his headset while staring at her in a way that looked sinister and specific. He no longer pretended anonymity, no longer appeared cheerful. Maya toasted him with her coffee cup. The Undertaker made a reckless exit from his car, attracting curses and the blares of car horns from several angry drivers. Maya shook her head and smirked. *So much for stealth,* she thought as he stumbled after the man she considered her angel of mercy. All in all, she thought her guards looked like comic book villains instead of real people posing an actual threat.

She knew she had her just-departed visitor to thank for her lack of concern, but as he retreated, so did his influence, and worry once again seeped into her consciousness. Especially when Jethro began marching in her direction. She watched his mouth form commands as he talked into his wireless, and she heard his words as if they were whispered in her ear, words that came with an explicit warning by their translator to take heed.

You need to know what's going on, Maya.

"Contact's been made," Jethro reported. "Looked like a lover but it had to be a front. Been here all month and never seen the guy before. May have passed a message. We're following."

Anger at the men she saw as responsible for her exile welled inside her like roiling lava, bursting her bubble of complacency and destroying her reprieve from all the pressure. Her inner competitor – the one that had made her an all-star on the volleyball court during college – hardened her resolve to face this challenge head-on.

All right, boys. I'm here to play offense.

Maya abandoned her coffee, stood up from her seat and deliberately held Jethro's gaze through the glass, her stare a refusal to be intimidated any longer. It felt good to be obvious, and she realized just how tired she was of all this, of pretending to be unaware, of all the stupidity and furtiveness, and especially how her current situation – her life in suspension – had no expiration date she could foresee. Whatever the fallout, she was done: done with waiting, done with trying to figure out why she was hiding and from whom.

Jethro paused and raised an eyebrow, discreetly moving a panel of his jacket aside so she could see his holstered gun. Then he smiled, the big creep.

Run! The panicked command echoed in Maya's mind… and adrenaline coursed through her body like a shot of jet fuel to a primed engine. She didn't pause to think, just bolted away from the window. She ran through the kitchen and into the back alley.

CHAPTER ONE

Seven years was a long time to be in a wrecked marriage. Maya likened her existence these days to a kind of permanent post-trauma, where she was consigned to forever tip-toe around in her own personal life, picking through her relationship with her husband for signs of compassion like she might search the debris of a catastrophe for something – anything at all – salvageable.

When she thought about their digression from where she was now, she determined her last and perhaps only feelings of optimism had occurred at the altar, when she'd believed fervently in their ceremony and all it represented. How she'd cried during their promises to cherish and protect, and how brightly her conviction in their future had burned. When Stu delivered his vows, he'd stood so tall and strong… she would never have believed such sincerity could fade. However, she fast learned it would last only as long as it took them to walk out the cathedral doors after the reverend pronounced them mister and missus.

"The guys are going to steal me for a quick pub tour before the reception, okay?" Stu whispered in her ear. "Mother!" he called over his shoulder. "Take Maya home to rest before dinner, all right?" He placed a swift kiss on Maya's temple and was gone, leaving her struggling to cover her anger with an over-bright smile.

Really? He was so hard up for a scotch he would abandon her on the church steps to toss one back with his buddies? She turned to her new mother-in-law to decline her offer of company and avoid the very real possibility of a bridal tantrum in front of her. Maya's best friend, Kate Blake – along with Maya's sisters, bless them – intervened.

"We've got you," Kate murmured so only Maya could hear, and then more loudly, "We'll see everyone at the dance!" She flashed the milling guests a grin, and along with the other bridesmaids, pulled Maya toward the church parking lot and into one of the cars.

Her girls had taken good care of her, too, plying her with humor and champagne until she set aside the bitter resentment that had her fuming and willing to skip the reception altogether. She even believed Stuart's disregard for her at the church was an aberration, although truthfully, she knew better. No one else was surprised either, Maya noted. Which depressed her.

But she'd pretended everything was fine, both at her wedding reception and all the public gatherings thereafter through the years. Stuart's willingness to leave her side for any and all excuses continued to embarrass her, even if she could plausibly attribute his departures to their busy schedules and need to stay in touch with a large circle of friends and associates. And she was determined to prove everyone wrong, to earn through forbearance if she must the casual, bedrock-like intimacy that drew her to the idea of marriage in the first place and convinced her she needed to keep trying.

She was thankful the palpable doubt she'd felt from her friends and family – and if she was being honest, herself – no longer distressed her to the extent it had in the beginning, when she was forever steeling herself against anger and tears; when she felt destroyed for days after one of Stuart's blithe escapes. His constancy in this area had inured her, eventually blunting the sharp stab she used to feel when faced with his lack of devotion.

Her medical training helped in a morbid kind of way, too, partly because medical school and residency took everything she had to give. She didn't have the intellectual or emotional resources to brood when she faced, every day, twenty hours of class and studying; or when she worked back-to-back twelve-hour shifts on rotation for her residency. In light of these demands on her time, she'd come to view her relationship with Stuart like she would a patient who came into her emergency room: it was anemic and listless but alive, while others were rushing through the doors with fragile aortas and potentially fatal knife wounds. She focused on the truly dying, telling herself she'd get to that other guy as soon as she could.

Still, over the years, she'd come to suspect there was nothing more she could do, that she would either have to leave – an unthinkable prospect – or accept her marriage as it was, which was barely a friendship. She never believed she would be the kind of woman to settle for an apathetic husband, partly because she'd assumed at first Stuart's love for her would draw them closer once they'd married. It hadn't. And that he didn't love her – at least not in the idealized way she thought he should – revealed more of her own ugliness than Stuart's. She knew her pride hurt more than her heart; and she understood her determination to stick it out was a testament to her desire not to fail, not because she loved Stuart as she should.

Early on, their home life had provided a sufficiently fascinating diversion from her dissatisfaction, enough for Maya to wonder later how big a factor public pressure had been on their efforts to carry on. Maya's in-laws were members of an elite social milieu in New York she knew nothing about growing up, aside from what most people knew of old families with big money. To Maya, the Evans patriarchs, like the Rockefellers or Vanderbilts, occupied the same place in American lore as other historical detritus she'd been forced to consider in grade school, like the rise and fall of riverboat commerce, or the washed-out and distant images of dead presidents on daguerreotypes. But the effect of the Evans wealth on her day-to-day life now was significant, and not something she could have understood until she was part of it, when their extravagances separated her from what she'd always assumed was reality. She and Stu had a housekeeper for crying out loud, a fact she vowed never to reveal to her parents. They wouldn't understand, and she could well predict their disapproval should they find out. If she was being honest, she shared it.

Maya had adjusted to a more intrusive public life, too, most of which revolved around her father-in-law, Thad. He was frequently pictured in the society pages, of course, but he was also chief executive for the country's largest insurance company; was in fact responsible for catapulting his organization into its premier market position via a massive public-private deal he was credited with creating. Stu had told her about it when they were engaged, reporting with pride on the intricacy of his father's campaign and how the effort had required more than a decade of legislative lobbying and aggressive political contributions. It brought billions to the company's bottom line and solidified Thad's candidacy for top dog.

Unfortunately, this meant Thad became the face of an unpopular kind of corporate policy, and subsequently a lighting rod for protesters and similar unpleasantness. Maya and Stuart weren't directly targeted, but close enough in Maya's experience. This meant they all had drivers and a security contingent whenever they went out.

Maya had stayed out of the limelight to sidestep the more disturbing attention Thad and those closest to him suffered, but she'd still had to change her habits out of caution. She never, for instance, took a spontaneous walk in the park or made an unaccompanied trip to the grocery store, not that she shopped for groceries any longer. For the first time in her life, she was fluent in the strange privacy characterizing interactions between the wealthy and their attendants, people who witnessed the personal lives of those they served without being included in them. She'd been so uncomfortable with these relationships in the beginning, was still plagued with guilt over the underlying premise: how another human being was hired to make her bed, fold her clothes, or put his or her life on the line for a job. She minimized interactions with these people as much as she could, sneaking her own laundry to the drycleaners to be washed or ironed, and keeping her personal clutter to a minimum so no one had to pick up after her.

She no longer fought the need for a security escort, however. On more than one occasion, Maya had witnessed thwarted physical attacks on Thad by crazed strangers, the kind who often appeared at public events Thad attended. Usually the attacks were verbal, comprised of a few protesters carrying signs in the hopes of capitalizing on media attention, and their real aim was to garner visibility, not inflict bodily harm. Then again, she'd been hurt once when she was between Thad and a man running to tackle him. Maya was knocked to the ground hard enough to sprain one of her wrists. Thereafter, she took better care when she was in public with her father-in-law close by, a situation she made every effort to avoid.

She was adopted by one guard in particular who, no matter how hard she tried to drive him away, faithfully showed up to both protect and torment her over the years, although she didn't believe he intended to trouble her as he did. But she wouldn't have been so loyal given how deliberately, relentlessly rude she was to him.

It was a defense. Mitch Donovan was hired by her father-in-law about a year after Maya and Stu's wedding, and since she'd had no complaints about the guard he replaced, she didn't understand why she needed someone new. The head of the Evans security team introduced her to him on a day Stu traveled for work. Mr. Donovan would be available whenever she or the younger Mr. Evans wanted to step out, and here were his pager and cell numbers. Mitch had been reluctant to shake her hand, which she'd found offensive until it happened, at which point she was overwhelmed by a sense of grief so acute her knees buckled. Mitch grasped her elbow to steady her, support she quickly shrugged off in her embarrassment.

"It's just... you remind me of someone," she blurted after a lengthy, uncomfortable pause. And he did. Something about his eyes, and a sheen of vitality she associated with a family she used to socialize with back in North Carolina, the Blakes. The likeness was superficial, but it made her horribly homesick, and if possible, even sadder over her empty, soul-sucking marriage.

Maya realized everyone was waiting for her to explain her strange greeting, or maybe they simply hoped she'd resolve the awkwardness she'd created. Sweat bloomed on her forehead and she became aware of the shallow, insufficient breaths she took, which she worried were too loud. She felt unanchored and bizarre and very much hoped she didn't look it. She checked Mitch's expression. It did not encourage her.

Her lack of composure was obvious. Worse, she felt like Mitch had shone a spotlight on her most private fears, ones she preferred to pretend she didn't have and most definitely wanted to keep hidden.

Her marriage was disappointing and unlikely to improve. Her absorbing career was no more than a convenient place to hide. And if she couldn't achieve happiness with an M.D. under her belt and marriage to a beautiful, wealthy man, something was very, very wrong with her.

And there it was, dang it, the path to the ultimate no-no of all her memories: Aiden. It was Mitch's fault for bringing him to mind, she decided, since he looked at her in the same penetrating way and exhibited the same physical markers. Aiden symbolized all her missteps up to now, his name synonymous with the more unpleasant consequences of her running away – from him and North Carolina and all the possibly destructive super-secrets he wore like a cloying aftershave. With just a glance in Mitch's direction, Maya saw starkly the unhappiness of her future as Mrs. Evans, understood too well what she didn't and never would have with Stu.

She despised Aiden – or at least, she wanted to – for stealing her peace of mind so thoroughly after her wedding, she'd never regained it. That awful dance at the reception, where every second felt like an accusation. His recriminations, issued without actual speech, were like an internal battering ram ripping through her insides from the center of her liver. *This marriage is a lie you cannot turn into truth. I'm the one you wanted. You've made a terrible mistake.* When Mitch Donovan shook her hand, his touch was a direct transmission line to the whole, miserable litany.

And no. Just... *no.* She would *not* feel that draw again, the attraction to Aiden that had solidified her decision to marry Stu when she was finishing college. Back then, she was struggling for purchase on adult life with very little hope she'd achieve it, thinking maybe she had it in her to go to medical school, and how, if she was lucky, she might be able to build a life with Stuart Evans. Stuart had been a guy who, unlike Aiden, didn't seem like he'd die without her. Stuart was maybe predictable by comparison, bland even... but he never freaked her out with intense, hungry stares that gave her the impression she was about to fall off a thousand-foot ledge. Mostly he never made her feel crazy, like she could suddenly smell the ocean, or feel a sea breeze on her skin; or think she wanted nothing more than to dive into the biggest, deepest body of salt water she could find. She hated swimming in the ocean. All she could think about when she waded in was a statistic on shark attacks, how most of them happened in three feet of water.

"There are about a gazillion things waiting to kill you out there," Maya explained once when her friend, Kate, questioned her on her saltwater reticence. "People don't belong in oceans. That's why God invented swimming pools." Kate snickered.

"Laugh all you want, Blake," Maya retorted. "I'll be your ER doc when you come in with shark's teeth lodged in your sternum. Or a Man-O-War wrapped around your neck. Don't think I'll forget this conversation, either."

Interactions with Aiden back then felt like a free-fall into chaos when she was already too at odds with herself to cope. And even though she'd refused what Aiden represented – by running to what she thought was safety with Stuart – the memory of Aiden continued to niggle away at her tenuous stability, no outside reminders necessary.

She couldn't afford to feel gutted every time she ran into Mitch the Security Guard. In fact, she wouldn't. Her unprompted self-negotiations concerning love and marriage were taxing enough, and she decided she'd do anything to preclude repeat panic attacks triggered by something she could control.

"I would prefer, Mr. Donovan, that you stay out of my personal space as much as possible. I don't want to be aware of you, so no casual comments, no taking my arm. In fact, if you must address me, don't make eye contact. Are we clear?"

Mitch's boss appeared stricken, but Mitch smiled at her indulgently, as if she'd made a weak joke and he wanted to make her feel better about it.

"Of course, Maya." He stared, without apology, directly in her eyes.

So much for her attempt at a firewall, which meant she'd just have to try harder. "That's Mrs. Evans to you," she snapped, pivoting on her heel and hurrying off.

Thereafter she went to heroic lengths to avoid him and repeatedly stated her request for a different escort when one was needed. Everyone except her – and Mitch she supposed, since he always showed up looking all confident and like he had her number – suffered from inexplicable amnesia in these situations; no matter who she spoke with beforehand, no matter how many times she complained about Mitch's unsuitability, no one listened to her. No one seemed to even remember her complaints, and Mitch was the one who came, without fail, to take her out.

"Did everyone in security get bashed in the head?" she finally asked him. "I don't want you around. Why can't you guys understand this?"

"Oh, I understand, Maya."

Eventually she gave up her public campaign against him and settled for being as hateful as she could to him personally. She texted her need to leave in thirty minutes, then either left immediately to make him scramble, or kept him waiting another two hours. She was dismissive and haughty, impatient and willing to criticize him for all manner of imaginary missteps. Mitch responded by ignoring her. Or he gave her probing looks that dared her to continue her tantrum, until she couldn't sustain her conviction, and her tirades died without the bloodletting she intended. Then she undid all her hard work with an apology.

"I'm sorry to be so spiteful," she'd mumble.

Mitch always forgave her, which made her feel even more exposed. "It's okay, Maya. I get it," he said, and then he stroked her hair, or squeezed her hand. She had to run – literally turn from him and run – to get away from what he made her feel.

In what Maya considered the most perverse irony of all, she came to find periodic comfort in Mitch's constant reminders of love, loss, and that guy back home who got away. Thad's extra-curricular romantic habits, which became much less discreet following his wife's death due to cancer, had grown to include Maya's husband, where Stu would play wing man with any number of suspiciously sexy young women, ones who didn't hesitate to drape themselves all over a married man – at their house or in public, it didn't matter. Maya seethed at what she saw as Stu's complicity, and because she thought he made her look weak in front of their friends.

"It's not like your dad's personal life is any of my business," she complained one evening as they prepared for bed, "but I don't understand why you're part of it. All those women… it's like you're double dating, and you're not exactly discouraging any of them." Maya suspected this was precisely the case but hoped she was wrong. This was the first time she'd brought it up, and she badly wanted her husband to take her in his arms and deny he was choosing casual affection with strangers over real intimacy with her.

Instead, Stuart bristled, and she knew she was in for a scolding. "Give the guy a break, Maya," he said shortly, his condescending tone one she knew too well. She could almost hear the words "you idiot" tacked on the end of his comment, and she slumped to sit on the edge of the bed. *Another dead-end conversation where I get to feel guilty over his indiscretions*, she mused. Should she point out she was concerned about his behavior, not Thad's?

"He's under a lot of pressure at work," Stu continued. "And

Mom's illness was a terrific drag, something I'd expect you to understand. He deserves to kick up his heels. I'm just along for the ride. It's like… I don't know. A father-son bonding thing."

Riiiight.

Her hopes for marital enlightenment sank for the nine hundredth time. She realized how, once again, she'd believed Stuart would act differently if only he understood he was hurting her. He had demonstrated – once again – her feelings were not a consideration for him. Even worse, Stuart's dalliances became more blatant after this conversation. This was when she came to welcome those pesky introspections Mitch Donovan prompted.

Maya was never aware of asking for relief, but whenever Stuart and Buffy-Number-Whatever went too far in her presence, she felt as though Mitch channeled Aiden, and her fantasy-man, himself, appeared to comfort her. Sometimes when she was truly desperate, she even saw him. In these situations, she no longer cared if Aiden was a made-up psychological defense; he eased the ache of betrayal and shame, and he saved her from making a scene that would have broken her carefully built image of a strong and stable wife, one confident enough in her marriage to overlook a little friendly flirting.

But inside she would be anxious and miserable… and then a moment later, she felt removed, in the same way she used to when she experienced what she thought of as one of Aiden's mind-wipes, and oh, what she wouldn't give to have *that* prescription on re-order. She could witness something offensive and then find herself unable to recall it, or the event seemed so absurd it no longer mattered. Best of all, she felt cherished after these illusions, truly loved. This sense of herself as attractive and worthy lasted for hours, and nothing – not Stuart's continued disregard for her, not his most puerile escapades with other women – nothing upset her.

Maya's favorite of these experiences followed a public demonstration she could not clearly remember. Perhaps it was a kiss Stuart shared with some female guest in their kitchen during a party they hosted, the woman in his lap, their hands inching beneath each other's shirts, while friends milled around as if the couple's behavior was nothing unusual. Stuart was no doubt drunk and would use that as his excuse, but Maya would have been appalled and angry and on the verge of tears…

The actual image of them had disappeared from her mind,

however, or maybe it was so overshadowed by the contentment that followed, she no longer cared. Aiden was before her and said... she didn't know what he said, but it launched a reverie that erased her heartbreak and removed all her devastation. By the time Maya was aware again, she felt better than she ever had after one of these compromises. In fact, she felt not only strong, but free, and as if Stuart's penchant for public fondling might never affect her again. Not her happiness, not her plans for her future, not her confidence in her own ability to love and care for another.

And she finally knew how it felt to be in Aiden's arms. Amid an intimate crowd and seconds from a volcanic emotional breakdown, Maya had the impression she'd been wrapped in a bubble, a protective cocoon insulating her not just from her own hurt and anger, but also the perceptions of everyone else there. None of the other guests appeared to even see her any longer, meaning no one scrutinized her response to Stu's make-out session, or worse, looked at her with pity. It was as if her mind manifested her most private wish, and the partygoers all disappeared so she could fully enjoy it.

This time, Aiden came to her like an avenging angel, one sent to protect her and dispense with her agony using violence if necessary. She breathed deeply as her trouble dissipated, lifting away like it was helium-injected; and she felt stable for the first time that evening. Maybe for the first time in months. She found she could also stand tall and open her eyes without dreading what she'd see.

She saw Aiden's shirtfront clenched in her fists, and Aiden's face when she looked up. Enfolded in his embrace, Aiden's voice calmed her, the concern he expressed healing the ragged cuts to the heart she'd received with each and every one of Stuart's tactless romantic displays.

She felt steady and strong, but also, despite Aiden's pull on her senses, aware of herself. Which was unusual when Aiden was around. She welcomed the clarity this time.

She faced her dilemma without a preconceived idea of how things should work out between her and Stu; and without censure, she evaluated her own contributions to her marital problems. She saw she was not responsible for Stuart's myriad discourtesies, but she was guilty of running scared from truths she should have faced years ago.

She was sorry for her dishonesty. She recalled her many misjudgments, starting with those she'd made in Griffins Bay as a senior in college. She regretted her unfair treatment of Aiden, how her efforts to drive away her own fear had compromised not just her, but him, as well. Her confession to him now, conflicting beliefs and all, was immediate.

She thought the words as she focused on his shirtfront. *I am so sorry. But I can't be here with you like this, won't do this to Stu. Even if he doesn't care, we're married and I won't betray him.* Then she raised her gaze to offer Aiden the first clean sentiments she ever had, with no attempt at evasion. *But you were right. I shouldn't have run from you. I'm sorry I wasn't brave enough.* She forced a few inches of distance between them and crossed her arms to keep herself from clinging, not just physically, but also to the hope of escape he represented.

Aiden cradled Maya's face in his hands and swept her tears away with his thumbs. "It's okay, love. I think you're going to get the chance to be brave again soon. I just want you to know there's more out there for you, that this doesn't have to be enough." When he released her, his devotion remained behind, a glowing warmth within her fortifying her against what she knew was coming. Which was the end of her belief that she could and should save her relationship with her husband.

This time, she knew how her frustrations with Stu would play out, and it wasn't with them together. Stu wasn't leaving her any choice.

BOOKS IN THIS SERIES

Printed in Great
Britain
by Amazon